Mysterious Dreams of the Dead

ALSO BY TERRY WATADA

FICTION
The Three Pleasures
The Blood of Foxes
Daruma Days

POETRY
The Four Sufferings
The Game of 100 Ghosts
Obon: the Festival of the Dead
10,000 Views of Rain
A Thousand Homes

NON-FICTION
The TBC: The Toronto Buddhist Church 1995 – 2010
Bukkyo Tozen: A History of Jodo Shinshu
Buddhism in Canada 1905 – 1995

CHILDREN'S BOOKS
The Nishga Girl
Seeing the Invisible: The Story of Irene Uchida – Canadian Scientist

MYSTERIOUS DREAMS OF THE DEAD

A WORK OF FICTION
INSPIRED BY TRUE EVENTS

TERRY WATADA

ANVIL PRESS • VANCOUVER

Anvil Press Publishers Inc.
P.O. Box 3008, Station Terminal
Vancouver, B.C. V6B 3X5 CANADA
www.anvilpress.com

Library and Archives Canada Cataloguing in Publication

Title: Mysterious dreams of the dead / a novel by Terry Watada.
Names: Watada, Terry, 1951- author.
Identifiers: Canadiana 20200185500 | ISBN 9781772141504 (softcover)
Classification: LCC PS8595.A79 M97 2020 | DDC C813/.54—dc23

Book design by Rayola.com
Represented in Canada by Publishers Group Canada
Distributed by Raincoast Books (Canada); Small Press Distribution (USA)

The publisher gratefully acknowledges the financial assistance of the Canada Council for the Arts, the Canada Book Fund, and the Province of British Columbia through the BC Arts Council and the Book Publishing Tax Credit.

Printed and bound in Canada

Dedicated to the *Sansei*: the third generation.

"The true mystery of the world is the visible, not the invisible." – Oscar Wilde

Prologue

1987

One of those rootless, forgotten nights. I leaned against the rail of a large table, surveying the debris field of reds and prized colour'd balls with their multiple point values, trying to put my long-ago high-school geometry to good use. The lacquered wood and twenty-ounce weight of my pool cue felt secure on the bridge of my left hand, its solid heft cool against my cheek as I calculated angles and aimed.

Playing pool was a good way to relax after a week of teaching classes at the University of Toronto and tutoring spoiled kids from Upper Canada families three evenings a week. I also edited professors' books from time to time. I made enough for entertainment expenses anyway. I had graduated with an MA in English in the early 1980s and was biding my time, a long time, before starting the PhD program. I needed the break from study.

While the Friday night crowd slid and squirmed around the room of Curly's Billiards, the RCA-Victor TV set with the fading and distorted picture blared out a newscast:

Police arrested four men of Armenian background today on suspicion of planting a bomb on the northbound Yonge-University TTC line last Tuesday morning. The Metro Toronto Bomb Squad found explosive material in a gym bag on the lead subway car. Witnesses became suspicious when they saw four men leave the bag under their seat before quickly exiting at the next stop. The bomb did not explode, and no one was hurt.

Four blurry men covered their faces to get away from the intense fixed stare of the cameras. Their dark skin and slicked back hair burned through the static of the television image. I imagined the garlic and parsley sweat-odour exuding from their bodies. My mother would never call them "Canadians."

I turned to concentrate on the bright-green sheen of the table; nothing could disturb me, not even the distraction of the PA system that suddenly crackled to life above me. "Line one for Mike Shintani," growled a voice that sounded like a hung-over Tom Waits.

I ignored the summons and continued lining up the shot, sliding my cue back and forth between my fingers, again, taking aim as I peered through the cigarette smoke-fog.

"Yo, Shintani, answer the damn phone!" Waits insisted from behind his counter.

Dave Watanabe, my opponent, partner, and ride, backed him up: "You'd better get that."

I scratched off the pink. Minus six points.

"Yeah, this is Mike," I answered on a convenient wall phone. "What is it?"

"Hi, it's Cathy..."

"Oh, hi, Cath. How did you know I was here?"

"Where else would you be on a Friday night? Dave with you?"

"Yeah, he just finished a double shift —"

"Did you read about Boku?" she said, unusually quick on the draw.

"Where?"

Another pocket of silence. "In tonight's *Daily Star*."

"Boku's in the paper?"

"Yes, listen to this." Cathy read the article slowly in that precise, yet hesitating, way she had, like the way she sits upright, so straight she puts a ruler to shame. She always stopped cold between sentences as if thinking about what to say next.

> A Toronto Canadian-Japanese man says he robbed the Canadian Imperial Bank of Commerce at the corner of Dundas and Spadina to defend the honour of his grandfather, who was interned during World War II. The twenty-five-year-old Kenneth Sugiura told District Court that he is willing to go to jail for ten years to protest the treatment 20,000 Japanese Canadians received in World War II. Sugiura had quit the faculty of architecture at the University of British Columbia in order to come back to Toronto to begin a business based on a new computer program he had developed while living in Vancouver. Bail has been set at $100,000.

"Are you kidding me? Are you saying that's Boku?"

"It sounds like him."

"Yeah, but…I can't believe it. Has he lost his mind? What kind of loser —"

"Michael!" Cathy chided abruptly.

"This has got to be some kind of joke. You know Boku."

Cathy started crying softly. I imagined her gently curved eyes squeezed shut. Her ex-fiancé was known for his practical jokes, but this was beyond the pale. Kenneth "Boku" Sugiura was born in the working-class ghetto of Spadina and Dundas but raised in the unremarkable suburb of Agincourt in western Scarborough, an enclave of accidental parks, split-level bungalows, and well-equipped schools. Like me, he had made his way through a conventional education to university.

"Cathy, don't cry," I said. She could be a pill sometimes. "There's gotta be a logical explanation for all this. Let me talk to Glenn. Maybe he knows something."

"You'll let me know what you find out?" she sniffled.

"Yeah, sure."

Dave sank a two-ball combination when I returned with the bizarre story.

"You shitting me?" my buddy asked. "He's not that kind of guy. Is he?"

"Well, the paper says he is," I confirmed, as I pointed to the article in a stray copy I picked up from a chair by the phone.

"Let me see that."

"That guy had everything going for him," I declared as Dave ruffled and folded the paper smooth. "He was gonna run IBM for Christ's sake. How many guys get that kind of opportunity?"

"Why are you so pissed?"

"I'm pissed … I'm pissed because …" I stammered. "He had it all and a fiancée … er … girlfriend." I faded for a moment of reflection. "You know Cathy?"

"For sure. She's a 10. Maybe an 8."

"Well, he's thrown it all away now."

It was true. Boku Sugiura had "had it all." He was the poster boy for *Sansei of the Year*. Now what?

1.

New Year's Day 1983

The 401, the McDonald-Cartier Highway, splits Scarborough, a suburb of ill-planned and dilapidated strip malls, green spaces spotted with hydro-tower scarecrows to ward off stray pedestrians, and blinking traffic lights changing without thought to method or madness. The house lights of split-levels and bungalows, their inhabitants dying a slow death, wink in the darkness of anonymous, yet similar, streets.

Though lacking in consumer amenities within walking distance, the planned communities with their cookie-cutter houses and nearby schools beckon the upwardly mobile. A generation born before or during World War II has migrated from downtown row houses to seek a clean life, a genteel life, in a well-appointed home providing comfort for their elderly parents nicely stored away in the basement, prosperity for their children, and security for their future retirement.

The promise is no more present than during the Christmas holiday season. Every other home outlined with strings of lights and representations of the nativity or Santa Claus with reindeers (same thing for some). The tree seen through front bay windows glitters with bright ornaments and sparkling bubble lights. The gifts underneath are decorated with shimmering paper depicting festive scenes. Aromatic meals permeate each house, from storage attic to finished basement.

For the *Nikkei,* Christmas is celebrated not so much for the religious imperatives, but for the chance that Japanese Canadians can come together free of government scrutiny. The real holiday for them is New Year's Day, the occasion when delicacies can be made and served and visits by friends and relatives happen in a unique manner all day long.

The old Japanese tradition of *Oshougatsu* lives in the Nikkei outposts. The *Nisei* have done well with the multiple-car garage and the cars to fill them adjacent to a five-bedroom house. Their elderly *Issei* parents are deposited in those basements with SONY Trinitrons and separate rooms with bath and toilet. Clammy or downright cold apartments, but it doesn't matter as guilt is assuaged, especially with the dehumidifier or heater chugging along twenty-four-hours a day. Their children, the Sansei, brood in their bedrooms filled with rock posters, a television each, and Sega video game consoles.

Oshougatsu is celebrated in the customary manner, but in a much more limited way than in the past.

Some Issei still go visiting to pay their New Year's respects, though how many friends they see depends, for one, on the fickle holiday schedule of the TTC bus. And two, how many friends are still alive. Tradition commands that only the men travel from house to house all day long, while the women stay at home to welcome the peripatetic guests in order to serve the *ose-chiryouri* and keep the nomads company. In their heart of hearts, the Issei know it's a useless pursuit — all that's left them is a deceased friend's dark and abandoned house, owned now by the insensitive, disrespectful, and traditionless children. So, most stay home.

The Nisei themselves negotiate with their relatives where New Year's Day is to be spent: a sister's place because it's her turn, or a restaurant like Sea Hi or China House, a Chinatown experience in a single building in a clean and safe uptown district. Both do business in the Jewish area of town. Most of the men would rather lie down on a couch in the TV room and watch the various college football games. The women cook and serve, naturally.

Precious few observe the old tradition of preparing osechi-ryouri, a custom that started in the late nineteenth century. The pioneer Issei mothers had brought the old New Year's recipes over from Japan and taught the Nisei like Boku's mom from the time they were born. Mrs. Sugiura had learned well. She had not taught her daughter of course — too much cheerleading and dating for Elaine. "Too Japanese-y," she would complain.

Sansei usually do what their parents do; some, however, venture out on their own in keeping with the old customs, though they no longer drop by unannounced or uninvited. If they dare do so, they are gossiped about and their parents will chastise them to no end. "Don't go to that Shiomi house again! Dirty-foul-mouthed gossipmongers talk stink about you ever since."

KENNETH "BOKU" SUGIURA, the eldest of the children, was in town from the University of British Columbia for the holidays. At five feet, five inches, Boku was short, but had an athlete's body. His winning and broad smile was a Sugiura family trait, and made him seem approachable, just like his sister Elaine. There was always a mischievous glint in his eyes, like he could be pulling your leg with everything he said. He was a good guy and a long-time friend whose company I always enjoyed and, in fact, I looked forward to having.

Since he had invited me, I made sure to drop by his parents' house in my rented-for-the-holiday-car at the top of the DVP during my usual Oshougatsu rounds (after visiting my favourite: Dave Watanabe's place). A mountain of sushi, Cumberland chow mein, *nishime*, shrimp tempura, Japanese style *char shiu* (very different from the Chinese), and other delicacies always graced Mrs. Sugiura's table.

The Sugiura family lived in a quiet cul-de-sac near Ellesmere and Victoria Park, in the middle of the suburbs. Their split-back bungalow was roomy with a side kitchen and a finished basement that served as an apartment for Boku's grandmother, on his mother's side, and matriarch of the family. I wasn't sure my friend knew anything about her. Grandma's story was a blank except that a rumour persisted that her husband, his grandfather, had died mysteriously somewhere in BC. But that was a rumour; he had died well before Boku was born. He couldn't learn anything from his grandmother. Her English was only slightly better than his Japanese.

Haruo Sugiura, the patriarch and Boku's paternal grandfather, began an exemplary life as a dry goods store owner on Powell Street in Vancouver. He and his wife Hanako had two sons, Herb and Daniel. Herb liked working with his hands and so went out to work, mostly local labour jobs. At some point he fell out with his father; they were so much alike. He took off for the Cumberland Mines. Daniel got himself into UBC to study English literature, only to be dismissed because of WWII. He then became a reporter for *The New Canadian*, a Nisei newspaper. Haruo and Hanako ended up in the Lemon Creek internment camp where Hanako died of an undisclosed condition. Haruo lost touch with his eldest son.

After the war, Haruo moved to Toronto to establish a carpentry business and, by the 1950s, became prosperous, which allowed him and Herb to reunite, reconcile, and settle in a third-floor walkup attic on McCaul Street. A good part of town for them since the first Buddhist Church was on nearby Huron St., its co-op for Japanese food was nearby at Dundas and Huron, and many Nikkei lived in the area. The apartment eventually became too small after Herb married and the couple started having babies. Haruo moved to a larger place on Huron Street. The downtown residence suited his needs. Herb took his family to the Greenwood and Danforth part of town before moving to the suburbs like most other Nisei. It was a sign of affluence, of having made it, as long as not too many moved into the same neighbourhood.

And that was all Boku revealed to me. Haruo died in the 1970s, a passing that affected Boku a great deal.

WHENEVER I WALKED into their house, I tugged at the cuffs of my Kresge's plaid shirt, feeling the roughness of the polyester material. I did the same that New Year's Day.

The house was still decked out with Christmas decorations: the six-foot tree dripped with tinsel and ornaments; opened presents underneath, tissue exploded out of the boxes; greeting cards strewn everywhere. The glass cabinet displaying Royal Doulton statuettes stood proudly in the corner as if not to be outdone.

Inside the front door, I found the expected mess of shoes on the floor. They were haphazardly organized; it's a wonder anyone could find theirs. I, of course, removed my own and placed them wherever convenient. There were many people visiting.

It was the shank of that Oshougatsu evening, and Boku's mom, with all the guests taken care of, sat with her son and me, watching us partake of the remains of the tempura shrimp and vegetables, sushi, and a rare treat: *kazunoko konbu* sent by a life-long friend from a cannery in British Columbia. The herring eggs on seaweed were farmed off the north-western coast of the province by the local Indigenous people. Eighty per cent of their crop went to Japan; the remainder went to Hawaii and California. A very small amount either stayed in Vancouver for sale, or came here through Japanese fishmongers, friends or relatives in the business feeling sorry for their big-city cousins back east. The price in the downtown Japanese grocery stores like Dundas Union or Furuya was prohibitive.

Though the delicacy represents fertility, I took the chance because I love eating it with *shoyu* and rice. I really had to control myself at the dinner table; otherwise, I would become the subject of negative gossip on the Nikkei grapevine.

Elaine, Boku's cheerleader sister with the long hair and smile that never quit, took off early in the evening to catch a movie with her then white-boy boyfriend. I was disappointed as I had missed her. Nisei uncles, aunts, and friends typically dropped by all day and a few of the men lingered still in the basement watch-

ing some college football while drinking beer and eating leftover
maki sushi and chips.

Mrs. Sugiura waited for a lull in the meal to say, "So, Michael,
I read in *The New Canadian* the NAJC is moving ahead with reparations."

"Sure thing," I replied.

"I hear you're involved in the campaign," she added.

"A little. I fold fliers and give workshops at information sessions
and school gatherings."

"Why are you involved in that?" Boku asked.

"Why not?"

"Because it's not right."

"Reparations isn't right?"

"It didn't happen to you."

"Of course not, but it did to our families."

"We did all right. So did your parents," said Boku.

"Yeah, but they could've had it a lot easier. If they didn't have
to start from scratch after they worked so hard to build themselves up, who knows where we'd be? Imagine a J-town in
Vancouver. How cool would that be? Everyone together in one
place, like the Chinese or Italians."

"What's so good about that?"

I couldn't think of a quick answer, but I said, "Well, you
wouldn't have to travel an hour and a half to get to church."

"Give me a break. Church?" he scoffed.

"Look, the point is everything was taken away from our
families, and why? Because of the way they looked."

"But they rose above it. They did it by themselves. Why do
they ... why do we need 'blood money' now?"

"What about the lost opportunities?"

"What opportunities? Whatever they lost, they got back."

As she served another portion of rice to both of us, Mrs.
Sugiura rejoined the conversation. She spoke in a measured
voice: "Your uncle was ruined."

"How?" Boku asked, surprised she had spoken.

"Uncle Dan was in his second year at the University of British Columbia. He had a bright future ahead of him when the war hit. He was asked to leave after December 7. I think that was the beginning of his end."

Boku fell silent. His face flashed red. Uncle Dan was always the family shame, but no one ever openly brought him up. He existed in the whispers and hushed conspiracies of the rumour mill. What made Mrs. Sugiura bring him up that night was anybody's guess. Boku told me later his mother's candour even surprised him.

I turned back to enjoy my kazunoko as Boku simmered in his thoughts. He appeared upset and scrunched his face.

2.

New Year's Day 1984

Oshougatsu, the following year, was a decidedly different experience. Like the year before, Boku had flown in on the Canadian Pacific redeye from Vancouver just before Christmas and had contacted me early Christmas Eve morning, waking me up. His laughter over the phone cackled and crackled, always mocking me in my discomfort. As luck would have it, we didn't have a chance to get together until New Year's Day.

When I arrived, something was wrong. There was no logjam of shoes on the floor of the vestibule. I placed mine beside the family's shoes. That was strange. Boku's younger sister was there, but didn't greet me with my anticipated enthusiasm. Elaine, her long black hair neatly edging her face, soft curved eyes, and broad mouth. Every time I saw her throughout high school, university, and Japanese language school days, she would hug me without fail with her comforting arms and inviting body. Her eyes would sparkle and then disappear as her smile grew wide. Tonight, she seemed a little upset and gave me a perfunctory hello. I missed the sensation of my face flushing red with her touch. Never did anything about it in the past. I was such a fool.

"Hey, what's with her?" I asked Boku.

"Who?" he responded.

"Your sister. Didn't you see?" I said as she scurried down the stairs to the television room. No customary hug, no warm body, nothing. All the Sugiuras hugged, except maybe the grandma. It was something I was never comfortable with and never initiated, but I enjoyed getting them.

"Oh, don't mind her. Time of the month," he said with a grin.

"Shut up," I growled.

Unlike times past, this visit was a subdued affair. Mrs. Sugiura dutifully set a place for me at the mahogany dinner table and filled the serving plates with freshly prepared tempura, sliced Chinese barbecue pork, and rolled sushi. No kazunoko this year. Her husband, Herb, busily banged dishes and pots about in the kitchen as if upset by something. Mrs. Sugiura left the table with a scowl on her face.

"What's going on?" I finally asked Boku. "Everyone's acting like someone died."

"Hey, watch what you're saying. My cousin —"

"Oh, Jesus, really? I'm really sorry. I didn't mean anything —"

"Just kidding," he revealed.

"You *baka*."

"I quit UBC," he said with a thud.

"You quit —"

"Keep your voice down. Everybody's upset as it is."

"You're in second year, for Christ's sake! Why'd you quit?"

"Can't say."

"You can't sit there, drop a bombshell like that, and tell me you don't know why!"

"I didn't say I don't know why. I said I won't say."

"Cut the crap," I said under my breath.

He took a long sigh as he held up a *futomaki*. "History must be ascertained and not studied," he announced rather philosophically.

"What?"

"History must be ascertained, not studied," he repeated.

"I heard you the first time. What's that mean?"

"I've become an epistemological detective." His voice was flat, mechanical, robotic — as if he had memorized the passage from some text and was reciting it back to me.

"An epis... what does *that* mean?" I said, my tone betraying my irritation. "Why are you talking like that?"

"Think back a year ago," he said with a grin that said he knew the punch line to some joke, but he wasn't going to tell it. "At Oshougatsu, I mean."

"What's last year got to do with anything?"

"Remember what you said to me?"

"No."

"About reparations. How you said I knew nothing about reparations, the internment, the war."

"I don't think I said —"

"I remember it clearly."

"Have you been angry with me for a year?"

"Who said I was angry? I admit, I was hurt, humiliated, mad for a time, but I got over it."

"It wasn't that bad," I insisted. Boku had given no indication at the time that he was so upset.

"Yes, it was."

I didn't think so; I looked anywhere but at him. Sansei just didn't do that. After recovering, I pressed to find out more. "Okay, okay, but why'd you quit?"

"I learned all that I needed to know."

"What does that mean?"

"I told you, I became an epistemological detective."

"Yeah, but what does that mean? Come on, man, fess up."

"All right, I'll put it in terms even you can understand," he said. "I'm a detective looking for the truth."

"What truth?" I asked.

"The truth about the internment."

"The internment?"

"Yeah, you think you know everything about it, but you weren't there."

"Oh, like you were," I countered.

"No, I wasn't. But my grandpa was. He rose above it all and became the man I respected. The man I loved."

"And so?"

"So, I want to ascertain history, not hear about it or read about it. I am a detective about to become my grandpa."

BOKU WAS AS CLEAR AS MUD. Confused, I gave up and descended to the TV room downstairs where two or three uncles and *baachan* sat watching U of M play Michigan State in some Fruit Bowl game. Elaine had disappeared deep into the house by this point, most likely to her room. She probably didn't want to hang out with the "old folks." Boku did the same.

According to the aunts, the Nisei men who lounged, drank beer, and snacked on chips, dried squid, and baloney slices all afternoon on couches (like seals and walruses basking on a rocky shore) were no better than *huks*. My mom used to say, "Only *hakujin* drink." As if to say the Japanese were better than that, they were above it all. Or should be. White boys were drunkards on New Year's Eve. They became good-for-nothing, watching football all the next day suffering their hangovers. "What kind of way is that to respect the coming of the New Year?" Mom observed. But I wasn't so sure my mother would think so highly of the falling-down-drunk *salarymen* in contemporary Japan. I supposed the Nisei male relatives were given a pass.

What Grandma, unable to understand sports, got out of the game was a mystery; she remained as silent as a tomb in her La-Z-Boy staring at the chaotic movement on the screen.

I usually asked her how she was in my rudimentary Japanese since I felt like she was being left out of the festivities. "*Obasan, ogenki desu ka?*"

She stirred awake with a start, turned her gaze toward me, and asked who I was: "*Ko no hito da re desu ka?*"

"Shintani Michael," answered one of the Nisei men in the room.

"Shintani? *Nihonjin, desu ka?*"

"Sansei."

"Shintani? I know you-*no obaachan*," she answered in accented and broken English.

And that was that. It was boring television, but that's what you do on New Year's Day. At least, I caught up with Boku's relatives if not with Boku himself.

3.

Summer 1987

Outside the pool hall, the humidity had turned into a light rain once Dave Watanabe and I walked to his car, a late model Chevy Nova with custom shocks and a killer Blauplunck stereo system he installed himself. The cold wetness felt good on my face as I continued to try and make sense of the news.

Dave Watanabe was seven years my junior, but we became fast friends back in the late '70s when I was involved in the Asian Canadian Student Movement at the University of Toronto. We helped put on the National Sansei Conference in 1977 at the Japanese Canadian Cultural Centre commonly known as the JCCC or The Centre, and Dave came out of curiosity.

Dave wasn't much for school and so got his Grade 12 and then worked at his father's place of business, a Jewish-owned dress factory and distribution centre in the Spadina/Dundas area of Toronto. Perhaps nepotistic but his father wanted to secure his son's future. He saw Dave becoming a middle manager, making a decent living one day. Dave's only obstacle to complete happiness was his girlfriend.

He was an east-end city kid, but his girl, Joanna "Joanie" Fujibayashi, was strictly Don Mills. A very pretty teenager with thick but short hair, short to be "different," she eventually grew into a confident and attractive woman.

The wide major street was empty of cars as we sped along, the streetlights streaming by. Bruce Springsteen played on the Blauplunkt, loud and earnest; the melodic strains of Roy Orbison underneath the anthemic power chords comforted me, inspiring me to drum along on the dash and sing out loud.

Dave lit a cigarette and cracked open a window. It bothered him when I coughed. Entertained by my antics, he smiled but was quiet as he drew on the cigarette and exhaled out the side of his mouth. I was a terrible singer, but I felt I had the spirit of rock 'n roll in my veins, especially howling along the asphalt of freeways and byways. *Baby, I was born to run...* Dave never sang, but he felt the same. Guess that was why we got along. Once on Eglinton Avenue, he suddenly turned onto the Don Valley Parkway and headed south.

I was surprised enough to stop singing. "You not picking up Joanie?" We always picked up his girl after playing pool.

"Nah," he said.

"Oh, it's like that, is it?"

He crushed out his cigarette like Bogart trying to gain some time before the interrogation at police headquarters. "We had words."

I remained silent as the Boss came around for another chorus.

"She's always ragging on me 'bout quitting my old man's and going back to school. Maybe community college."

"Well, okay. But not everyone's right for post-secondary."

"That's what I been trying to tell her. I'm too old for school."

"Yeah, well..." I rolled down the window to feel the night air. It had stopped raining.

"I don't want much outta life. The three 'Cs,' you know what I mean?"

"What's that?"

"Car, condo, kids," he informed. "I know, 'kids' starts with a 'K,'" he sneered. "Children, all right? But not right away."

I had heard this throughout the many years of their courtship. Dave and Joanie had met at the JCCC when they were kids themselves and Dave had just made his driver's license. As a volunteer parking attendant at the annual bazaar, he was in his usual leather jacket, shades, and hanging cigarette, when he struck up a conversation on a break. So unlike him since he preferred letting others talk, like me for instance. But she must've been something to him. She was inside the building behind one of the kiosks looking pretty and selling "trinkets" to hakujin browsers. They weren't Sid Vicious and Nancy Spungen, or even Sonny and Cher (God forbid) by any stretch of the imagination, but they seemed right for each other. He drove fast, sneered at "adults," and listened to rock with the radio on eleven. She knew cars, even with her suburban roots, or maybe because of them.

And they had some really good times. The usual date-like occasions like the movies, the annual Auto Show at the Canadian National Exhibition grounds, or a dance at the JCCC. But also barreling up to Wasaga Beach in his car for a weekend stay at a friend's cottage; cruising Yonge Street on a Saturday night on a full tank of gas; or playing pinball at some all-night sub shop on the Danforth. What sealed the deal was her uncanny knowledge of cars. Dave would point out any vehicle passing by or parked in the street and she would rattle off make, model, and year. Like she had turned to *Car and Driver* and recited the description. It helped that her Nisei dad owned an automobile repair shop.

Joanie began to get serious about their relationship. Somewhere in their early to mid-twenties, she complained that "David's" (as she called him rather formally) entire life revolved around his parents' lives and being Japanese (Japanese Canadian actually): he still lived at home where his mother cooked a mean steak or Atlantic salmon in shoyu and she made him lunch to take to work or school every day; she even washed and ironed his clothes; he worked for his father at the clothing factory; he hung out at The Centre where his father was on the board of directors and president more than a few terms; and he had only ever dated Sansei whom he referred to as "Centre Girls." Add to that his dentist, his doctor, his auto body shop mechanic (Joanie's father's shop of course), and G&G Electronics, his stereo and TV store — all were Japanese Canadian.

Joanie was more egalitarian in her patronage. She was Christian and went to a church in her suburban neighbourhood; she was nearly done at university studying sciences so she could have a career upon graduation; and she went shopping with her friends at major malls or in outlet malls in the United States. It was ironic, though, that most of her friends, certainly her best friends, were Nikkei from the JCCC. Like most of us, they had Canadian friends: workmates, classmates, and neighbours. And they enjoyed their company, but they preferred to be with Nikkei.

I admired and laughed along with the grad student wits like Douglas Cowling and Jennifer Head. I wasn't white, but they made me feel like I belonged. They addressed me as Michael, after all. Still, I found I preferred to be with Dave and his family on the weekend.

"We're going to get married at the Buddhist Church and move in with your parents!" she complained to Dave as he told me. "I can just see it."

"So?"

"I'm not Buddhist!"

"So, we'll go to the United Church!" The Japanese United Church on Ossington housed in a building right out of the Victorian age with thick brick walls and dark interior.

SHE WAS RIGHT about our Nikkei world. I grew up without a physical community right outside our door. Oh, we ate mostly Japanese food, essentials like rice and tofu bought at stores like Dundas Union, Furuya, Sanko Trading, and Sandown Market, but we missed a Powell Street Japanese Canadian community in pre-war Vancouver. It was instinctive since neither of us had lived back then; in fact, I had never been to that west coast city (not sure about Dave).

But we knew. We missed our parents' Sunday mornings on Vancouver's Cordova Street or Jackson Avenue listening to the shouts of good friends in Powell Ground, the sound of Christian hymns in Japanese, the chanting of the Heart Sutra by Buddhists, voices mixed in a competition of choirs. We missed the open and

smiling faces that greeted us everywhere: the light of eyes sparkling in the noon-day sun. We missed the ubiquitous heavy aroma
of tempura, chicken teriyaki, and sizzling *gaijin* beef from places
like the New Pier Café or Ernie's lunch counter, places I heard
Nisei talk about. We missed the connections found nowhere else
in the world. And we missed the salt carried by the fractured
light and wind of the sea that nourished us, that created us. We
missed a home.

So we manufactured one with what was left, scattered and
distant though it was.

"YOU'VE GOT TO get out in the world," Joanie would advise, riding shotgun in Dave's Chevy Nova on nights with me dutifully
sitting in back. "Go to college and then get a career. Not a job —
a career! At least get up by yourself and make your bed every
day!" she would tell Dave.

"Yeah, yeah, yeah," was all Dave would mutter in response.
Sometimes when her opinions became a little too exuberant,
he'd growl, "Cool your jets." That was a real Dave thing to say.
Still, there was a great love and affection between the two, no
matter what, and I kept that within my soul, fearing that this was
going to be a deal-breaker.

4.

Autumn 1990

She was asleep as she rose into the air with arms spread wide, poised as if about to fly. Angel wings unfurled tracing the horizon. Her eyes sealed by the night, she reached upward and began to soar — right through the cloud ceiling and into the open dark blue. The sky bruised easily. But the stars jeweled her neck as she climbed higher and higher.

I called out her name, "Chiemi!" Odd since I sensed I hadn't seen her before that moment. She turned and smiled before waving goodbye to me standing on the ground. I began crying.

— Summer 1935

"Why'd you stop?"

"That is all that there is," Naoko said in her staccato and syntactically correct pronunciation. "On page, that is all."

Naoko Ito, an international grad student at the University of Toronto, sat hunched over the diary in front of her computer, like a sentinel on a parliament building. Not that she had gargoyle looks. On the contrary, she possessed more than conventional Japanese beauty. With a perfectly round face, full red lips, inviting mouth, and modest breasts, but short shapely legs, she had stunning looks. Her page-boy haircut suited her and half-encircled her face.

I HAD MET HER at a U of T foreign-students mixer late summer of 1990. I was no longer a student, but an instructor indulging in university life, which suited me since I could meet and greet students between my classes and evening tutorials.

I had made many connections through the Student Movement days on campus and so attended the many student parties and gatherings. Jon Fleming, faculty coordinator and fellow student during my MA studies, invited me to this particular occasion.

"Mike, how're you doing?"

"Fine, Jon, fine."

He was a lanky man with a full head of red hair and a winning wit. It was a requirement in the English Department, it seemed.

"Are you coming to the staff meeting Tuesday?"

"Yeah, but I don't want to. Just another opportunity for the Dean to exercise his ego."

"True, but it's organized by Jennifer Head."

"So?"

"She gives good Jennifer!"

A winning wit.

Some hakujin friends said I should move out of my mom's house, get on with my life, and find a real career, make some real money, get married, and move to the suburbs. That seemed ludicrous to me. That wasn't Japanese. Seeking the conventional, too, bored me. Besides, I did admit I was always looking for my "significant other."

As I navigated the swirls and eddies of mostly female Japanese students and white-boy huk hustlers fueled by some Oriental fantasy, I spotted Naoko sitting with her friends on the one couch in the room. The secondhand piece of furniture was probably commandeered from Hart House for the International Student Union, a building that would've looked "fab, gear, far out" in the 1960s, but, so many years later, now suffered from anachronism with its broad yellow and green Mondrian panels and signage in a psychedelic font.

Right from the get-go, Naoko struck me with a strange but compelling attraction — not the love-at-first-sight kind, but something rather metaphysical. She was older than most visiting students, maybe in her late 20s — she was doing graduate work after all. She had more than a mature intellectual beauty about her; an intensity emanated from her, yet I couldn't put my finger on the source. The attraction emboldened me to approach her, something I seldom did before. I felt much older than most of the female students, but soon discovered the age spread between Naoko and me wasn't so bad. I wasn't some huk letch with a "Madame Butterfly" fixation. At least, that was what I told myself. The tingling within me increased the closer I got and the longer I remained in her presence.

She was completely fascinating. I had a funny feeling about her. I was moved to look at her ears out of some unknown and intuitive urge; maybe it was the fact that I was reading *A Wild Sheep Chase* at the time. She exposed one when she curled her hair back with a finger, but there was nothing unusual about it.

"Hi, I'm Mike Shintani."

"Shintani-*san*?"

"Call me Mike, everybody does."

"*Mis-tah Mai-ko?*"

"No, no, no, just Mike."

She bent her head down and caught glimpses of me with sly and slight movements of her eyes. Very formal, very Japanese. Direct eye contact would've been rude. She didn't utter a sound after that, as if pinned by some code of silence.

I decided to do my best Lou Reed and slouched in the sofa while asking if she knew the song playing: "Walk on the Wild Side." She shook her head slightly, still not uttering a word.

I almost left when she suddenly spoke, "Are you student here?"

Relieved at the response, I took advantage of the moment. "Yes, kind of...I mean I'm an instructor in the English department until I start the doctoral program."

OVER A BOWL of wonton noodle soup in the nearby Golden City, my favourite haunt in the old Bay Street Chinatown area, I observed her shining face with the gaze averted as we continued our conversation. I usually ate there with Dave, Glenn, or Boku, or a combination thereof; it was nice being with a woman. I think Radar, the sole waiter in the place, was surprised.

Naoko told me she was a visa student from Yokohama, spending a year or two learning English (though she could speak, read, and write well enough as I soon discovered). She was also working on her doctorate about the *matsutake* mushroom and its cultural implications for Japanese Canadians of all things.

Her father was some corporate honcho in Tokyo, making more money than he knew what to do with. He was recently assigned to Canada and so his daughter could go to a foreign country to study any obscure subject and learn English to boot, something many Japanese wanted to know. What was charming about her was her lack of pretension. She may have had money, but she didn't want others to know it. Very Japanese.

Her mother was an elegant corporate wife. The photo of her Naoko showed me was of a confident woman in a formal kimono. She did not smile, of course, but I could tell by what Naoko added that her mother was perhaps stern, but generous, with her time for her family.

I revealed my Nikkei experience to her: my grandparents and father in Vancouver, the logging camps, the fishing industry, the war, the evacuation, the internment, the exile when Dad met Mom after the war. I also said my grandmother had died of cancer during a trip home to Japan. Not that I went through any of it, but I must admit to knowing more about the experience than my fellow JCs, though Boku knew some of his family's story, because of the "rap and bull sessions" of the Asian Canadian Student Movement, an offshoot of the larger University Student Movement of the 1970s.

In the pre-war days, my grandparents lived on Powell Street, my father a junior bank official of some kind, my grandpa a grocery storeowner. Photographs of Dad show a man choked by his sports coat, crisp white shirt, and bow tie, having surrendered to the conventional and shackled by race, a "Jap" with a higher education and limited opportunity. His best friend, Uncle Kunio, once told me he swore too much. Now that was a surprise. I never heard him swear. Not ever. He was too much of a quiet man for that.

Once I told that to Naoko, she relaxed and laughed for the first time in my presence, though I didn't understand the joke. It was then I noticed her eyes; when she gazed at me, they were intense, bright. They sparked with their own light source from within. Or so I imagined. I'm not saying she was a space alien, but her looks were quite arresting, even supernatural, I'd say. Again, I felt her power, the core of her being. A touch of the metaphysical at my shoulder made me steady myself, though there was no chance of falling off my metal chair. But I did drop my spoon into my soup, the hot splash hitting my face. I winced.

Naoko laughed again. "That alway happen," she said.

"What?" I asked as I wiped away the broth and soothed the burn.

"When people see my eye, they alway do something."

"Oh, yeah, I can understand why." Then I asked, with a smile, "Can you see in the dark?" I knew it was a stupid, stupid thing to say as soon as I uttered it.

Though she seemed a tad surprised, if not shocked, she said nothing in return.

"I'm sorry, I didn't mean..." While turning away from the extraordinary, I decided to tell her about my recently discovered father's diary.

ROY SHINTANI, my *otousan*, had been flying shotgun in a hired Cessna in 1971 when the plane crashed north of Marathon, Ontario, a town resting on the hump of Lake Superior. A search party had found the wreckage but not the bodies. He and the hired pilot were inexplicably lost. I was fifteen at the time.

Okaasan said rather cryptically that he had been on a search. For what, she didn't say or didn't know. She obviously didn't want to talk so I let it go. After my undergrad years, I started looking through his possessions: letters, photographs, official documents from his bank job, his books (mostly pulp science and detective fiction), Nisei Club newsletters (a club formed in Toronto in the 1950s), old issues of *The New Canadian*, nothing much from the War Days; Mom was a packrat and kept everything. I did this to discover the character of the man.

In the basement, I found tucked away behind the furnace a cardboard box marked "Moose Jaw 1947." *Moose Jaw?*

In the box, there was a bound set of postcards as well as old photographs and a few other things — a palm-sized smooth stone specifically. The prize was his journal, all written in Japanese. That was the second anomaly I learned about the man: he was fluent in Japanese.

I could not read any of it, despite my seven years at the Orde Street Japanese School (more like seven years of *gesha* and recess), but it seemed to be a hit-'n-miss accounting of his life during the war years, ending in Moose Jaw. Why he was in that obscure Prairie town was a mystery. I knew, or rather I assumed, he was in one of the camps in BC. I couldn't fathom why he would settle in Saskatchewan afterward.

"How did Otousan know Japanese?" Mom was sitting in her sewing room at the back of the house. She was surrounded by material piled high, waiting to be used.

She answered, "Your otousan was a smart man."

"I know that. Just where did he learn?"

"We all had to take Japanese after school, six days a week. You went, all the good it did you." She scowled and half turned away.

I grimaced and disregarded the calculated comment. Japanese language school, even at one Saturday morning a week, was an inconvenience. As a little kid, I used to cry at the prospect of a Saturday without *Bugs Bunny* cartoons or *Three Stooges* shorts.

My mother wouldn't even look at the diary. So I devised a plan. At the university I looked for a translator, but what they charged was way above my pay grade. Most justified their rates by pointing out how difficult a job it was because the handwriting was at times illegible and the Japanese itself was "old style" — Meiji period diction and syntax. I put the project on the back-burner. Then I met Naoko.

She was willing to do the job out of interest's sake. I quickly took her up on the offer and we met several times in her apartment or in Robart's Library, "Fort Book" to students on campus. As it turned out, the book was a dream diary. More impressionistic than factual.

It was filled with passages like this:

Chiemi looked down at me and I fell to my knees. She continued to float higher and higher, yet I saw her face clearly. The farther she rose, the closer she seemed.

A prickling sensation swelled in my stomach and I tightly held myself in. The nearer she came the more intense the feeling. I keeled over. On the ground, I lifted my head for what felt like the last time and saw to my amazement her full face.

Her eyes ... her eyes ... were lovely almond eyes but one pointed below the other. They appeared off-kilter. Not hideous, but intriguingly positioned. They peered into me and grabbed hold of my soul.

—July 1940

5.

Summer 1987

G olden City, a Chinese restaurant of beginnings and endings. The food was cheap and readily available. During my radical student days, it was considered "soul food."

The eatery was hunkered down along an anonymous stretch of dilapidated buildings in the original Chinatown on the south side of Dundas between Bay and University. Beside it was the fabled Dundas Union, the eastern Canada reincarnation of Union Fish, the old Japanese-Canadian-fisherman's outlet store on Powell Street in pre-war Vancouver. The Toronto store stuffed its shelves with products from Japan; the business was eventually enhanced with a delivery service. A dark-blue van followed a route to Japanese-Canadian households around the city to offer a wide range of staples like rice in hundred-pound bags and fresh tofu in open cans and specialties like konbu, fine *nori*, *sembei*, and a thousand other items. A very useful service until the driver retired or died in the late '80s. Anyway, the Nikkei by that point lived too far away in remote suburbs to make it profitable.

Golden City was one storefront wide. Inside featured a narrow but deep space that ended with a three-step stone staircase polished black by grease up to the kitchen. From what could be seen from one of the wobbly metallic tables, the backroom was a dark shadowy cave with the corner of a dingy stove visible with well-worn pots and black patina'd woks hanging above. Next to the collection and mantel was a tired sink cracked and rusted beyond use. From time to time a withered cook in a soiled apron appeared, pressed a finger against the side of a nostril, and blew out a rope of snot that splattered the steps below. He ignored the pool of phlegmatic discharge as he slouched away.

In the restaurant's front end, ducks, chickens, and pigs hung collared on meat hooks in the grease-smeared picture window. The carcasses glazed with char shiu, oyster, or some other exotic culinary secret sauce shone brilliantly as if to distract the mind from the cruel execution by knife and crispy fire they had recently endured.

The checkerboard floor of black and dingy tile was slick in spots, cracked, fractured, and torn up in others. A narrow groove nearly down the centre acted as a pathway from the kitchen to the tables. "Radar," as Boku had nicknamed him, was the sole waiter.

Here was a runt of an immigrant man worn away by his frustrated dreams. He spoke a form of English that seemed crippled at the best of times. To his fellow workers and owner, he conversed in *Toisan*, a guttural dialect from southern China. To customers, whether they were Chinese or "Canadian," he grunted, gestured, or mouthed a few words, some recognizable, some ambiguous, most unintelligible. He was a man of few words on many levels.

Why Boku had named him Radar was not clear at first. He bore no resemblance to the *M*A*S*H* character other than the fact that he was short. He certainly wasn't from Korea. His square head with a flat-top hairdo was greased to an excessive sheen — rivulets of hair shone even in the dull light of the restaurant. The overhang of his Peking-Man forehead forced him to squint even with his thick, black-rimmed glasses. The acne scars, a prominent part of the geography of his face, acted as testament to the establishment's unclean state. His body was compact, and he wore the same soiled white jacket, shirt, bow tie, black slacks, and polished but scuffed Oxfords every time we were there.

Boku swore that Radar had the ability to predict what customers wanted to order; hence the nickname. But I argued that that was easy. White people always wanted sweet and sour, fried rice, and egg rolls. "Number 5 with *two* egg rolls." Add chicken chow mein and maybe chop suey and you had a "special occasion." We too consistently ordered the same thing: wonton noodle soup or a rice dish with char shiu on top. To mix it up, though it never tripped up Radar, we sometimes wanted beef and greens on rice or duck or chicken on rice. Nevertheless, our limited range of choices was cheap, fast, filling, and delicious. Boku never took those facts into account.

Just as important as the food was the music. It was the late 1980s and people were starting to forget the Beatles, Chicago, and the Supremes. The hits of the Sixties and Seventies! So we found refuge in Golden City with its odd combination of Cantonese chow mein and the Rolling Stones, the Animals, and the Kinks playing overhead. Our soul food and our music: it was Nirvana on Earth.

TWO DAYS AFTER CATHY'S CALL, I ended up with Dave at Golden City once again after cruising Yonge Street with my good buddy. After the film *American Graffiti*, the car-cruising craze had hit across North America. Any town with a long main drag saw even an anemic weekday night come alive with caravans of cars driving up and down that street. Parties of two, three, or more guys and gals screamed out car windows or sunroofs and the like. Very few men flew solo. Loud stupid conversations between some drunks, some stone-cold sober, flowed between vehicles. Some with bottles of beer often hurled out of adolescent protest. Rock 'n roll played by wise-cracking DJs the soundtrack.

Toronto was no different. Gas was relatively cheap; clubs and other entertainment were not. So why not drive up and down the Yonge Street strip? Nameless pedestrians walked the concrete sidewalks like a meandering, disorganized pilgrimage. Where Mecca was was anyone's guess, but intense neon lit the way. Several cross streets offered vehicles an opportunity to turn around and head in the opposite direction or even away from the action to a Chinatown sanctuary or a sad, tired Fran's Restaurant on College

Street or St. Clair Avenue. Open twenty-four hours, Fran's played host to midnight denizens like hookers, pimps, pushers, and druggies — the perfect spot for young-adult hipster gypsies.

Dave, Joanie, and I often made the trek on a boring Saturday night — sometimes Dave and me alone on a Sunday with nothing else to do. That night I was too preoccupied with Boku to care about the street theatre. Dave took us way up to Eglinton and took a wicked right and headed for the Don Valley Parkway — a chance to open up the Nova for him, a chance to think for me.

While roaring down to the delta of the DVP, Dave aimed his car at the off-ramp at the Gardiner and we merged into the cross-town expressway easily. The streetlamps were still pale as the moon rose on the horizon, a canopy of lights to celebrate a summer *Nighttown*, a Joycean term I adopted to describe China-town. Exiting into the base of the downtown core, Dave remained silent as he adjusted the Blaupunkt's volume. Springsteen thundered through *Thunder Road* as the streets narrowed with the ap-proach of Chinatown.

Dave and I sat at one of the tables up front. The barbecue meat carcasses seemed suddenly struck by *rigor mortis* that even-ing. The antiquated air conditioner stuck into the wall above the front door chugged, sputtered, and complained with its furtive effort to cool. Radar didn't care as he trundled along the rail-groove in the floor.

"Hello. Hello," he opened in a friendly voice. He magically produced three cups of water, each plastic glass clouded from overuse. "You wait for friend?"

"Wait, there's only two of us," Dave corrected. Only Boku called him "Radar" and never to his face.

"Yeah," I interjected. "We're waiting for a friend."

Radar shrugged his shoulders, said something indecipherable, and slinked off.

Dave screwed up his face and asked, "Who you expecting?"

"I called Glenn at Curly's. Should be finished his tennis game by now and on his way."

Glenn Tabuchi was one of The Boys, a loose confederation of friends formed in our childhoods, at the Toronto Buddhist Church, the one who knew he wanted to be a chartered accountant, a CA, since Grade 9 at Jarvis Collegiate, the two-hundred-year-old high school.

He was also one of "those guys": easy good-looks, athletic in a middle-class kind of way (tennis was his game, racquetball a close second), and an inarticulate shyness around the ladies. Charming. Good enough marks to get into the U of T's business admin program right after first year. He graduated with honours and passed the CA test while enrolled in the MBA program. After finishing with his education, he quickly joined the firm owned by Tak Nobuto, a well-known Nisei accountant, as a junior employee with a lot of potential. Lucky guy living the life of Riley. He even had an apartment while the rest of us still lived at home. We couldn't afford not to, or so we reasoned.

His Achilles heel may have been his lack of general knowledge. Though he approached genius status in math, his studies were rather narrow. Never read a book, never offered an opinion much above how "the game" was going on television. *Sports Illustrated* was his Bible; the sports section of any newspaper his encyclo-pedia. Knowing his limitations, he wisely kept mum on politics, philosophy, religion, or literature. But he had an appreciation for the arts (though he spat out "artsy" every time the topic came up), probably because of one of his many past girlfriends was a Korean Canadian who worked for Citytv.

He may have been ignorant about the world, but he was cool. One of us. Maybe I was the only one who criticized him, since I majored in English literature. Damn it, he could get most any girl he set his mind on. Though he had many throughout his "sexual career," he was honourable about it: one of his ex-girl-friends dubbed him a "serial monogamist."

Everyone wanted to be Glenn's friend, something about his way. People felt his silence signified intelligence. Maybe it did. His money didn't hurt either since really none of us had any to speak of. Everyone wanted to be a hanger-on, hoping maybe some of his charisma or good fortune would rub off onto them.

Glenn walked into Golden City just after Radar left us alone. Dave and I were hungry and couldn't wait any longer. We were just about to wave Radar back when Glenn joined us. He was in his tennis whites, Polo shirt, Adidas shoes, and carried a matching bag with racket in hand. His hair was wet, but styled in a shag cut like Jimmy Connors, the champ.

"Hello, ladies, how's it hanging?"

"Glenn, that doesn't make any sense," I remarked.

"Why?"

"Never mind."

Dave turned away and scowled into his sleeve. He had no love for Glenn, but he tolerated him for my sake more than anything else.

"You hear about Boku?" I asked.

"As a matter of fact, I did. From Cath," he answered casually. Before continuing he turned to a magically present Radar who brought three plates of food: two char shiu on rice and one beef and greens on rice. The waiter was amazing — maybe he was psychic. Or maybe he had supernatural powers.

"I called him," Glenn revealed.

"You what?" I asked, surprised.

"I called him.

"Where? In jail?"

"At home. He's out on bail."

Glenn was audacious, I gave him that. I never would've done such a thing, even if we were the best of friends. I immediately felt the sting of guilt.

Since that New Year's argument in 1984, I had seen Boku only a few times. He lived his life and I lived mine. I will say he seemed confident in himself back then. He was at peace with his calamitous decision to leave school. I wondered if the bank robbery was part of it.

"What did he say?" Dave rejoined.

"Nothing really, so I suggested we have dinner together. You up for a meet?" he asked me.

"Yeah … yeah sure," I said trying to evaluate the consequences, though I had a feeling there weren't going to be any.

"Yeah, he asked for you."

I didn't respond, but I was more than a little curious.

"How about Wednesday? Bumpkins at 7:30?"

"Sure … sure," I said, retreating into my thoughts.

6.

Autumn 1990 – Winter 1991

My father was an "elegant" writer? Naoko assured me that he was. Her use of the word "elegant" seemed unnatural, forced. But she went on to insist, "He use beautiful words," a definite exaggeration. They reminded her of "a soft rainfall." Very poetic on her part, I thought. She also added that the dreams were progressive, one picked up where the other left off. She turned to me with her exquisite eyes and I believed her.

> *Grey skies, its clouds frayed until empty without her winged-*
> *self swooping through the heavens. How I longed to see her*
> *again. Yet her hanging black tresses tickled my nose in my sleep,*
> *and I chuckled. I could not see her. She was a ghost to me now.*
> *– December 1940*

Lyrical, certainly.

Chiemi obsessed me. A familiar energy emanated from an indeterminate part of my body. I reached for my father but held nothing but air.

MY FATHER, A QUIET MAN, had led a routine life. Every workday, he rose from bed at precisely 6:30 in the morning, without an alarm clock, without my mother nudging him. He silently selected his clothes for the day, a conservative suit, perhaps blue, certainly grey, a suitable bow tie and dark patent-leather shoes. In our 1950s kitchen, small, low-lying counters, under-lit and dingy, he ate breakfast by himself, a bowl of cereal (sensible shredded wheat, of course), a small glass of orange juice, and a cup of coffee, no cream, maybe homo milk. He was off to work by 8:00 on the dot.

He worked for the Canadian Imperial Bank of Commerce, first as a clerk before working his way up to assistant manager — at the branch right on the corner of Dundas and Spadina — and then at head office in the downtown core in some high-class position. It was like he picked up from where he left off in Vancouver. World War II must've felt like a minor inconvenience to him.

In 1950, he and Mom bought a house on Sullivan Street in the centre of what was to become the new Chinatown by the '90s. Our house was the only detached one on the entire length of the street. Every other home was part of a long stretch of row houses, usually with a small fenced-in garden in front and a small, hemmed-in and cramped backyard. City maple trees lined the street, mature with branches that reached for the heavens. We could've moved to the suburbs, but my mother said they simply didn't want to. I supposed they felt an obligation to the Jewish landlords and neighbours who had given them their first break with a rented room and a job after the Toronto restrictions on Japanese Canadians were lifted.

On weekends, he just seemed like any normal dad, allowing himself to sleep until 8:00. After a luxurious breakfast of sizzling eggs and curling bacon, cooked by my accommodating mother, he then puttered in the backyard garden, disappeared into the basement from time to time, and took care of outside chores like buying the groceries or cleaning eaves. My parents walked to and from the Japanese stores from Bay to Spadina on Dundas.

I liked the area. Chinatown was traditionally hidden behind City Hall downtown, but by the 1960s and '70s, its strictly immigrant residents began migrating to the Garment District where we lived. The rent and house prices were far cheaper. So only a scattering of white faces roamed the local streets.

The Art Gallery of Ontario anchored the east end of Sullivan

Street, where it butted into Beverley Street, the border between high culture and immigrant frugality. I made many friends, mostly Chinese, some Jewish Canadian. The Tabuchis owned a confectionary store on Sullivan at Huron, smack in the middle of that stretch of working-class homes. North of the store, the hustle and bustle of Dundas Avenue claimed its aortic status in Toronto.

As kids, I always hung out with Glenn and sometimes his younger brother. I don't think his parents liked me coming in because Glenn always told me to help myself to the candy and bags of potato chips. His father just glared at me and his older son as I did so. His eyes stabbed me with guilt. Didn't stop me, but I felt guilty about it.

At the Toronto Buddhist Church, a streetcar and a short walk away, I would catch up with The Boys on Sundays and make plans for the following weekend. Don't know why, since we all lived in different parts of the city. Glenn and I lived downtown. Boku's parents started at Spadina and Dundas, but then Boku and his sister were born and then initially raised in the city's east end before moving out to Agincourt; other families followed to West Hill, Rexdale, and Etobicoke. We got together most Sundays, though by the mid- to late-1980s, The Boys became mostly Glenn, Boku, and me. In the '90s, no one came to service.

AT THE MOMENT, however, I was just fine being with Naoko. I chose to be with her on Sundays. We spent many weeks since that party together at her place poring over the pages and inputting the translation into her computer and printing it out. At least, she did. Other issues came to my mind. Why did he write everything in Japanese? He studied business at UBC, not Japanese. He could speak, naturally enough, because his parents, my grandparents, spoke little else. But as far as I knew he didn't write Japanese. And who was Chiemi? Did she even exist? My eyes throbbed with pain the more I thought about it.

Bloor Street outside and below Naoko's apartment was grey with dirty city snow, the imprint of civilization. The winter wind fluttered awnings, flags, and banners. People bundled in heavy coats shuffled along the sidewalk careful not to slip and fall on black ice. Cars skidded along the asphalt.

Naoko's one-room student apartment was across from the Country Style Hungarian Restaurant, the last of the Eastern European diners that dotted the street and represented a refuge for poor students who wanted a nice night out with friends or a date. By the '90s, Country Style with its basic 1950s dining furniture and old-world posters and paintings on the walls upped its prices without modernizing, save for the refrigerated dessert cabinet at the front. Really fit in with the Bohemian-chic style of the neighbourhood.

Her apartment looked like a place furnished by a student on a budget. Rickety, rescued wooden chairs, skeletal and painted beige. There was a perfunctory kitchen area kept clean as most Japanese would keep it. The bathroom, just off the kitchen, was another story, but it was old and worn from years of rentals. The apartment was a throwback to the 1970s when I was at university as an undergraduate student, but there were unique features that were strictly contemporary. Her desk had no use for chairs since its legs were cut low to the ground, a touch of hip Japanese style. Only a *zabuton*, patterned with some Edo-period design, offered sitting comfort. The bed too consisted of just the mattress, *ofuton* style on the floor. It brought back the old days in The Camp, a commune house of the Asian Canadian Student Movement, when I was considered a radical, an *Aka*. I liked the cool factor of her place so much I refurnished my own bedroom in my mom's house.

There were makeshift shelves of piled red bricks and two-by-four planks found somewhere on a renovation site or garbage pile, lining the bottom third of the walls. Loads of school texts, but there were some novels and books of poetry: the *Norton Anthology of English Literature*, Joyce's *Ulysses*, Faulkner's *Light in August*, Eliot's *The Waste Land*, and Stevens' *Collected* to name a few. I don't know if she had read all or any of these, though some were well thumbed (perhaps from a used bookstore), or even if she understood what she did read; it was an impressive library, nonetheless. We never discussed any of the books. What was curious was her field of anthropology, not English literature, yet no texts on bones and antiquities, prehistoric civilizations graced the shelves. Not even one on mushrooms.

She adorned the walls with culturally appropriate posters — Bruce Lee, Kurosawa's *Seven Samurai*, Haruki Murakami's *Dance Dance Dance*, and Yukio Mishima in military uniform, *hachimaki* and drawn sword. When I asked about the latter, "Mishima-*sensei*..." was all she said in a wistful and sad manner.

A record player sat glumly on a milk crate, gasping for breath in the onslaught of the oncoming digital age. It had two small detachable speakers and a heavy, crude needle that could rip a vinyl record into pieces within a dozen spins. It was one of her "hiding luxuries" as she called it. Albums strewn about featured no title beyond 1976.

So, what was with this Tokyo girl living on the edge of retro-poverty? I mean her father, as I found out, was a VP of Mitsui Corporation, assigned to its Canadian head office in Montreal as president. As an only child, she would've been indulged by her parents; I could only reason that she wanted to make it on her own. Either that or they had a husband in the wings for her in Japan and she exited stage left but quick. Don't know for sure, since she never revealed her past to me except surface facts. I didn't mind, I liked it. She was intelligent, unpretentiously beautiful, and politically aware, or so I fantasized. Made us part of the Radical Chic — like John and Yoko.

Our time together was heavenly. By midwinter, I walked into the apartment with a proprietary sense and we settled quickly with a bottle of beer each at her low-riding desk. She put on *Sweet Baby James* followed by *Blue*. Seemed appropriate somehow as she flipped the pages, calling attention to the sentences she wanted me to understand.

Most times I was distracted. Her perfume, a patchouli and flower mix, materialized like an uninvited but welcomed guest. After a while, it seemed to wrap around me like her arms. The closer I sat to her, the aroma of her smooth, unblemished skin and plentiful black hair usurped the hippie patchouli. Then there were her eyes. The tingle became ever-present.

She seldom looked at me full in the face, but when she did, I was drawn into the bright rapturous depths of those eyes. I was sure she knew it too, but we did nothing. I engaged instead in casual innuendo, like complimenting her every chance I had or "accidentally" brushing against an arm or leg. We also talked about her eyes and their effect on people, men especially.

"Don't you know how they make men feel?" I asked cautiously.

"It make them drop things." She smiled knowingly.

I smiled at the intimate reminiscence. "Aren't you curious as to why?"

She concluded the subject by not answering and returning to the diary. I let it go, sensing her discomfort.

THERE CAME A NIGHT I couldn't stand it anymore. I pushed the diary away and took her in my arms. Overwhelmed, I kissed her urgently. I risked it all. *Go for broke!* Passion took over, electricity crackled. She didn't cry out, shudder in revulsion, or push me away. I felt myself shaking so I closed my eyes and went blind, except that I saw her prism eyes, glowing and staring at me. The tingling intensified and crushed my heart.

The soft padding of her footsteps led me to the mattress futon. As she slid out of her Bob Dylan T-shirt and worn blue jeans, the curves, hills, and valleys of her shoulders, breasts, and hips completed what I had only imagined before. We fell to the mattress. Sensations of pleasure ensued.

Afterwards, we lay in a heap within a white landscape of Egyptian sheets and pillows, another luxury she didn't deny herself. Her skin glowed, steaming and cooling in the bare apartment air.

I turned my gaze away from the architecture of her legs to her window, a source of light, the separation of worlds: warmth and cold, colour and grey. A single layer of smudged glass held back the streetscape: hard, inhospitable concrete and asphalt; tired buildings leaning into the wind; trees bent in defeat; men trundling toward jobs inside bike repair shops, countertop diners, and used bookstores; women swallowed by oversized coats cowering with babies in carriages and heading home to frigid hallways and empty bedrooms.

The window held in a fantastic dimension of serenity, mystery, and smooth female touch. It was marked by hipster privation — funky furniture, Japanese herbal teas, and crunchy packets of Sapporo Ichiban, all underwritten by parental coffers. It was a bastion of countercultural artifacts, the Last Poets chanting a hypnotic East Harlem rap, Patti Smith chewing and spitting out poetry. It was Naoko's apartment, replete with kisses, intertwining limbs, our naked bodies.

And my father's words.

> *Shamed into carrying a card that labelled me, branded me as the enemy, I looked for salvation. Invisible ropes kept me from standing up straight; they pulled me down to the ground with every effort. The frustration of my tightening fists resisting the tension made my face flame red with torment. Did I hear the fluttering of wings? No dreams. Not one dream. Just a blank blackness fills my sleep.*
>
> *I ache for a dream ... of her. To see her rise before me, envelop me in her embrace and draw me to the glory of sunlight and balmy breezes.*
>
> *– March 1941*

7.

Summer 1987

So it was that Glenn and I waited for Boku outside our latest favourite resto, Bumpkins, a unique French *boîte* on Parliament Street in the heart of Cabbagetown, on that clear night in that summer of crime and confusion. The meeting was really happening. I don't mind saying I was nervous. I had to hand it to Glenn, he had the balls to talk to Boku after his arrest and new-found notoriety. It would've been too much for me, risking embarrassment and shame for him and me.

Bumpkins was the centrepiece of the area's gentrification. Houses renovated by yuppie incomes and tastes reflected a cognoscenti that shunned the upscale, overpriced, and stuffy places in Leaside and Rosedale. They wanted civilized and different, simpler yet stylish, dining emporiums. No china ware and champagne crystal eateries for that crowd.

Bumpkins had been a favourite of ours since late-university days: unpretentious, relatively cheap, yet it appealed to our heightened sense of culinary sophistication. It was decorated in the rustic South-of-France style, or so we presumed. The walls were made of knotted wood rescued from dilapidated barns. The floor consisted of unadorned wooden slats. Picnic tables were lined up in two parallel rows, one butt-ended to the next. There were no strangers in the place by the end of the meal.

And there had been the ever-present Edith Piaf. Her insistent and plaintive pale-blue French voice filled the place with much love, sorrow, and painful loss.

The menu was rotated through the week, giving the impression of different fare every day with ingredients bought fresh that morning at the St. Lawrence Farmers' Market. The ever-changing chalkboard remained testament to that. We always tried to hit the night they served garlic scampi — light yet meaty, miniature lobster tails. The prices were remarkable. The most expensive dish was $5.00, perfect for a university student's budget when he wanted to splurge. Not bad too for those of us at the start of a career.

Boku's love of the restaurant had extended to the waitress Kiki, who was the cook and co-owner's wife. He claimed she reminded him of Brigitte Bardot with pouting lips, curvaceous body, and long, thick hair (brunette in Kiki's case). She also had a fiery personality, which made her even more attractive to my criminal pal. She was constantly fighting with her husband in the back kitchen. Hardly private arguments, she could be heard crying from time to time, something that in the past had alarmed Boku.

"Maybe I should do something," he once said with conviction. He stood up in anger.

"Stay out of it," I had advised.

He had sat back down with a worried face.

While waiting for Boku, Glenn and I mostly remained silent, failing to address the proverbial elephant in the room.

"This place ain't the same," Glenn finally said.

"Yeah, it's changed. Kiki's gone. The menu too...different." The place was under new management, a couple of the waiters took over, and they tried to maintain the feel of the place, but it proved impossible. Food costs had just become too high to keep prices low. The scampi was gone. The chalkboard was still there, but it never changed. No one even made a gesture to the past by erasing the board occasionally. It hung as a plaque to the glory days. It was like some petroglyph unreflective of what was on offer.

"What the hell is beef heart?"

"Beef heart?"

"Yeah, it's right here," Glenn said as he pointed to the item in the printed menu. He clenched his jaw, upsetting its clean line.

"I guess it's heart of beef," I said, smiling.

"Hey, wise guy, I ain't eating something that was beating yesterday," he declared as a new waitress, a pretty girl with scrubbed Maritime looks, lit our tea candle.

"Hello, ladies," interrupted a familiar voice. It was Boku, neatly dressed in an Applebee plaid shirt, khakis, and brown loafers. He didn't look worse-for-wear given his recent jail time.

"*Hello, ladies*?" Glenn questioned rising to the jocular tone. "That's my line."

"Hey, I'm not the one sitting with his boyfriend by candle-light."

Our dinner started well. It somehow felt like the old days even without Kiki. Boku ordered the mussels as an appetizer for the table: a wonderful treat with the morsels swimming in butter, garlic, and sea broth. It was accompanied by fresh, crusty French bread, no butter as was the custom of the place. Olive oil only. As a main course, Glenn feasted on the pasta; Boku yearned for the traditional scampi, but settled on chicken caesar salad, and I dared to order the beef heart.

"It tastes just like steak!" I claimed.

"Settle down, Nancy," Glenn admonished.

I called for white wine in a carafe. It came with a bottle of lemon infused water, the first restaurant in the city to do so.

While eating, a beaming Glenn launched into a vivid description of his new apartment off Spadina, north of Chinatown — "Around Davenport," he emphasized.

"Hey, near the church," I observed. "You'll be there more often then."

"As if," he answered.

It was all light and flowers until dessert.

"So, Boku," Glenn started casually. "Why'd you do it?"

Boku laughed immoderately at the abrupt change of subject.

Glenn and I looked at each other, nonplussed by the outburst.

"Glenn, you are something," Boku said as he chortled and then choked on his crème brûlée. "You cut through the bullshit faster than a pig snuffling for truffles."

"What're you, a poet?" Glenn rejoined. "Your parents make bail? Of course, they did. Man, you owe them so much. So, why'd you rob a bank? Come on, give. It's not like you need the cash."

"I'm an epistemological detective," he stated rather flatly again.

As Glenn screwed his face up, I interjected, "You said that before. You're still playing the detective, are you? But what does that mean?"

"I did it to be my grandfather."

"What does *pissing* have to do with your grandfather?" Glenn asked out of his woeful ignorance.

"You should read more," Boku rejoined. "Epistemological."

"Never mind him," I said, dismissing Glenn with a wave of the hand. "What do you mean 'be' your grandfather?" I could feel my face flushing red. I hadn't understood that line in 1984 and I didn't understand it now.

"He was wrongly arrested for something he didn't do."

"When?" Glenn asked.

"World War II."

"Wait a minute, you robbed a bank to get the money your grandparents lost because of the war?" I asked.

"Yes and no."

He was as clear as a San Francisco fog. "What kind of explanation is that?"

"I wanted to ascertain his experience," he continued. "It's a philosophical investigation."

"Again, what?"

"Why're you talking like that?" Glenn asked.

Boku ignored the question. "He was arrested and jailed because of his face. It wasn't for anything he did."

"Yeah, so?"

"Well, I was arrested for something I didn't do. Just like him. And I'll probably be convicted and put in jail just because they said I did."

Glenn's brain must have been reeling, as mine was. With puffed cheeks, Glenn breathed out slowly.

I looked at Boku, scanning his face for the tell of a joke. He was known for his pranks, after all. He wasn't this time. "What are you talking about?"

"They say I robbed a bank. You both think I did simply because they said I did."

Glenn said, "You mean the cops?"

"Yeah, the cops."

"Take it easy, Glenn," I assured. "Let Boku talk."

"I really had no intention of robbing that bank ... taking or keeping the money."

"But you just said you did it to avenge your grandfather."

"Calling attention to the original crime against my grandfather by the powers-that-be was enough to get it into the papers, but I had no desire to take the money."

"This is crazy," Glenn proclaimed in exasperation. "How much you get?"

"For what?"

"Robbing the bank, idiot."

"Glenn, I told you I didn't rob the bank."

Leaning closer to Boku, I wanted further clarification. "But you tried to rob that bank."

"So they say, so you say," he said pausing before continuing. "Did I take any money? No. Did I try to make an escape? No. Did I even put up a fight? No."

"Then why'd you do it?" Glenn asked with a raised voice.

"I'm ascertaining history, not studying it," Boku said conclusively.

Glenn ignored the assertion and asked, exasperated, "How could you do that to your mother?"

8.

1990–1991

Naoko became much more relaxed around me. She looked me straight in the eyes, smiled when she saw me, and revealed her thoughts.

"*Mis-tah Maiko*, I have strong feeling for you," she began. "I feel you are like your father. I mean, sensitive and full of thought."

"Okay, but I doubt it. And call me 'Mike,' okay?"

She smiled. She just seemed like a different person.

If truth be told, I had "strong feeling" for her, too. The allure of those eyes grew beyond my first experience of them. That tingling within me grew stronger as time passed. Once during a winter afternoon when the sky was thick, yet clear, like blue honey, I caught her profile in the light as she moved to put the kettle on for tea. A warmth came over my body. It was almost overwhelming. She turned to face me, and her eyes grew in my imagination until they seemed like hypnotic discs. I filled up with wonder.

I talked about her to Glenn more than once. I didn't dare introduce him to her, and for good reason. After one long confessional about her, he took me aside to ask if she had any friends. I was incredulous and tried to put him off.

"What in the world would you have in common with a Japanese student working on her PhD?"

"Hey, I like smart chicks."

From that moment, I vowed never to inflict any of The Boys on her.

I did take her home for Oshougatsu 1991. I was nervous of what she might think, a man in his thirties living with his mom. Then again, the Japanese and Japanese Canadians really don't expect their children to move out until they marry. Naoko was out, but she was a student; she got a pass, I'm sure.

The pewter sky was oppressive as we shuffled along Sullivan Street from the Art Gallery streetcar stop at Beverley Street. The sidewalk was hard, brittle, and unyielding, but the bare trees bent over slightly as if to welcome us. The front yards and gardens were empty since there had been no snow since last November when the first fall came as a flurry, but didn't stick.

We walked hand-in-hand (or rather glove-in-mitten) even though it was as cold as a "well-digger's ass." From within her heavy coat and hood, Naoko kept looking at the house numbers zipping past, anxious to find my mom's place. I peered into the surrounding darkness, imagining the shadows of "Little Tokyo" accompanying us.

It actually wasn't called "Little Tokyo" or "Japantown" or "J-Town" back in the 1950s and '60s. It was just the neighbourhood where we first lived. Every Nikkei individual and institution started life in Toronto there. The Watadas lived on McCaul Street; the Ishidas, Matsubas, Kiyonagas, Nakamuras, Sugiuras, Tabuchis, and so many more lived on adjoining streets. The first Toronto Buddhist church started in a row house on Huron St.; the Reverend Tsuji and his wife lived in the crowded space; the planning of the Buddhist Church on Bathurst took place there, as did that of the Japanese Canadian Cultural Centre. Members of the various *kenjinkai* and the political arm of the community, the Japanese Canadian Citizens' Association, met in the back-room of the Nikko Garden Restaurant. *The New Canadian* and the *Continental Times*, both on Queen Street near Spadina, kept churning out weekly issues with community news for a shrinking subscriber base. Nikkei businesses sprang up within the confines: the Tsuji brothers opened an auto repair garage in a back alley — illegal, but it made money; a Japanese and later English language bookstore operated by Kameoka-*san* ran out of his house on Sullivan St.; the Kawasaki's corner store, with three young brothers always fighting, sat at Huron and Dundas; the food co-op nearby operated by the Buddhist Church eventually turned into Furuya, a Japanese grocery store, with a sombre Mr. Ishida as the butcher and a smiling and friendly Mrs. Ishida on the fish counter; perched above was Nikko Garden, the first formal-dining Japanese restaurant in Toronto, owned and run by Gus and Jim Kadonaga, brothers who hated each other (so much so that Gus acted as maître d' while Jim worked in the back, or was it the opposite?); the farthest outpost east was the Ginza Café, at Bay and Dundas, where anyone could get *teishoku, ochazuke,* and *denbatsuke* at the long counter. Other Japanese grocery stores opened and spread out around the nexus of Spadina and Dundas: Sandown Market, Sanko Trading, and the venerable Dundas Union. Harry Sugimoto, his family stuck in a house on Dundas so narrow you could touch each wall by spreading your arms, would soon open Danforth Cleaners in the east end when he made a little money. Dr. Kuwabara, family doctor, and Dr. Nakashima, a dentist, were together at Spadina and Bloor. The Nikkei youth also had fun: the Nisei Club staged parties, like the Harvest Dance, the Sadie Hawkins Do, and the Christmas Social, at the Hagermann Hall located right in the heart of the original Chinatown, much to the dismay of their Issei elders who frowned on "touch dancing"; bowling and ice-hockey leagues formed; Sansei attended Japanese language classes twice a week at the YMCA at College and Yonge.

The Nikkei would not move into the suburbs (near and far) until later when racist tensions and restrictions eased. If they ended up living in the same neighbourhood, never mind street, it was by pure happenstance. Most families did not want to be "Japanese Canadian" by that point. All the Issei, Nisei homes, businesses and institutions were gone or virtually gone by the '90s, becoming ghosts haunting me as childhood memories does everyone.

The New Year's feast had become a little sad, with no one coming over to visit; friends and relatives stopped just before the 1990s. Mom made a small amount of sushi: futomaki and *agezushi* only. She also prepared a smattering of tempura, morsels of char shiu (bought at Golden City no doubt), and a plate of chow mein (Japanese Canadian style). There was a pot of steamed rice, a staple. We weren't iconoclasts after all. But gone were the days of abundant delicacies, though Boku's mom and others still put on the hog. I stopped going given what happened to my pal. Besides, I was no longer invited; and I understood. Too embarrassed since I knew too much.

Naoko was all smiles as I opened the front door and we took off our shoes in the hallway. I followed her down the long dark hall to the dining room in the back. Okaasan greeted her with as much warmth as she could muster. My mother's eroded face, thinning hair, and the slight stoop of her back slowed her down to a shuffle.

Naoko bowed and said something in Japanese while presenting her host with a bouquet of flowers.

I could see Okaasan was pleased, surprised, even uplifted by my girlfriend. She always encouraged me to bring home my romantic interests, though I always suspected she wanted to check them out, make sure they were the "right kind." *You can marry anyone you want as long as she's Japanese,* she used to say. Though it was early in our relationship, I decided to bring Naoko home. She was the first, and it felt right.

Okaa made the effort to bring clean plates to the table when Naoko jumped up to help. "No, no, you sit. Michael, help me," she commanded.

"Oh right, sorry."

We spent a pleasant hour or two celebrating New Year's and my perceived escape from celibacy. With the final *ogochisou-sama*, my mother pulled me aside. "Michael, you had better be careful with this one."

"Why?"

"Well, she's Japanese."

"I thought you'd be pleased."

"Yes, but you aren't used to such girls. They are different from 'Canadian' girls. They're not spoiled Sansei."

"You're nuts, Ma." She wanted me to date Japanese, and now that I was, she seemed to be telling me to dump her.

"Michael!" she said and grabbed my arm.

"Yeah, Ma."

"She's not what she seems."

My mother was always having visions; she was "sensitive" to otherworldly forces. She knew I was going to break my leg, for example. The evening before my football game back in high school, she pleaded with me not to play. I dismissed her warning, since it was a championship game. And as foretold, I broke my leg, tackling the fullback for the opposition.

The worst of her predictions came the night before Dad left for Northern Ontario. She had a dream and woke up screaming. I hurried to her bedroom to find Dad comforting her.

Four ghosts had risen through the floorboards at the foot of her bed, and started nattering at her. What they said was incomprehensible, but she knew something evil had entered our lives.

My parents argued about it the next day, but Dad wouldn't hear of it and departed.

It wasn't like Mom went to fortune tellers in Chinatown, but she was always worried about things based on her visions.

I had no idea what her warning about Naoko meant, but I was so happy I dismissed her perception as superstition. I will admit there was something about Naoko and her effect on me.

IN GRANGE PARK, bleak with the burden of winter and the lateness of the evening, Naoko and I huddled and walked to the University Subway. The chill of dark winter enveloped us in a lace of frost, the distant houses and building lights in their crystalline sparkle made the air brittle, skin-scraping, and fragile.

I wondered what Okaa meant by her warning. I dismissed it as a symptom of old age.

"The osechi was very good. Very authentic," Naoko offered.

I knew she was being polite.

After a pause, she continued, "Your okaasan is very nice, but she is sad."

"Yes, I suppose she is. Don't know why, other than Dad being gone."

"Does she know about diary?"

"Yeah, kinda. She won't even look at it."

She fell quiet before she spoke again. "Why not?"

"Don't know. It probably has something to do with his death . . . crashing in a plane north of Lake Superior."

"Why he go there?" she asked demurely.

Why indeed. The thought of it brought back old feelings, old mysteries and questions, old pain.

"Don't know. Searching for something, I guess. Maybe Mom will tell me, at the *proper juncture*," I said in a mocking Wodehouse tone.

She smiled and turned away for fear of prying. In point of fact, I just didn't know the truth. No one can ever know his father completely, but I craved to know a little of my father's truth. The danger for me, the fear I had, was that the truth would ring hollow.

As I kissed Naoko goodnight before her apartment door, I noticed that the tingling feeling within me was gone. I turned and headed back home.

IN THE DAYS and weeks thereafter, as Naoko and I went deeper into his words, we discarded most of the text since it was either too hard to decipher or seemingly unimportant. What we did salvage struck an odd chord with me. It was as if Dad was conveying a message to me, though there was no direct address to me or anyone else, family or friends. By this point, I was intrigued enough to keep urging Naoko for more and more information.

I could only go so far and came to a dead end. It was then I decided to talk to Mom.

"I didn't know Dad knew Japanese," I asked her one late afternoon when the light had dulled, and rain clouds threatened. She sat in her favourite chair knitting.

"He spent some time in Japan," she said curtly.

"When was that? I don't remember him going."

"Before you," was all she said.

"Can you give me some details? Like why, when, and where?"

"Ask your uncle."

She meant Uncle Kunio out in Vancouver. He was my courtesy uncle, since I had no real ones.

"Right...who's Chiemi? She's all over the book." I stretched the truth to make my point.

Mom's face froze in a kind of surprise and subdued horror.

"Okaa? Who is Chiemi? Someone you know? Someone..."

She curled up into a ball of silence and avoidance.

9.

Summer 1987

After that bizarre dinner at Bumpkins, Glenn and I retreated home in his car. Boku's cryptic words continued to swirl in my brain: "epistemological detective," "ascertaining history." I got it, he's a detective looking for truth — the experience of the internment. To be his grandfather. But where did he get such phrases? It wasn't natural from him. Did they justify what he did? He did rob a bank. *They say I did; you say I did.* I repeated his words over and over in my head. He really believed he didn't rob a bank. It must be a smokescreen. He was lying to cover-up his true intention. Maybe.

Glenn decided to stay in the old neighbourhood that night; he must've been feeling confused and insecure and needed to be close to his own. I could see Boku's actions shook Glenn to his core. "My mom gave me so much. She did everything for me," Glenn had once said.

We talked, but drew no closer to understanding Boku's motives for robbing that bank. He didn't need the money.

"Is he psycho or what?" Glenn blurted out after we parked and walked toward our respective homes.

"You always say that," I answered. "Everyone is 'psycho' if you don't understand them."

"Right, as if you don't."

"Sorry, I don't mean to be critical. I think Boku has lost it. He's delusional. He tried to rob the bank, but he didn't because he had no intention of robbing it. He won't admit the obvious. If that's not delusional, I don't know what is."

"Do you think he's crazy?" asked Glenn.

"I can't believe it," I concluded. "And don't go around saying he is."

"How could he do that to his mom?"

WHEN THE SUGIURA FAMILY could afford a down-payment for a semi-detached house in a suitable area, they had moved out of their third-floor walk-up on McCaul Street to Old Riverdale, in a side street south of Greenwood and Gerrard, a long-time working-class neighbourhood. Boku's paternal grandfather, Haruo, stayed in the Spadina/Dundas area, while his maternal grandma came to live with them once they moved to Scarborough when the Sugiura grandchildren went to university. I don't know where she was before, most likely in the Huron Street area, though I never saw her there.

Both Boku and his sister Elaine attended Jarvis Collegiate, like Glenn and me. They didn't live in the district, but their parents wanted a "good education" for them at a top-flight, but inexpensive, school. As I said, I fell for Elaine when I saw her doing *Alabama* with the rest of the cheerleading squad. Gyrating hips and doing the splits were pretty sexy for high school.

I had first met them and all my other JC friends at the Toronto Buddhist Church. We were in the various youth clubs: The Boys and The Girls Clubs, Taruna, Jr. YBA and TYBA, short for the Toronto Young Buddhists Association. Though the church welcomed all who were interested in the *dharma*, most of the members were Nikkei. Our parents and grandparents wanted us to remain Japanese and to know something of our culture and traditions; thus, the church founders made the place as Japanese as possible so that only the most rabid of Japanophiles ever dared to walk through the front doors.

Boku's grandmother also wanted her grandchildren to be Japanese; she said so in no uncertain terms. *"He will not be Canadian! He will remain loyal,"* she had pronounced in her best Japanese. Not sure why she was so nationalistic. Japan, after all, had lost the war.

By the time Boku, two years my junior, and I both made university, his family had fully established themselves in the burbs, but maintained their connection to the downtown church. They dutifully made the hour-and-a-bit trek by car every Sunday. Parking was scarce, but they managed to attend.

Boku seemed like any normal kid, though I didn't really hang out with him until well into high school. Maybe I wanted to get an "in" with his sister. I don't know, but by Grade 13, we were the best of friends, though he was forever pulling pranks, especially on his friends at church: like stirring a spoon in hot tea, leaving it awhile, and then taking it out to press against someone's hand (usually mine). It scalded the skin. My reaction? A swift punch to his shoulder.

His favourite practical jokes involved feigning homosexuality. He would surreptitiously grab one of The Boys' hands and then try to kiss him on the cheek. Perhaps he enjoyed the discomfort produced, especially in Glenn. He was lucky no one reacted with more than a punch to the shoulder.

Perhaps he was gay, some speculated. Others, like me, disputed that, especially when he started dating Cathy. A church girl and high-school classmate, they hung out together at the church, like everyone else, but they didn't start dating until near the end of university days. She took physical education and Boku majored in computer science. In hindsight, I suspect he hooked up with her because it was time, pressure from his grandmother, and Cathy was convenient. She would have him.

Was he overcompensating? Some of The Boys thought so. I did notice some changes in Cathy's appearance at that time: she started wearing heavy mascara and eyeliner, long eyelashes and ruby-red lipstick. No low-cut tops, but she wore micro-miniskirts and she unbound her usual ponytail to let the hair fall and pool on her shoulders. She also started teetering on high heels, even when going to class. It simply wasn't her. I did ask her why, but she just shrugged.

One day, I caught up with Boku in the university Student Common Room at Hart House.

"Hey man, what's with Cathy and the Halloween makeup?" I was subtle in those days.

"Yeah, doesn't she look great?" he answered with as straight a face as a Catholic in confession.

"What do you mean?"

"Just like a hooker."

"Wait a minute. You want her to look like —"

"A hooker, yeah."

"Why?"

"Get her away from her fresh-faced-high-school-jock look. You know what I mean? We're in university for Christ's sake."

Maybe he was overcompensating, but then a visible change came over him. Perhaps it was Cathy's rebellion that started it. She was tired of the unnatural look — unnatural for her anyway. She got to the point where she just wasn't comfortable in the streetwalker garb. Shame became the better part of valour. Boku acquiesced to her complaint and soon broke up with her.

BOKU BECAME A different guy. From the moment he entered the University of Toronto, his ambition was to become a doctor, like two of his uncles, Mickey and Yogi (yes, named after the Yankee heroes). But he developed a different view of life after Cathy.

"Doctors," he said with disgust, "all they want is money. You take my Uncle Yogi. All he ever talks about is his boat, his Rolex, and his trophy huk wife."

"Never mind that," I interjected. "Why'd you dump Cathy?"

"No reason."

"Come on."

"She doesn't know how to use *hashi*."

"Really, she could learn if it's that important to you."

"She acts like a real princess. She ordered beef and greens on me and just let it sit there. Didn't take one bite. And she smiled at me the whole time!"

"That's the reason?" I didn't believe it was merely over a rice dish at the Golden City.

"She's just too ordinary," he concluded.

"Ordinary? Is that why you tarted her up?"

"Hey, shut up! That's no way to talk about her."

"But you said she —"

"I was wrong!" he snapped. "I was wrong."

I had never seen him so worked up about Cathy. I knew he loved her; he just couldn't see a future with her. What Cathy wanted was a conventional life: two cars, condo at first, and then two kids, just like Dave and Joanie, only she added two vacations, the eventual ranch-style suburban house, and maybe a cottage up at Wasaga or some place. Boku was to have a good career, not a job, and come home every day for dinner with weekends off. Medicine would do, ideally, with the extra Wednesday off. They could join a country club to play golf or tennis as leisure activities, be active at the church and JCCC, and maybe join her parents' Nisei bowling league (they needed younger members). She could shop at some high-end mall like the Bayview Shopping Centre (never the exclusive couture-infested Yorkville, since that was below Eglinton Avenue) and he could take care of the family Accord or Camry. A Mercedes or Lexus later.

But not Boku. "What a waste of a life!" he contended. Instead he had a taste for something else, something out of the ordinary, possibly be of service to mankind. Social services, CUSO, Red Cross? No, too socialist as he put it. Something more in my line of thinking he joked — whatever that meant.

The first manifestation of the "new" Boku came a week later when I again ran into him in the Student Common Room. I didn't notice it at first, but eventually I spied a golden crucifix around his neck.

"Hey, what's with the Jesus T?" I asked.

"The what?"

"The crucifix," I said, pointing to the object shining in the harsh fluorescent light.

"Have some respect," he chastised. "I've joined the Catholic Church."

"The Catholic...? Are you nuts?"

His was a strictly Buddhist family. His paternal grandfather had been a prominent member back in Vancouver. He helped establish the first temple in Canada. His mother was the president of the Toronto *Dana*, the women's club, and his father was a stalwart of the *Sangha*, the men's club. His sister would date white boys, sure, but she would never consider getting serious with one — he would have to be Buddhist at the very least.

So Boku becoming a Catholic was as incongruous as... well, me becoming one.

"I needed something in my life," he explained.

"So, you picked a religion that doesn't even let you read its manual?"

"What are you talking about?" he said angrily.

"You know, you can't read the Bible. The priest has to interpret it for you."

"Christians read the Bible."

"Catholics don't."

"Shut it. You don't know."

"I mean it, man. What do your parents think?"

He walked away flashing a grin back at me.

I stood awestruck and then called after him. "You didn't tell them?"

"I'm off to Mass."

Boku, in retrospect, was forever doing stuff like that. Maybe he was truly searching for meaning, or he was just doing it to upset his family and friends.

Catholicism as it turned out didn't do it for him, so he turned to Anglicanism, Catholic-lite as I put it. Then he explored Amway, fantasy sports leagues, and even philately. I believe he would've joined the Red Hat Society if they let him. Then he found something he could sink his teeth into, so to speak.

IT STARTED WHEN Glenn, Boku, and I attended a dance at the JCCC back in the winter of 1982. The West Room, which constituted half of the bottom floor of the Centre, was decorated like an early 1980s disco. The room pulsated with the likes of Donna Summer, KC & the Sunshine Band, and the Bee Gees' *Saturday Night Fever* soundtrack. The crowd was large with Sansei.

The girls were alluring with long hair, flashy clothing, and heavy makeup. Trend-following girls wanting to be stylish women. They waited patiently in groups for something, anything, to happen. The boys stood against the painted cement block walls scanning the room for a dance partner, possibly a life partner.

Glenn strode in with the confidence of a made career, a late-model sports car, and a sharp-looking, narrow-lapelled jacket and thin tie from Le Château Men's Wear. He immediately spied me and Boku sitting at one of the large foldout wooden tables. The dance floor at the vacant end of the room throbbed with a loud bass line and flickered in the strobe and multi-hued lights.

"Yo, girlfriends, what's happening?"

Boku nursed his beer, but he seemed agitated as if something was bothering him. "That's getting a bit tired."

"What's with Sally?" he asked me. "He on the rag?"

"Shut it, Glenn."

"All right, but I'm not gonna say anything about you two holding hands in the dark," he said with a grin. After a pause waiting for a reaction, he continued, "So what's doing?"

"Nothing much," I said.

"Why aren't you out on the floor?"

"No one inspires."

"No, I meant you two together." He laughed.

"Didn't you hear me?" Boku snapped. "You're not —"

"You aren't funny, Glenn," I said calmly.

"Hey, so so-or-ry," he sang. "I didn't mean anything by it."

"Sorry, Glenn," Boku apologized. "I'm just tired of this...this being stag hanging out with guys all the time."

I wanted to remind him of Cathy, but that was a wound freshly cut.

Glenn smirked in a mischievous way. "Let's make this interesting, then."

"What do you mean?" I asked.

"Let's have a contest. Ten bucks from each to the one who can pick up the ugliest girl."

"Are you ever going to grow up?"

"C'mon, Mike, it'll be fun."

"Count me out," I said, and left the table. Glenn, like Boku, liked to play practical jokes. The difference lay in the quality of the joke. Boku's were somewhat witty, if cruel. Glenn's were crude, if sometimes cruel. A heated discussion soon attracted my attention. It was between Dave and Joanie.

"You never want to do anything out of your comfort zone," Joanie accused.

Dave just shrugged.

"What's the controversy?" I asked when joining them.

"Dave wants to keep working at his father's place instead of going to college."

"It's good money," Dave insisted.

"Yes, but there's no future."

"Sure, there is. Look at my old man. He's manager, got a company car, four weeks' vacation, pension coming —"

"Yes, that's good for him, but you can do better with education."

"I got an education."

"High school. What can you get with that? Tell him, Michael."

"Aw, I'm getting a beer," Dave said as he stood to leave the table. "You want one, Mike?"

"Sure." I hunkered down with Joanie.

"See what I mean? He just shuts down and walks away."

"Yeah, but you've got to give him some space. Let him think it's his idea. You've sown the seed, now see if it grows."

"Mike, you win!" came a voice shouting over the din.

I turned and there was Glenn grinning at me. "Win what?"

"The contest," he explained, slapped my shoulder, and guffawed as he walked away.

"What was that?" Joanie asked.

"Nothing, he's just an asshole."

"Michael!" I always upset girls.

Later that evening, I punched Glenn in the shoulder hard. Before he could retaliate, Boku made a proposal. "Let's have a real contest."

"What?"

"In two weeks, let's meet at a restaurant, each with a date. The one who hasn't got one has to pay for everyone."

I balked. How was I going to pay for such a meal, since I didn't have any prospects? At the time, I was living on a TA's stipend while finishing off my MA thesis and doing whatever tutoring I could pick up.

"It's a challenge, I know, but it's better than an ugly-girl contest. That was just cold."

"You know me," Glenn answered. "It'll be a snap."

"Yeah, right," I said. "Wouldn't it be funny if you're the only one flying solo?"

"So, you're in?" Boku asked.

"Okay, okay." It was set then: two weeks and we would meet at Bumpkins with a date.

"One thing," Glenn warned as he turned to leave, "guy dates don't count!"

"Asshole," I said, stopping myself from running after him to smack his guffawing face.

AS IT HAPPENED, I waited with Cathy just inside Bumpkins at the appointed hour. I didn't care how Boku would feel. Didn't know what I was going to say to Cathy or Boku for that matter, but damned if I was going to pay for everyone.

I liked Cathy, just not in that way. We had known each other since Toronto Buddhist Church and high school days. Yes, Boku was right, she was a jock with a princess complex. Always wearing her hair in a ponytail, she usually wore Reebok sneakers, a Polo golf shirt, and a sweater that was tied around her neck, so the arms could drape demurely across her breasts. I liked her short skirts, displaying well her pampered, but working-class-athletically-muscled legs, but she sat so prim and proper her back was as painfully straight as the spine of the CN Tower.

She expected certain things. Every door had to be held open for her; every date must be dressed appropriate to the occasion; every date must come with a corsage or a single rose if nothing else; every date must include transportation (streetcar tickets at the very least); every greeting must be accompanied with a compliment; there must be no swearing during the evening; every movie must be her choice; every bill must be picked up by her date.

She lived just south of the Art Gallery of Ontario, in a semi-detached house with a green roof needing replacement, so picking her up wasn't much of a hardship.

Eventually Glenn came along with another of his long line of quickly forgotten girls, and we waited. After a half hour, there was no sign of Boku. It was clear he wasn't going to show.

We sat down at a window table and enjoyed the evening with the house specialty: scampi. The conversation was civilized even if Glenn stewed in his anger.

10.

January 1991

The rain caught me by surprise. I felt it even in my sleep. It hurt, every drop a needle point piercing the skin. Blood-water flowed in rivulets, spreading to cover my face, chest and arms. But then the liquid evaporated into a light illuminating the room. And there she was, Chiemi, full of an aching, grievous beauty. Her sadness emanating from within. As I stood, my heart beat a riot of emotion and chaos. She started to fade, and I collapsed before her indistinct image. Darkness replaced the light and the calm of sanctuary came over me. I awoke to a different reality.

— December 7, 1941

Naoko and I decided to concentrate on only the dates that seemed significant, though at times that was a difficult task. December 7 was easy enough. Other dates not. Interpreting the imagery was still the hard part, if not impossible. I could see the Japanese Zeroes as the rain. The light? The darkness? Anyone's guess.

And who was Chiemi? The mystery drove me mad. Mom was the key, but that was easier said than done. The two of us were profoundly alone in the world. And ever since Dad died, I'd catch her in her bedroom facing the wall and sobbing softly. At times, I thought I heard her chanting.

I was so sad for my mother. If I missed Dad to my very soul, how did it affect my mom? In many ways she was lonelier than I was. There was nothing I could do to comfort her. Every time I tried, she would have none of it. Was this a Nikkei trait? We weren't a samurai family, though most thought they were.

I HAD GRANDPARENTS, most of them in Japan, but all banished from Canada after the war and most died before I was born in 1956. I know Dad's mom died of cancer, because we got a letter from family there. I had one grandfather here, my mom's father, but I didn't know him well, and he passed when I was very young. I did know he came back to Canada, after the voluntary exile to the homeland, in 1945 or thereabouts. Perhaps that was the first riddle: since he gave up any claim to Canadian citizenship, how did he get back into the country? Don't know what had happened to his wife, my grandma. My guess was that she died in Japan like Dad's, and so Grandpa moved back to Canada to be with family.

Other kids were spoiled by their *ojiichan* and obaachan — chocolates and ice cream cones whenever they visited. Toys bought on a whim. Extra rice at dinner. "You've got to grow tall!" All I got was a pity treat because I happened to be a friend of their grandchild. After I grew up, I saw that to be a parent was to say "No" most of the time, and my dad was good at that. I understood; I just wished I had a grandparent or two who owned a corner store like Glenn's family and who said "Yes" occasionally.

Besides absent grandparents, I had no aunts, uncles, and therefore cousins in Canada, some lived in Japan, but I didn't know them. I did have "courtesy" relatives: friends of the family who gave me Christmas and birthday presents, but never their favours when it counted, since I wasn't their responsibility; I wasn't related no matter how much I pretended I was or yearned for it. Reality always set me straight.

Life became worse without my dad. I missed out on all the activities: father/son banquets with the Boy Scouts, playing catch in the park, going to hockey games on early mornings, family birthdays, and community events. Not that that ever happened with my dad during my childhood, but I liked to think it would have. He wasn't that kind of father. I do have a recollection of walking with Dad hand-in-hand in a snowstorm in a park somewhere. I thought his hand was so big I was safe. To this day, the memory is agonizingly clear.

Most importantly, I missed all the advice he might've given me about life. Neither he nor I ever brought anything serious into the conversation, though by my teen years, I could've used his wise take on issues. He was a quiet man.

I often gazed at family photographs, looking for clues to the past, looking for a ghost of the present. Some of the photos were taken before the war, many after, but none during or just after, especially during Dad's unexplained trip to Japan. Still, the subtle features of his face drew closer to disappearing altogether. His voice too subsided to a whisper. I barely remembered its intonation.

With no one to talk to, I fell into a cup of silence in my own house. The past was a cast of anonymous people populating vague events and incidents. They were pictured in photographs, some so clear I could almost step in and be a part of the scene, but remained mute, impotent. No descriptors underneath or on the back.

Photos of my early teen years and before were properly collected and mounted in albums — mostly of my birthday parties held at home with one or two friends, Mom hovering over us with cake and ice cream. My father was never in any of them. He must have been behind the camera. There were a few of community picnics, organised by the Japanese Canadian Citizens League or the Buddhist Church, and the Eaton's Santa Claus Parade, oddly enough, since I had no memory of being there. But they too remained anonymous.

After Dad's death, I became entombed by the silence; I could do nothing but stare into my mother's worn face, scanning her features, the eyes and collapsing cheeks, and watch the crevices turn into ravines.

THE ONE CONVERSATION I had with Mom about her family was back in the early U of T days. She wasn't so bad then. The *Powell Street Review* staff, a Toronto community journal for Sansei, held a conference in 1974 a few years after my father's death and put up a photograph exhibit of the internment. These were the first to be publicly viewed.

I was astounded by the powerful black and white images of snow-covered shacks, evergreen mountains dwarfing the camps below with the exiled who could've been my relatives huddled in front of the shacks, clothed in heavy coats, coarse pants, and boots, their faces dripping with distress and confusion; in other pictures, they stood on railroad platforms or waterside piers. Yet the stories were like the wisps of smoke coming out of the cabin chimneys, rising and disappearing.

I shook with rage in front of the photographs. I felt two feet tall, my stomach churning with acid. My hands began to sweat. I imagined my eyes would start bleeding.

I couldn't stand the deep pockets of alienation around my memories. I was compelled to talk to Mom. She always had ignored me whenever I asked about the past. I expected the same this time around, so when I approached her, I took a different tact.

"How did you meet Dad?"

Her answer was quick and sharp. "Baka!" More like a bark than a clear expletive. The term for *idiot* holds more power and significance in Japanese than in English. I immediately withdrew, knowing I had crossed some unseen line. My mother was distorted with anger, shame, and vibrating secret shadows.

Her anger upset me. It was an innocent question.

After a long moment, she softened. "*Bocchan,* you don't need to know such things," she said in Japanese.

"But, Ma, I want to know."

"*Aho,*" she scoffed, trying to dismiss me.

"Just tell me what part of Japan we're from."

She slowly revealed that my maternal grandparents were from Kagoshima. She then continued, a surprise to me. Her father was in Canada at the time when he called upon his father to arrange a marriage for him. Grandma emigrated from the same *ken*. An arranged marriage? My hands felt cold as I rested them on my knees. I knew arrangements existed, but for other foreigners, not modern Canadians like us. Then I reasoned that maybe we weren't Canadians at all. I had been fooling myself all these years.

I stayed at it to get more information. She mumbled a little more. Haruko Otani (my mother) was born in Steveston, BC, back in the early 1920s. After high school, she worked in a cannery. She met my father at a *Bussei* dance for Steveston exiles in Hamilton after the war. Why a city boy was there, I had no idea. Mom said she didn't know either. But there he was; they met, dated, and fell in love.

Dad's family were from Fukuoka. He was born in Victoria, BC, around the same time as Mom. He moved to Vancouver for university and work. When the government demanded the Internees choose between resettling in Japan or venturing east of the Rockies in the mid-1940s, both sets of grandparents decided to move "home." Nisei were told to give up their citizenships if they went with their parents, so my parents stayed because they knew Canada; it was a case of the Devil-You-Know. We never heard from the grandparents again, except my maternal grandpa who moved back to Toronto, and the letter telling us about Dad's mom.

She did confirm Dad's involvement with the JCCL, the Japanese Canadian Citizens League, the political arm of the Nikkei community. She also hinted at other incidents of activism in one form or another, but I couldn't get more from her. She clammed up like an oyster.

That was about all, but I knew I had to press for more. Later.

The rain caught me by surprise. I felt it even in my sleep. It hurt, every drop a needle point piercing the skin. Blood-water flowed in rivulets spreading to cover my face, chest and arms.

"Your father...had deep feeling, *ne*?" Naoko asked demurely. "I mean, the rain and hurt."

"Yeah, Pearl Harbor. Your boys..." I knew that was a mistake. "Sorry, I didn't mean that."

She seemed to ignore me. She continued to translate. I interpreted the imagery. We saw Kurosawa movies; we had Asian-only meals together. In her apartment we listened to Joni Mitchell or Gordon Lightfoot and went to bed. Sometimes we lay on the futon with our backs to each other and remained silent for a few hours. Eventually, either she or I turned off the light and gave in to the pull of sleep.

But then there came a change in my father's writing that affected Naoko and me profoundly.

11.
1982

No one saw Boku for weeks after the Bumpkins bet debacle. I thought he was ducking us because he owed us a meal, but then I finally ran into him on campus in the St. George Library.

"Boku! Where you been, man?"

"Shh. We're in a library."

"Thanks for the news update, you simp. But where you been? Glenn's madder than a hornet kicked in the ass."

"Yeah, well, I been busy. And I don't owe you guys a meal," he said.

"Tell that to Glenn."

"Mike, I met someone."

"Oh, really, who?"

"Well, I was at the laundry. You know, the Chinaman's at Greenwood and Danforth?"

"Don't be a racist. It's called Atta Chong."

"Yeah, well, I met Dominique there."

Dominique, with no last name apparently, was from French Guiana, a freshly arrived immigrant to Canada. Boku met her while retrieving his dry-cleaning, a holdover habit from when his family home was near the laundry. Perhaps out of desperation to find a date for Bumpkins, he girded his loins (figuratively, I hope) and asked if she'd like a coffee. To his surprise she said yes.

She was married and unhappy. According to Boku, her husband was a brute, beating her at the slightest provocation, which prompted her to leave him. Boku instantly felt sorry for her. Maybe he thought of Kiki at Bumpkins.

In any case, from coffee to a full-blown affair took only a

matter of days. They started living together shortly thereafter and moved to a shared apartment somewhere in the west end. Boku drew money from his OSAP grant and loan to afford it. How long that would last was anyone's guess, but he was in love. Practical reasoning went out the door.

"So, you see, I couldn't come out to Bumpkins. We can't be seen together in public in case it got back to her husband. He's stalking her."

"Who else knows about this? Do your parents?"

"I told them I was seeing someone. I even told my dad she was brown."

"Not black?"

"No, no, no. You know how he is. As it was, he asked, 'How brown is she?'"

We burst out laughing, prompting the librarian to ask us to leave. Outside, he promised he would introduce Dominique to me sometime soon.

In the following weeks, I went to class, tutoring indifferent freshmen, and tried dealing with Glenn. I met him one Sunday at church. A rare occurrence.

"Calm down, man. So what if he owes us? It was a meaningless bet in the first place."

"He agreed to it and he lost. Now you tell me he's shacked up with some Nigerian."

"French Guianese. Close."

"Whatever. He owes me."

"Forget it. Let him off the hook, will ya?"

"Why should I?"

"Because he's our friend."

"Christ, someone is only as good as his word. How can I ever trust him again if he doesn't pay?"

"You can't trust him because of a stupid bet? Grow up, man."

He paused and stared at me as if contemplating the implications of what I had just said. "Let's go eat at the Bloor Inn. Service is almost over," he said.

"Yeah, sure. We gotta wait for the girls."

"I got a hunger on for a banquet burger and a Coke and it's on you."

"Wait, what?"

"Only fair, you're Boku's friend," he said with a smile. "And you're mine."

We were standing in the lower lobby of the Buddhist Church like The Boys always did when we were teenagers during Sunday service. A modern church back in the 1960s when the Nisei raised the money to build it, the place served the community well. The congregational, made from pure blond maple (very Canadian), was large, able to accommodate up to three hundred. The ceiling was high, the altar designed by a devout Nisei professional artist and adorned with a golden statue of the Buddha, and a scroll with calligraphy said to have been written by Abbott Rennyo. The basement was finished with a painted grey cement floor, kitchen, and break-out rooms, and equipped with close-circuit TV for overflow during popular funerals. The area was easily converted for Sunday school, committee meetings, bazaars, and holiday dances.

Only Glenn and I were there, the rest of the gang had long abandoned our Sunday ritual for sleeping in and other concerns. Many of the girls of our set, however, still showed up on a regular basis at their parents' insistence.

At our height, there must've been about twenty to thirty of us, probably more, who met every Sunday out of a sense of loyalty or duty. Certainly not out of religious fervour. But we hated the sermons, made unappetizing by the religious moralizing, complex language, and increasingly long homilies.

We skipped the service and dutifully waited in the lobby dishing the dirt, shooting the breeze, until the minister showed up in the upper lobby in front of the doors to the congregational, waiting to shake hands and thank parishioners. Though a Buddhist church, the hierarchy and members used Christian terms to make the religion more palatable to Canadian tastes — after all, the Buddhists were expelled from Vancouver because of the way they looked, acted, and what they practiced.

To the minister's credit, he never chastised us for loitering. Reverend Tsuji, the long-ago first minister, once told me, "The Buddha is always near." It didn't matter where we were, in other words. The current *bousan* patiently waited for the last *gatha* to end, and the folks began to filter out to go to the basement for a light lunch prepared by the Dana or *Fujinkai*.

But ever since senior high school, we didn't go for the free lunch — not cool. "What am I, six-years-old?" Glenn would say in protest. We and a contingent of The Girls would head off *en masse* down Bathurst to Bloor Street, the delta of greasy-spoons and pool halls. We either went to the Bloor Inn or Peter's Café, both diners featuring red Naugahyde booths, a long soda counter with pies and cakes in a display case, and an open kitchen for burgers and fries, and a back kitchen for dinner specials like the half-barbecue chicken or the Blue Plate, a holdover from the war, no doubt.

So there we sat that Sunday in two or three booths with an assortment of The Girls with names like Laurie, Elaine, Joan, and Caroline. The Girls, as opposed to The Boys (the terms derived from the Girls and Boys Clubs at the TBC we all joined as kids), made the long trek from the suburbs downtown with their parents every Sunday. They were all very pretty, with long hair and a flip in their bangs to keep their freshly scrubbed faces clear. They wore little makeup, maybe a touch of lipstick, some blush. They dressed stylishly, but not outlandishly, mostly smart, if not enticing, minidresses with white nylons and black Mary Jane shoes. Above all else, they had a polish that distinguished them from the Chinese immigrant girls whose numbers were steadily increasing in Toronto. I could always tell a Sansei from an FOJ (Fresh off the Jet).

I always liked being around Sansei girls, secretly wanted to date one or two, but that was not to be. Known them too long to be mature around them. The girls, too, didn't much like us

Sansei boys. Probably for the same reasons; but maybe, there was more to it. I had heard that to them, Sansei boys were just that: boys, and not men. Somehow aggressive huks were. I always thought the girls couldn't help it. Most movies, TV shows, magazines, billboard ads, and everything else featured white men as the heroes. What chance did Asian men have?

Back in the day, I did ask out one or two of them, but no luck. When I asked, they laughed until they saw I was serious. Then they said those fateful words: "I like you as a friend." At least they didn't say what their preference was. Ah, well, we were all teenagers back then. What could I expect?

To tell the truth, I had zero confidence when it came to females. It took a great deal to ask one out. I blamed my father. No advice, no guidance, no opinion was ever offered. My mother was the "mum" housewife. My father — not a modicum of encouragement or advice, hardly ever a word — the distant parent. We never had a heart-to-heart talk. But then I lost him, absolute silence taking his silent place.

The Girls would only stay for lunch since they had mall shopping in the afternoon. Gossip and outfits were their main concerns. By the beginning of the 1980s, Gonads Gotanda, Sad Ebisuzaki, the Lump, Fats Yoshimura, and other members of The Boys never showed up for church, their nicknames an immature desecration of a Nisei affectation (with nicknames like Blue, Fuzzy, and Blackie). On a rare occasion, many of us met on a Saturday to play touch football. On a Sunday afternoon, however, neither Glenn nor I could even muster enough of us to play a good game of snooker at Bloor Street's Eight Ball Pool Hall or Diamond Billiards, which was upstairs from Peter's Café.

But as the Buddha taught, *change is constant* and *life is suffering*. Glenn and I made the best of it while grazing on our burgers with everything on them, fries with gravy and coleslaw on the side — the classic Hamburger Deluxe. Inevitably one of the girls brought up Boku.

"Michael, what's with Boku these days? Haven't seen him in a long time."

"Yeah, not since he and Cathy broke up," another added.

I had to be careful not to spark a locust swarm of gossip.

"He's shacked up with a Black girl," Glenn blurted out.

"What?" said a chorus of stunned voices.

"No," I insisted. "Glenn doesn't know what he's talking about."

"Yeah, he met this Nigerian."

"Will you shut up?"

The swarm began with swirling questions.

"She's not Nigerian" was all I could say while glaring at Glenn who shrugged his shoulders and went back to his soda.

The swarm turned into a plague.

12.

February 1991

nisei

nisei   *mass*

   Nisei mass evacuation

Nisei Mass Evacuation Group

nmegnmegnmegnmeg nmeg

                −1942

An actual poem by my father, and in English? I never... Postmodern, free verse, like so many contemporary poets. Was he emulating e.e. cummings? Did he even know cummings? Or were they doodles, random notes on the page? Like the last line indicated. Or was it concrete poetry? When did he write it? 1942 as it says or much earlier? And why in English, and not in Japanese? Finally, what or who was the Nisei Mass Evacuation Group?

Naoko had no idea, but she did have a strange reaction to the words. Her eyes lifted from the page and gazed at me. The pupils stared at me, fixed independently with the brightness of her consciousness and will. Her glare did not so much as touch me, as it hit me like starlight does in its remoteness, distance, and frigid temperatures. My stomach instantly caved, and my brain was paralyzed with fear as my legs quivered with weakness until I nearly blacked out.

When she snapped out of it and released me, I sat stunned. I somehow mustered my strength and stammered nonsensically, "You...you...all right?"

"Yes, why do you say like that?" she said.

"You...you...seemed out of it." I had no idea why I said that.

"No, nothing wrong."

I let it go, not realizing that our relationship had profoundly changed.

Naoko's lips grew pale in the days to come. Her beautiful, smooth skin slowly, almost imperceptibly, became translucent. Her eyes were as intense as ever; maybe they sparked with a sharp beauty I hadn't noticed before, but her body started to distort, started to be...to become transparent. As absurd as that may have been, an urge within me surged through my being, making me feel as if I should grab her, hold her, to prevent her from disappearing. But I did nothing; then the sensation was over. *Must be my imagination*, I said to myself. I dismissed it immediately since everything appeared normal again.

Nisei Mass Evacuation Group. I made a beeline for my mother. I was determined to get an answer even if she balked and shut down. She did, naturally.

"Come on, Ma," I barked.

She was as stony silent as ever, sitting like a mute, meditating Buddha, indifferent yet holding the entire universe within, in her comfortable but worn chair. She was in the darkest part of the house, in the back in a small room off the kitchen. Daylight served as no illumination despite it being mid-afternoon. She had been dozing the winter away.

"You've got to tell me. It was important enough for Dad to write it in his diary." I would not be denied. "You do this to me every time," I said as I threw my arms up in the air. "Give me something. It's my right to know."

She sat without moving. She then closed her eyes, drew a deep breath as if resigned to her fate, and said, "The NMEG was a protest group of Nisei during the war."

I was nonplussed not only that she answered, but by the response itself. "Protest group? Dad? I thought he was in the JCCL with Uncle Kunio," I said, not really knowing anything. The JCCL could've been an anarchist group for all I knew. "He protested? You mean he didn't cooperate like all the others? I always imagined when the order was given, he went with everyone else like sheep to the camps. *Shikataganai* and all that." A flurry of questions ensued. My poor mother.

"You are young. You have no idea what happened back then. You have no idea what shikataganai means."

"It means 'nothing could be done,'" I explained.

"No, it means I have no choice," she said defiantly.

I had no idea what she meant, so I brought the subject back. "Tell me, was Dad part of the Nisei what-do-you-call-it group?"

"Nisei Mass Evacuation Group. And yes," she said finally, "he was a member."

"But he was in the JCCL. You told me so."

"After," she interrupted. "They kicked him out. The JCCL, I mean."

I ignored that little bomb for the moment. "What did this group do?"

"Ask Uncle Kunio."

"Mom."

"No, I mean it. I don't know anything about the group or your father's part in it. Uncle Kunio was there. He knows."

"But Uncle's in Vancouver."

That ended the longest conversation I ever had with my mother. Oddly enough, as I backed away from her, I thought I saw in Mom that same transparency that was in Naoko — only for a split second, but it was there. She was growing fainter. I shook my head, and everything stopped.

I QUICKLY RUSHED back to Naoko's apartment. Bounding up the stairs, I felt the urge to yell out her name, like in one of those 1960s British movies with Michael Caine or Albert Finney. But I resisted. I came to a resounding halt when I opened the door and found no one home.

I shouldn't have been upset. She had probably just stepped out to the corner store or something like that, but I had a bad feeling about her absence. I was exhilarated, disappointed, and worried all at the same time.

My father had been part of a group protesting the Canadian government's high-handed and racist treatment of Japanese Canadians. Or so I assumed. It answered a few questions about my past. Pointed thoughts ran through my brain. *So how could Naoko not be here to hear my news? She must concentrate her efforts on finding more references to the Nisei Mass Evacuation Group. But where is she?*

And so, I waited as daylight crept into dusk. At some point, I opened the fridge and pulled out pickled ham and lettuce to make a sandwich. I found a beer and helped myself before putting Joni Mitchell's *Hejira* on the record player. The pale blond music poured into the living room as I sat at Naoko's desk to stare at the words of the diary in front of me. *Cold Saskatchewan blues.*

My Uncle Kunio came to mind as I crunched on my mystery-meat sandwich. He wasn't my real uncle, of course but, like so many of my parents' friends, he was my courtesy uncle. He was still living in Vancouver, having moved there from Christina Lake (a self-supporting camp for the Japanese Canadians, I later learned) via Kamloops in 1950. His wife, Aunt Marion, and his daughter had died about a decade ago, both of breast cancer, so he kicked around alone in his big house out in Kitsilano. The last time I saw him was at a memorial for the two in Toronto — once a jolly big man, he had been reduced by the tragedy and his advancing age. He always had a warm handshake, a smile, and half hug for me. And on that occasion, he rallied to greet me the same way, but I could feel his trembling soul.

Uncle was born in Victoria, BC, in 1918. His family owned and operated the Shimizu Rice Mill, located on the outskirts of Chinatown. His mother and he moved to Powell Street to get a "proper Japanese education" at the best school in BC. Uncle, later, was the only one at the age of seven to move to Japan with his grandmother to further his education there. With a Japanese education, it was commonly believed, he and the other oldest sons might be able to have a career, given the employment limitations imposed by racist Canadian and BC governments. He returned in 1932, a *Kika-Nisei* and worked until he enrolled at UBC. After graduating, he started out in Steveston for a bit. He then moved back to Vancouver and started seeing my aunt, a "Kitsilano gal," and they had bright plans despite the fact that he couldn't find a job in his field of physics and math.

He and Dad had known each other during the early days. They met at Japanese School on Alexander Street. Otousan was like a little brother to him since they were two years apart in age. They hung out together just about every day, I was told, until Uncle left for Japan. Remarkably, my dad did let on that it was one of the saddest days of his childhood.

Because of their close friendship, they got into many fist fights. Uncle never understood Dad's penchant for fisticuffs since Dad never won. Dad couldn't help himself, Uncle guessed. Apparently, Otousan had a temper that went off like spit on a hot griddle. Something I never knew until my aunt's funeral, something I only half-believed. But then there was the revelation that my dad swore a lot. Never saw either trait in the man.

I made up my mind to somehow get to Vancouver to talk to my uncle.

BUT WHERE WAS NAOKO? Did I really witness her slow disappearance? Had she evaporated into nothingness? Impossible. The streetlight streaks from the frosted window grew wider and longer as darkness folded into the hours of the day. I lay on the bed reading by a lonely lamp until my mind started its cascade to sleep. I pulled the sheets over me, turned off the lamp and curled into a comfortable position.

I grew worried about Naoko but was too tired to do anything about it. Must've been the beer, even though I only had one. She hadn't forewarned me of her absence. But then in my half sleep, I heard her, or so I thought. I sensed myself come to a seated position, telling her excitedly about my conversation with my mother: all about my father, my uncle, and the Nisei Mass Evacuation Group. When I ended, I heard an audible pause before she spoke.

"Ah, the beginning of enlightenment," I heard her say.

Must've been a dream, I thought as I awoke. Only the hum of sparse traffic was in the air. I was still lying in the cold darkness, but then I sensed a presence.

"Naoko?" I asked quietly.

No answer. I peered into the black fabric of the room, straining my eyes to the extent of their power. An airless vacuum reigned. What happened to the random light and noise from outside? I dismissed the anomaly, convinced and irritated that something or someone was still there. In the next second, I saw a glimmer of light. It grew quickly into a shimmer. I sat on my knees waiting.

Out of the haze of light, I made out a figure and, to my amazement, I realized it was Naoko, naked and as sensuous as I'd ever seen her. She moved toward me. Her breasts shone a golden colour as did her shoulders. Her hair smooth and flowing emitted an exotic, sultry scent, like patchouli and plumeria blossoms. Her lips bright red and parted, her eyes sharp and penetrating. She reached out to me and I responded while fighting the heat in my loins, which seemed to be weighing me down. My clothes fell away as I stood and lurched toward her. The tingling in my body returned.

As we reached out for one another, her face fractured, like a Picasso portrait, and her sex opened to me, drawing me into its moist, mysterious interior. The aroma nearly overwhelmed me. A strange and foreign pain then engulfed me; my skin ripped open and blood gushed forth, but I didn't care. We embraced. Hungry mouths, intertwining limbs, and flowing saliva, we rolled and fought and loved for hours, it seemed. Yet throughout it all, I saw her shining eyes rise and revolve around me.

A peace descended as I lay on the cool sheets in the dénouement. A disembodied voice whispered in my ear, "Goodbye."

13.

Early Spring – Fall 1982

The extension phone sat like a black toad basking in the sun on my old, battered desk bought for a bargain-bin price at SS Kresge's when the department store meant something to the neighbourhood. We had but one telephone throughout my childhood. It hung off the kitchen wall like a huge bat. In my early teens, when phone calls signified freedom and social success, I would thunder down the steps from my room, grab the banister pole at the bottom, and swing around to change direction toward the kitchen. I would slip and slide along the red and grey linoleum hall floor to the kitchen to pick up the receiver before the caller hung up. We didn't have an answering machine. My father deemed it frivolous to have both. "You have two ears and one mouth — how many phones do you need?"

That would mean two by that logic. As for the answering machine, he just declared, "You're not that busy." I never said anything; that would have been insolent.

When Dad was lost to us, I finally installed, at my own expense, an extension in my room, along with an answering machine in case I was too wasted to bother, was disturbed by calls from Mom's friends (like Mrs. Miyamoto, the community caterer, who was always giving us food), but I rarely missed any of my own.

When I was enjoying a tranquil sleep on a day off from school in early spring 1982, the amphibian came to life. I let it go. That is until Mom came to my door encouraging me to take the call. "It's that friend of yours... what's-his-name? Boku? Boku Sugiura."

"Okay, Mom... thanks," I said in a haze. I picked up the telephone to hear an agitated voice.

"Mike, can you come meet me for a coffee?"

I woke up fully. "Yeah sure, what for?"

"There's something I want to tell you...about me and Dominique."

"What? You got her in trouble?"

"Shut up, you asshole. I'm serious. Can you meet me?"

He was serious. "Sure, where?"

"In an hour. Carrot Common. The coffee shop there."

THE CARROT COMMON was a small co-op of stores on the Danforth. Smartly designed, the place contained a health food store, bookstore, a Japanese restaurant named Michi's, clothing stores, and a Timothy's Coffee Shop. The place, dominated by the colour coffee-brown, was practically empty when I got there at about eleven in the morning. Boku sat at a corner table for two, nervously massaging his ceramic coffee cup.

I hadn't seen much of Boku after that day in the library. So, when I finally did see him, he looked despondent.

"Mike! Thanks for coming," he said looking up from the table. His face was pale and drawn from a lack of sleep.

"No problem," I said as I discarded my heavy coat. Despite the date, it was still cold outside. "What's up?"

"It's Dominique."

"What about her?"

"Well, we broke up."

I stayed mum. *That was fast*, I thought. What had it been, four, maybe five months?

"Yeah, we decided there wasn't much there. And I made a decision."

"What's that?"

"I'm moving to Vancouver. To go to UBC...finish my degree there," he said. "That was the other thing. She didn't want to go with me."

"So, you decided on this on your own."

"Yeah, I need to get outta this bullshit town."

"Why?"

"I just do."

"You called me just to tell me this?"

"I figured you would understand."

I didn't but I didn't let on.

The floor was wet with the melted slush of customers seeking refuge, the windows clouded with steam. The cool early spring weather conspired to keep him bundled and unidentified.

We sat for the next hour, Boku nursing his coffee while I ordered coffee and assorted pastry out of guilt and to share. I could not offer any advice, but I could see he was hurting, no matter what he said. As it was, I thought of her as another one of Boku's "projects." Someone fragile he could take care of.

I had never met Dominique. I didn't know if she actually existed. No one had ever met her, his parents, his sister (as far as I knew), Glenn, me. Why would he make her up? Why would he lie to me? To validate his life in his mind? Was he delusional? If I were in his position, would I make up a Dominique?

I TURNED MY overcoat collar to the cold Danforth wind as we faced each other to end our meeting. All I could say to Boku was goodbye and I wished him luck. I shook his hand, but he wanted to hug as Sugiuras do. So we did, and he was gone.

When I next heard from him, just after the new school year started, he revealed in a letter that he had done a completely Boku thing: he had applied for computer science at UBC while with Dominique, I gathered. When he was accepted for that September, he left his girlfriend and Toronto behind.

What made it a "Boku thing" was the fact that he flew to Vancouver without making any arrangements for housing or transportation. He just landed, took a bus, and wandered downtown for a day before settling in the mouse-infested, but affordable, Patricia Hotel on East Hastings Street. He stayed there until registration day.

I must say, the university was very tolerant, even helpful, according to Boku. A kindly older woman named Agnes on staff made sure he found accommodation right away. She went on to set up a bank account, food service vouchers, and locker for him. She even gave him a tour of the campus and faculty of architecture. In a letter, he nicknamed her "Agnes of God," a nod to his Catholic period, I supposed.

The next letter, I received, a couple of months after he left, gave a hint to his future plans.

> Dear Mike,
> Am settled now at UBC. Within the first week of classes, a thickly jowl'd Chinese guy came up to me speaking in his twisted, tortured way. I stepped back since his hair was as greasy as his skin. I eventually figured out he wanted me to join the Chinese Students Assoc. As if! I turned him down, insulted that he would even think of me in that FOJ club! How would I ever fit in? I like the food, but they are so uncool, so creepy. Some of the girls aren't bad.
> Now that's something. You find a good-looking Chinese chick and you really have something. Maybe I'll go to a dance or two.
> I think I've found something. I have to take an arts course as part of my program. At first, I couldn't see the need of it for computer sciences. Anyway, I enrolled in a philosophy course. The prof required The Fountainhead by Ayn Rand. You know her? Sure you do, you're an artsie, as Glenn would say.
> In any case, the book and lectures in the class opened my eyes. You know what the problem with the world is, Mike? Collectivism.
> We'll talk about it during Christmas break.
> Thanks for listening to me about Dominique. I appreciate your strength.
>
> Later, girlfriend,
> Boku
> October 1982

14.

February 1991

The bright morning light from a steel sun pouring through the window opened my sore eyes. It was not what disturbed my sleep, however. I heard the clatter of a disengaging lock, the turn of an old doorknob, and the creak of the door opening. *Naoko?*

"Hey, who are you?" a grizzled voice said. "You a squatter?"

"What?" I replied groggily. A wizened man stood above me. Though the man had a kind look about him, with a whisker-spotted chin that seemed to have separated from the rest of his face and drooped to the ground, he seemed not too pleased to see me.

"You can't be here."

"This is my girlfriend's place," I said, irritated.

"Who? No one's been here in months."

I shook my head clear. I lifted my head and focused my eyes on the room around me. It was empty, every stick of furniture, all the posters, all the Joni Mitchell albums, all the Japanese kitchen utensils gone. The appliances remained, unused and sad. Even our bed, gone. I was lying on bare floorboards, fully clothed. The walls were an unpainted canvas; the cupboards, open drawers, and shelves empty; the kitchen stripped of cutlery, dishes, pots, and pans; the floor bare. I suddenly felt debris on my face and so I brushed off what felt like stipple.

What's going on here? Where's Naoko? Was I in the Twilight Zone? *Submitted for your consideration . . .* I searched for an answer as my tormentor resumed. "You go on now. Get outta here now and I won't call the cops."

"Who are you?"

"I check on the place for the owner. Now, I'll let last night slide, but you gotta go."

"Last night? Yeah, what happened last night?"

"How should I know? I just know you slept here for free. Probably broke in. How long you been in here? You homeless or something? You don't look like a druggie ... or a rubbie for that matter," he said.

"No ... no, I'm not either of those things. Listen, were you here yesterday, during the day, I mean?"

"Ain't been here for a month."

"How about a month ago, was there a Japanese girl living here?"

"A what? The closest was a Singhalese, and he was a man. That was maybe two years ago. I told you nobody's been here in months. The last one was Eye-tai, I think. Yeah that's it."

A what and who? I climbed to my feet with difficulty. Feeling a fever rise in me, I broke out in a film of sweat.

"Listen here, young fellah, if you're done the third degree, I'm afraid you got to go. Don't make me call the cops."

"Yeah, yeah," I grumbled in total confusion. I picked up my winter jacket and headed for the door.

"Hey, wait!" the caretaker commanded. "Ain't you forgetting something?"

I looked at him pointing to something on the floor in the middle of the apartment. It was Dad's dream book — like a magical talisman or a tome of secrets and incantations, it had appeared out of nowhere. Everything else was gone, why not it?

Sensing the palace guard was getting nervous, I scooped up the book and fled the building.

LIKE THE DAY I MET with Boku about Dominique back in '82, I breathed in the cold, fresh air of hipster and ethnic Bloor Street and tried to clear the fog in my head. I looked up and down the street, desperate to see something familiar, maybe Naoko. Where could she be? I started running eastward, picking up speed as I went. This was too freakish an experience. I couldn't have dreamed the last six or so months: Naoko, the hip Japanese apartment, our meeting, our work, our dating, our lovemaking. She was real, right?

I peered at the sky to make sure there was only one sun. Had I been in an alternate universe? Was I in one now? The *otaku* in me came out: too much Aldous Huxley and Murakami Sensei.

It occurred to me that maybe she went to the university, her faculty. I suddenly stopped in my tracks. *I am such an idiot. All that time together, I could've asked. Maybe Mom was right.* She was a graduate student, that I knew, but in what? I was so wrapped up in my father's diary and her beauty, I realized I didn't know much about her studies. Yes, she mentioned she was studying the matsutake mushroom and the Japanese Canadians, but what discipline would that be, anthropology? Wait, didn't she mention anthropology? Or was it sociology? History? She could be in any of them.

I checked out all three on St. George campus. I asked several people but found nothing, except at the faculty of anthropology on Russell Street just off Queen's Park. It was an old Victorian building with a solid rock foundation and an arched entranceway.

At the reception desk, I asked the secretary if Naoko Ito was around. She looked at me with a blank face and said, "There's no Naoko, but there is a Naomi Ito here."

"Is she around?'

"I think she's at her carrel upstairs."

I approached the carrel with some trepidation. I turned the corner and found a young woman, thin with long hair and glasses poring over a text. She looked up at my interruption.

"Oh, I'm sorry," I said. "Do you know Naoko Ito."

"No," she said with a bland Canadian accent. "I'm the only Ito here."

I stood outside on the university grounds. I suddenly recalled my mother's warning at Oshougatsu. *"She's not what she seems."* What did she mean by that?

I had to find out and started running. Breathing clouds of smoke, I caught the subway at University and then the streetcar at Bathurst. Naoko didn't seem to exist. At least, no one knew her on campus. I wondered if this was all a con. Was Naoko a confidence artist? But what was the point? I have nothing of value. *A free meal at my mom's?* I made it back home within a half hour — at least TTC luck was on my side.

I found Mom in her sewing room upstairs on the sunny side of the house. Bent over and huddled in a corner, she reminded me of her advancing age and her *tanuki*-like existence. She was labouriously knitting another of her endless sweaters. She wove them, and no one wore them, especially me.

There was something off about her. I noticed, like the other day, that the lines of her figure seemed distorted; her hair not as salt and pepper, more a fading grey. There was something indistinct about her. Was she disappearing like Naoko? I shook it off with the sense of the absurd overtaking me.

Mom looked up and the pupils of her eyes were circled by a grey, almost blue, mucus, like an oyster encased by its juices. "You-*ka*?" she said.

"How long have I been gone?"

"How long? Overnight, I think, maybe more. I go to bed never worried about you."

"Do you remember Naoko?"

"Who?"

"Naoko! Japanese girl. I brought her to Oshougatsu last time."

"Oh, yes, the *honto* girl."

I was taken aback by her use of my slang for a "real Japanese" person, but I let it go. "Ma, what did you mean when you said, 'She's not what she seems?'"

"Did I say that?"

"Yes, you did. What did you mean?"

"I said, I don't know. Not sure I even said it."

"Okay, okay, but you remember her?"

"Of course, I do. You think I'm going *ga-ga* or something?"

"Ga-ga?"

"Empty in the head, *kichigai*, senile?" she said, pointing to her temple.

"I know, I know. You watch too much TV."

She just harrumphed and continued her knitting.

"Look, Ma, you remember Naoko, right?"

"I said so, didn't I?" she said with a touch of anger.

"I'm not going crazy then," I concluded, holding my head as it cleared. For a moment there I was feeling that Naoko was the story of my life: I finally meet the girl of my dreams, only to find she's imaginary.

"Why, what happened? What did you do to that poor girl?"

"What? No, nothing. I didn't do anything. How can you ask such a question?"

She fell silent.

THAT SILENCE PREVAILED and attacked my thoughts as I brooded in my room. The afternoon sun was as intense as that of the morning, but it didn't intrude on my thoughts — not like the absolute quiet of the house. To calm myself, I put on Santana's *Abraxas*; that exquisite opening of wind-chime tintinnabulation, screeching guitars, crystal piano notes, and primordial drumbeats put me in a pocket away from the surreal.

Yet my thoughts twisted and turned within the singing winds and crying beasts. Where was Naoko? Why had she left? I would've called the police, but all her possessions had been taken as well. I doubt that a kidnapper would've been so thorough and in one night, with me there. Maybe I was out longer than I thought, but Mom said I was only gone one night. What was going on? Maybe I imagined the whole thing. But it felt so real.

My head rattled with pain, swirling in confusion. An elaborate deception, perhaps? But who would've done such a thing?

The sun shifted along the contours of my bedroom walls. I sank deeper and deeper into the dark end of the day. Black air surrounded me, buried me. It was as if I had tumbled into a well; the depths enclosed and swallowed me whole. I was alone face to face with a creeping sense of emptiness. I couldn't escape — my thoughts my lone companion.

The walls of the well became the limits of my existence. At least I wasn't alone. A cockroach crawled precariously up my wall, an insect with little consciousness save an instinct for survival. It doesn't think and so isn't aware of other worlds. Lucky bug.

I looked up and saw the distant and cold light of a full moon. Soon it faintly illuminated what I came to realize was my room. But the roach floated in front of me. It started to glow just as the events of last night's encounter with Naoko flourished in my brain: both violent and exciting. The glow was soft at first, but then grew in intensity and expanded until the light reached out and grabbed me, pulled me in, and I seemed to be absorbed into a hallucination, a dream...

I FOUND MYSELF in a diner, sitting next to a stranger. He was familiar somehow. The walls were covered with vinyl album covers from the 1960s. *Disraeli Gears, Bridge Over Trouble Waters, Frank Sinatra at the Sands, Everybody Loves Somebody, Meet the Beatles, Elvis: for LP Lovers Only, Tijuana Brass*. They were stapled to the wood; *Such a waste*, I thought. A long counter with stools in front separated customers from the coffee, soda drinks, and dessert pies. At its far end, the open kitchen bustled with cooking and plating. I smelled the food. Strange, I couldn't see any cooks or staff. Metal tables with Formica tops and Naugahyde chairs littered the worn linoleum floor. There was only one customer sitting at the far end of the diner. I was naturally drawn to that person.

The closer I got, I noticed distinguishing features. She was a woman, her hair was long, her hands below the table. *Naoko!* I rushed forward out of excitement more than anything until I stood beside her.

She suddenly lifted her gaze. Her brightly lit eyes confirmed her identity and froze me to the spot. I tried to say something, but couldn't. She then smiled and let go of her grip on me.

"Naoko, is it really you?" I asked as I sat down.

Silence.

I looked around and suddenly remembered. "This is the Terminal, isn't it?" — a restaurant at the corner of Coxwell and the Danforth, relatively close to Atta Chong Laundry, in Dominique's old neighbourhood.

"What happened to you? Why'd you leave me? Where'd you go?" She remained silent and still. I wanted to reach out and shake her, but something held me back.

She then stood up, revealing her body. Thin in the right spots, curved and alluring in others. She took a few steps to leave.

"No," I said, feeling an impulse to follow her. But I couldn't move. "Don't go, talk to me. Tell me how I ... why ... why'd you leave me? Why?"

By the third "why" she was gone, but I heard her voice like a trail of perfume. One word echoed and faded: *"sintamanti."*

I AWOKE IN my room, the cockroach gone like Naoko. *"Sintamanti"* entered my head. An unfamiliar word, if it was a word, in a confused state of mind. I looked in my *Oxford* and found nothing.

Boku then came back to me. At the time, his actions seemed surreal, even his imprisonment for bank robbery. But I knew where he was, even though he had disappeared, and I hadn't spoken to or heard from him in three years. Maybe he was a cockroach now, living that metamorphosis in blissful ignorance.

Reaching the bottom of my mental well, I decided to act to confirm Naoko's existence. *I must ascertain history*, as my erstwhile criminal pal once said to me. I called Glenn, and after apologizing for the late hour, he said, "Yeah, what kind of question is that? Look, I never met her, but you talked about her enough."

All right, at least he and Mom acknowledge her existence.

"How come you never intro'd me to any of her friends? You know, the smart chicks? Why are you talking about her anyway? She's not real, is she? Trust you to make up a girl you're 'seeing.' She isn't one of d'em blowup dolls, is she?"

I hung up.

The next day I was still unnerved by what had happened. I arranged to meet Dave at the Golden City. Radar approached us and I asked, "You remember the girl I was with?"

He glared at me and quickly retreated to the kitchen.

"Man, what's wrong with you?" Dave asked.

"She's gone, Dave. Naoko. Gone in the night."

"What're you talking about?"

"I don't know. I woke up in her apartment and she was gone."

"To where?"

"I don't know. The freaky thing is everything is gone. Furniture, books, utensils, everything," I spit out.

"That is weird," he concluded. "What a way to breakup with someone."

Like Glenn, Dave confirmed that he heard me talking endlessly about Naoko, but had never met her. Mom had met her. And Radar, though he didn't admit it.

While we ate our beef and greens on rice, Dave confessed something momentous. "Joanie and I are breaking up."

"What? Why?"

"All the things we been talkin' 'bout: my lack of ambition, my need to hang out at the Centre. Whatever. She wants a ring and a mortgage."

"A what?" I asked.

"A mortgage. I told her I can't afford it, and you know what she said?"

I shook my head.

"'Everybody's got one. You go into debt.' That's what life is: barbecued and mortgaged," he concluded.

He sank into a sullen mood. His eyes were near tears, but he held them back. He pulled a cigarette from the pack in his shirt pocket. He lit up as he continued, "She felt like we should date other people and, maybe in a year, we get back together."

"C'mon, Dave, you know that ain't gonna happen."

"Yeah, I know."

I couldn't imagine a world without Dave and Joanie together. Then again, I couldn't imagine a world without Boku or even Glenn. I thought about offering to talk to Joanie, but I wasn't good at that kind of stuff. Joanie and I didn't have that kind of friendship. Maybe there was something I could do for Dave. Buy dinner. Play some pool. Just be there for him. At least I forgot about Naoko for a little bit.

THAT NIGHT, I again sat on my bed in my room thinking about Naoko. I surrounded myself with all the translated pages of my father's memoir. I certainly couldn't have done all this without someone's help, a native speaker. My mother could have, I suppose, but she was obstinately opposed to even looking at it. Naoko had to be real.

I took some time to consider what to do next. I was an assistant prof at the U of T, but the pay wasn't great since I only had an MA. A real translator was out of the question. Going to the International Students Union Building seemed a backward step; besides, my contacts had long since dried up — they had probably graduated.

But then I thought about Uncle Kunio. I could go to Vancouver and show the diary to him. Maybe he could shed some light. Maybe Mom would lend me the money.

15.

1982

ollectivism? The word came back to haunt me. I was confounded by it back in 1982. We never talked about it as he had suggested. I guess I was too busy talking about reparations and embarrassing him somehow.

Boku enrolled in computer science at UBC in 1982. By Oshougatsu 1984, he had quit. The only reason he gave his parents was that he had learned all he needed to know.

To say the least, his mother, as he told me, was upset. She saw her son as having thrown away his life. She curled up on her bed with her back to the open doorway. Many nights, Boku stood quietly backlit by the hall light, peering into the room.

"Come on, Ma. It ain't that bad," he said a few nights after announcing his decision to quit.

"I told everyone...you were the first in our family...your obaachan wrote to the Japan relatives. I dreamed of your graduation," she said in hiccupped sentences.

"You shouldn't've told anyone."

Like our house, silence fell like dusk on a late summer's day in the Sugiura household. Always so much left unsaid. The burden of history silences the Nisei, my parents' generation, and the burden of silence is borne by the children. No one reveals the secrets to anyone, not even family. And secrets once forgotten signify loss.

At times, I fancifully envisioned the Nisei coming together right after the war in some huge, cavernous horse palace like at the CNE or PNE, to swear to fall silent for our sake, the children. *Kodomo no tame ni.* Problem was such a secret came as a major shock to us when finally told. Laurier famously proclaimed:

"Canada is free and freedom is its nationality." Then to learn that our government labelled, exiled, imprisoned, and then stole the property of its own citizens, my parents, Boku's, Glenn's, Dave's, The Boys', The Girls', that of all our parents and grandparents, profoundly warped our view of the country, deeply affected the lives of three generations. And probably into the future.

Not many "Canadians," as my mother called white people, believed my generation was affected. We didn't suffer internment; we didn't suffer the label of *Enemy Alien*. *What are you complainin' 'bout? You got a nice house, an education, and a promising future.* Heard it all the time. For that, we were expected to keep quiet and mind our Ps and Qs, like the good little Japanese children we were brought up to be.

But the burden of history became the torment of loss. Most, like Glenn, remained blissfully ignorant and grabbed the carrot dangled in front of us. We did live the good life. Others, like Boku, paid the price for self-obsession. And I? I chose to protest. Shikataga-nai. I had no choice.

IN 1982, I was twenty-six and finishing my MA. I based my thesis on Ezra Pound's *China Cantos*. I wanted to work on Asian Canadian Literature but there was precious little to justify a whole thesis. The *Cantos*, at least, had an Asian theme. I waited. Perhaps more books would appear once I arrived at the PhD level.

Jon Fleming and I became good friends during that time. I liked his style. For our class together on James Joyce, he always wore a dark suit and had a glass of red wine in hand. He sipped as the professor lectured. I started to do the same, only I preferred white wine. Made the three hours and Joyce's dense intellectualism tolerable.

One day, he stopped showing up. I wasn't as confident as he was with the wine, so I left it at home. I thought his absence unusual, until I became bored of the classes and skipped the odd one. Then I met him in the student lounge. "Jon, where you been, man? You missed a hell of a lot of classes."

"What are you talking about? I've been attending," he claimed.

"No, you haven't."

"Hey, you're the one who hasn't been. You're never there when I am."

It turned out, when I was there, he wasn't, and when he was, I wasn't. We laughed heartily.

I hardly knew what collectivism meant.

I soon met Gary Konishi on campus. He and the Kawabata sisters, two attractive women dressed all in black and wore no makeup, were handing out pamphlets about the Yellow Seed North, a group ostensibly against racism. I noticed the three only gave the pamphlets to Asians.

The N-Seed met mostly in Gary's apartment, or in the basement of the Toronto Buddhist Church on Bathurst. Gary's father was the Assistant Minister. The young activist was a graduate of the U of T with a BA in History. He had gone to grad school, but soon quit because the "imperialist curriculum tries to co-op us with capitalist propaganda. We may be the *wretched of the earth, but we won't be fooled.*" He stressed the words of Frantz Fanon to emphasize his "hipness." He was not a handsome man, with a square head, beginnings of a Fu Manchu beard, and long, mostly unruly, hair, but there was strength in his upright posture and a fierce intelligence in his eyes.

I was interested in stopping the "subjugation of the third world's peoples of North America." Which meant, I assumed, me. I had been part of the student movement: anti-poverty, anti-racism, anti-imperialism, anti-injustice. But I didn't hate the Beatles — in fact I was a big fan — but I pretended I did to demonstrate solidarity with Black musicians.

What brought me to the meetings was the promise to meet intelligent females of substance, like the Kawabata sisters, their long hair acted like curtains to the wondrous sight of their beautiful faces. Their black clothes emphasized their slim figures. I admired their minds as well. They listened for your position and called you out for misspeaking or exposing of attitude. I was called a "chauvinist" more than once and even received a slap in the face on one occasion. I suppose I deserved it.

Gary's apartment was a one-room walk-up in a house on a side street off Greenwood Avenue in Old Riverdale (down the street from Atta Chong's). It was furnished simply with the usual bricks and boards for bookshelves. The chairs were second hand, rescued from used furniture stores or curbside. Posters and paintings on the walls screamed out injustice and protest. *Viva Che!* Black men and women in chains, barbed wire fences around Asians, that kind of thing. And records played incessantly: not the pop hits of the Top Forty — no Beatles, Stones, or Kinks (white rip-off-the-Black-man's-music bands) — but obscure (to me anyway) Black musicians like Roland Kirk, Sun Ra, the Last Poets, and Chris & Joanne's *Grain of Sand* — the first Asian American album. The indoctrination process was clear.

Gary always appeared in a *dashiki* (to stand in solidarity with the Black man's struggle, no doubt) and hachimaki (to identify with our struggle, without a doubt) as if to remind us of his catchphrase: *"Don't call me 'Oriental,' I've been stepped on long enough."*

He was never rabid in his rap; he didn't want to overthrow the government or anything like that. He wasn't a Marxist either, often criticizing artists like Chris & Joanne for their collectivist lyrics. *Is this what Boku meant?* Gary just wanted to make Asian Canadians aware of the racism inherent in a white-power structure.

What caught my eye in Gary's apartment was a small collection of black-and-white photographs of New Denver. Jerry-rigged shacks burdened with heavy snow and ice. There was one of a 1940s family standing, on a train platform was my guess, in the middle of their luggage.

"They're copies from the National Archive," said an unknown female voice.

I turned to meet a tall woman in glasses and short hair. She was dressed all in black. *Must be the uniform*, I thought.

"Gary kept these after the 1974 Asian Canadian conference he organized in town."

"Yeah, I remember seeing them back then. I was in first year and heard about the conference. I went to hear a musician, Terry Nakamoto, when I saw the collection."

Despite my young age, I got a lot out of that conference. It was held in a three-storey Victorian house on Mutual Street, near the Ryerson Institute of Technology. Gary and other Asians had rented the place and nicknamed it "The House." For the conference, Sansei and Canadian-born Chinese came together to explore their Asian Canadian identity over a week. Paintings and photographs adorned the walls, a sand sculpture covered the floor of one of the rooms, poets read their work to us, Dr. Alan Hotta flew in from UBC to lecture on the Sansei artist, and Terry and Martin sang their songs about the internment camps. Their purpose was to move the Asian North American Movement toward solidarity.

Besides Terry, I was taken by the odd reading by David Fujino, a beatnik poet in a beret and goatee. He held court on a sofa chair and gesticulated about the "Ni-sai, the I-sai and San-sai. You dig, man. You dig?" Others who talked about their artwork baffled me. Yet I found the whole experience exciting. It was all new to me.

My head spun after I sat in on the "rap sessions" about racism and identity. It was a heady experience that I couldn't fully appreciate because of my age.

GIGI CHAN was like the Kawabata sisters, a sharp mind and keenly aware of the nature of white society. She, however, was kind and much more tolerant of my ignorance. To a point.

"What does 'GiGi' stand for?" I asked. It could've been Chinese for all I knew.

"Gillian," she said. "Easier for my parents to pronounce than 'Gillian.'"

"Why did they name you that in the first place?"

I got no answer, just a cold stare.

"Why do you need to identify as being Asian?" I asked. "I'm just a Canadian."

"What does that mean?" she asked. "We've been oppressed for so long we're used to the white man dictating how we identify ourselves."

"I don't feel oppressed," I insisted. I felt I was being backed into a corner. "No one tells me how to identify myself."

"What do you mean? Look at how you're dressed."

I wound myself up and said, "What's that got to do with anything?" I could see she was getting angry, but I pressed further.

"I'm a student and I like Polo shirts. I have a variety of them in all different colours. I like slacks and penny loafers. No jeans. I don't want to look like I'm out on the street. I'm striving to be a yuppie for the middle class." I didn't mean to, but my voice was rising.

GiGi just stood and scowled at me. "You're a jerk!"

16.

March 1991

Vancouver lay below me like an oyster in its half-shell. The shimmering mountains surrounded the city, protecting it from outside influences.

The Nikkei dressed not for style, but for solidarity with Japan's rural past. The *hakama* were particularly fetching. The Nikkei had a "lifestyle," rather than a life.

I couldn't believe that my mother had given me the money to visit Uncle Kunio in Vancouver. Oh, I knew she had the money, what with Dad's insurance death benefits, pension savings, their savings, and her redress money. I didn't want to take it, but she insisted. When I told her of my plans, she simply reasoned, "Yes. You should talk to Kuni-*chan*. Stay with him and he'll tell you what you want to know. I'll call him. What else am I going to do with all that cash just lying around?"

Who talks like that?

"KUNI-CHAN" LIVED IN KITSILANO. West Broadway, the main street, was now a long strip of high-end boutiques, smart townhouses, and *haute cuisine* restaurants. "Yuppies" strolled along the avenue on an unusually sunny Sunday as I zoomed along in my rented car to my uncle's house well off Macdonald Street.

Leafy trees lined the quiet side street. It was wonderfully shady, the comforting shadows fracturing the rare March sunlight. Something about it felt supernatural, which put me in mind of Naoko's disappearance. She was never far from my thoughts. Maybe that caretaker, the grizzled old man, was part of a bizarre plot. But no kidnapper would bother taking the target victim and every lick of furniture and clothing. I took the old man at his word that Naoko didn't exist for him. If I went to the police, they'd probably lock me up in 999 Queen Street, the city's loony bin. But I knew Naoko was a real, live woman. And what did the word "sintamanti" mean, her last word to me? I promised myself to research it later.

So there I was in Vancouver during March Break holding on to the only thing left of Naoko: her translation. Maybe my uncle could take my mind off things by enlightening me about my father.

"Michael! So nice to see you. Come on in." Uncle greeted me with a wide smile and raspy voice. "Leave your bag in the hall so we can visit awhile." Uncle Kunio lived in a typical Westside house. A broad veranda in front and vegetable garden in back formed the perimeter of a wide, wooden house with a gabled roof. Trees on the street protected it with a heavy canopy against the steady rain of the spring months.

Uncle had put on the weight of his years, the stoop to his back was well pronounced. Dark bags under his eyes sat like luggage on a train platform. His skin crinkled whenever he smiled. He was the picture of sadness and regret. The passing of his loved ones — wife and daughter, double breast cancer victims — such a tragedy had added stress to his life.

He used to be a snappy dresser with three-piece suits and fresh ties, a smart-looking fedora perched on his head, but now he favoured the convenience of track pants and plaid shirts. His slippers scrapped as he shuffled into the depths of his place.

There was a specific smell in the air as if age and carelessness had come to settle with him as housemates. Since he was alone, I assumed, stale cooking smells and old-man perspiration took over. I didn't mind since there was lots of room for a house guest or two. I was very happy just to see him again.

"You want some tea and *kakimochi*?" he asked. "I remember how you ate them when I visited Toronto."

I smiled. "Sure, but let me get them." I walked quickly to the kitchen before he could.

"All right. The tea's on the counter and the kakimochi is in the cupboard above."

After some effort on my part, the hot-water pot sat on the stovetop waiting to boil, and I served the rice crackers in a handy bowl. They were stale, but I said nothing. The metal and linoleum table was comfortable enough as I gazed at my father's best friend from Steveston days, the days of their childhood. No, he wasn't my true uncle, but he might as well have been. He always treated me like a nephew. Gave me money for my birthday and Christmas every year like clockwork. Still did.

"Uncle, I've come here because I found a diary. Otousan's diary."

"Oh?"

I took from my carry-on bag the original copy and Naoko's translation, and passed them to him. He gazed intently, not overly surprised.

"Who translated?"

"A friend." No use going into that surreal and strange tale.

"I knew you couldn't have done it," he said with a crooked smirk. He read over a few pages and then fingered the book.

"Mat-chan's dream diary. He was forever scribbling in it. Never showed anyone the contents, not even me."

Mat-chan? Never heard anyone call him that. Then again, I never heard anyone, my mom especially, call Uncle "Kuni-chan."

"Can you read from where my friend left off?" I asked.

"Well, no, not really. Besides it being Meiji Japanese, his handwriting wasn't the best. Don't know how your friend got as far as he did."

"She," I corrected.

"She's good," he said, as he shot me a knowing look. "My eyes aren't what they used to be. Can't read more than a half hour at a time."

"Don't worry about it, Uncle Kunio. Maybe you can tell me something about Dad."

"Sure, what do you want to know?"

"How come he was so good at Japanese?"

"He went to Japanese school here."

"Yeah, but so did you and my mom. Everybody did, didn't they?"

"Yes, but your dad studied. Everybody else went for recess."

"But you studied in Japan. You were born in Steveston, and Mom told me, you went to Japan to study."

"True, my obaachan took me. But, now, I'm an old man and I've forgotten most of it. Trouble was, I didn't keep it up after the war."

After I steeped and poured the tea, we settled into a West Coast mellow mood. "What camp were my parents in?"

"Your okaa was in Tashme and your dad was in Angler."

"Where's Angler?"

"Your dad was arrested in Vancouver and sent to Ontario. First to Petawawa, and then to Angler, north of Lake Superior."

"Arrested? For what? Isn't that kind of ridiculous given the internment, I mean?"

"Your dad was a *ganbariya*."

"A what?"

"Ganbariya. A die-hard."

"You mean, like the movie?"

Uncle smiled before continuing. "They were a group of men who protested the internment."

"My father?" It did seem rather absurd, my conservative, ultra-quiet dad a protester. Though he confirmed Mom's contention, I really didn't believe him, but he went into the story about the Nisei Mass Evacuation Group, again what my mom said, and the more extremist groups, some who believed that Japan was to win the war in six weeks, tops. This group was known collectively as the Ganbariya. "You're saying my father was one of these men?"

"He was always a hothead. A firebrand. He was capable of rash action if pressured. He once walked into the offices of the

Big Cheeses, the ones responsible for the Evacuation."

The Evacuation — the euphemism for the forced exile and imprison-ment of the Japanese Canadians.

"Yes, sir, without a by-your-leave, he walked in there and demanded that they evacuate us in family groups and not divide us up like so much *maguro* at Toshi's," he asserted.

"My father? My father did that?" The image of my mild old man, whose face would crack if he raised his voice, formed in my imagination.

"There were many ganbariya. The NMEG was a bunch of hotheads — your father included, but ... they only wanted what we wanted: fair treatment for us Canadian citizens."

Turns out they all were willing to go to the camps to prove their loyalty, but as intact families. Don't know exactly what they did to work at getting their wishes, but apparently my father was heavily involved. I could see my uncle tiring as his head started to droop.

"My group was the Japanese Canadian Citizens League," my uncle added, as if revived by this memory. "And we wanted the same thing, of course." His eyes fell to half-mast as he said bitterly, "Etsuji Morii became the head of a government com-mission for some unknown reason. He was good at bamboozling the government. I guess he told them he best represented the community. That was a damn lie!"

"It's all right, Uncle," I said, surprised at the outburst.

Uncle Kunio composed himself and clasped his hands on the table before him. "That was the last straw for your father and his pals. They broke away and formed the NMEG."

Then he went on to talk about the radical die-hards, the Nationalists and the Yamato Boys. They became rabid in the Angler concentration camp, feeling the betrayal the Canadian government perpetrated on the Japanese Canadians throughout the internment. According to hearsay, my uncle said they wore hachimaki, bowed to the morning sun, and chanted and sang patriotic songs to the Emperor in the camp.

"Are you kidding me?" I said. They were not the shikataga-nai types. "How come I've never heard about this camp?"

"Nobody talks about it," my uncle said.

Yet another secret. I suppose the barbed wire and the machine gun towers made the internment experience that much more shameful.

The Yamato Boys were the true dissidents. The group, according to Uncle Kunio, was led by mostly Kika-Nisei, Japanese Canadians like my uncle educated in Japan, who did everything they could to disrupt the Canadian war effort while looking forward to Japan's victory over the decadent and weak West. They held sit-ins and marches, beat up and intimidated Canadian loyalists in the community, and even staged a riot or two in Vancouver and Ontario.

"For some reason, don't ask me why, but your father joined this group." Uncle was not one of them, despite his Japanese education. *What kept him away?* I wondered. Maybe it was Auntie Marion.

The general public, and in fact the Sansei generation, always thought Issei and Nisei passively accepted the evacuation, internment, and expulsion from the coast. I was shocked. I was led to believe they endured the taking and selling of their homes, possessions, and land for pennies on the dollar. They also took the exile from the West Coast in their stride without even a whimper of protest. But the revelation that such a group existed shifted my perspective. And then to find out that my father was part of this? He was the Nisei poster boy for suffering in silence. I knew about the NMEG because it was in his journal, but to be involved? What the hell was he thinking? Who was this man I called Father?

"I truly don't know why, Michael. I was at Christina Lake with your aunt," he said. "After the war, I lost track of him even more. I didn't hear anything about him until he showed up in Toronto in 1949, I think it was, just after the Toronto restrictions were lifted. Then he met your mother and got married, found a job somehow, bought a house, and eventually had you."

"Mom said he went to Japan about that time. Do you know why?"

"He told me he was looking for someone. Didn't say who. Don't know if he found her."

"Why do you say 'her'?"

"A lot of us went back there after the war. Mostly women."

He went on to tell me the government gave Japanese Canadians a choice: stay and move east of the Rockies, or give up your citizenship and go to Japan. Many Issei chose the latter. Though Nisei wanted to stay, they had to obey their fathers — daughters especially. I then imagined all those Nisei girls quietly weeping on the docks waiting to board their ships. Some, I assumed, had sweethearts they gave up. Others were fearful of what awaited them: a strange land (where they had never been) ravaged by war and poverty. Uncle told me, in the beginning, a few starved to death in Japan or came close. I'm sure the Nisei stood waiting with a heaviness weighing them down, thinning them out.

But who was Dad looking for? Chiemi maybe? Maybe she went there. Would I go to Japan to find Naoko? Mystery piled on mystery buried in mystery.

I decided I didn't want to press Uncle too much more; he was looking very fatigued by that point. I needed to talk to others in Vancouver. I first set my sights on finding out about this Morii guy, someone my uncle hated that was for certain. I just didn't know why. I figured he'd be a good starting point in understanding my father's world back then.

17.

1984

After the bizarre New Year's when Boku announced his departure from UBC, Mrs. Sugiura asked me at church to talk to her son. I was there for *Shusho-e*, the first service of the year. I did meet him soon enough in our favourite confessional — the Golden City cathedral — a week before he was to leave for Vancouver to "take care of business." Move out of his dorm room, I guessed, finish off his paperwork, and say goodbye to whomever. Agnes of God, perhaps, or an anonymous Chinese Canadian woman.

The restaurant was more like a nineteenth-century morgue than a church, the shadowy tables like slabs for corpses, the kitchen in back as ominous as a coroner's laboratory, the muted lighting suitable for a secret autopsy. Even Radar wore the shroud of death; his face, drained of colour, was a masque of the *rue morgue*. Saying nothing he scurried away.

As strange as Radar's behaviour was, the cold quickly took our minds off the ghoulish waiter. We seemed to have brought winter from the outside into the place. Our heavy coats could not keep the chill from our bodies as we sat at the worst possible table: right beside the staircase that led to the washroom abyss in the basement. The aroma of urine and Ajax crept up the stairs and sat at the top like some gruesome attendant too old and worn out to bother with hygiene.

"Why pick this table?" I asked Boku.

"I like it," he replied. I think he liked my discomfort.

I sat down, tolerating the cold and smell. "Why'd you quit?" There didn't seem to be any reason to beat around the bush.

Boku laughed at my abruptness. "Who are you, Glenn?"

"Very funny, but I'd like to know. And don't give me that crap about learning all that you needed to know."

"Well, I did."

"Sure, you did. You need to finish, to get the degree to get a career. Not a job, a career," I retorted. "What're going to do now?"

"Hey, you still going for reparations?"

"It's called 'redress' now and don't change the subject."

"Redress, reparations, no matter what you call it, it's all collectivist bull-crap to me."

"You said that before and I still don't understand what you mean by that. Are you gonna answer my question?"

"Redress is wrong!" he said angrily. "You have to ascertain history before you can talk about it."

"Is this part of your detective work?"

"What?"

"Seriously, what're you gonna do now?"

"I have an idea. It involves Cathy."

"Cathy? What about her?"

"You see her around?"

"Yeah, once in a while."

"You seeing her?" he asked abruptly.

"From seeing her around to seeing her. What kind of jump is that?"

"Just wanna know if you've betrayed me."

"Betray? Don't be a *bakatare*," I said. "You wanna get back with her? You've got to be kidding."

"So, you are seeing her."

"No!" I had seen her in the past at church dances in the Christmas-lit Social Hall in the basement. Maybe had a dance or two with her — slow dancing to the song "I'm Leaving it all Up to You" by Dale and Grace.

But Cathy and I never went out, not since the stupid bet-date at Bumpkins. "You wanna get back with her?'

"Thinking 'bout it. I got a plan."

"What kind of plan?"

"Can't say. You'll jinx it."

Before I could assuage his doubt, Radar appeared out of nowhere with a bowl of wonton noodle soup for me and a plate of beef and greens for Boku. We hadn't ordered the food, but it was welcomed, nevertheless. The man was psychic.

"Hey, man," I observed, "beef and greens! Appropriate, huh? Eat it all now! You want a fork?"

"Shut up, you bastard," he growled.

After my laughter subsided, we ate in silence for a good long time. I then noticed the cold again. The front door wasn't open, but the temperature in the place had dropped even more than when we arrived. Boku at some point sighed deeply and I could see his breath. The cloud of steam rose into the air like a premonition. I shivered. The ghosts of Nighttown were intruding.

THE TORONTO BUDDHIST CHURCH basement bustled with activity. Middle-aged women in aprons and smocks danced an amazing choreography in the back-kitchen, preparing lunch for members and customers who paid a cursory sum for a *bento* of rice, teriyaki chicken, and *tsukemono*, or Nikkei style chow mein and grilled salmon. It was February, dreary and cold, and *Harumatsuri* — time to look forward optimistically to *Hanamatsuri* and warmer weather.

The public knew it too, packing the church for a taste of the exotic. Never mind the spiritual reasons for the celebration, they were more than likely drawn in by the aromas of tempura shrimp and vegetables or the barbecue smoke of the plump chicken breasts, wings, and legs. There was the pervasive smell of burning incense to remind everyone of the Buddha's presence, but that was lost on the uninitiated. The surrounding community simply never understood the goings-on within this little Buddhist church inexplicably located in the west-end working-class neighbourhood of Bathurst north of Bloor.

Perhaps some were taken in by the stereotypes. I chewed out my fair share of ignorant white boys who asked, "Where're the *gee-sha* girls?" Most others were looking for bargains amongst the trinkets and baked goods upstairs in the intensely scented *hondo*, or paying for a tasty meal of unfamiliar food or food they only had once a year.

Every large Nisei hand-built wooden table protected by a white paper covering was loaded with customers. The latecomers stood against the white concrete walls surveying the landscape for finished meals and people with multiple packages and bags shuffling to leave. Once a space was spied, they rushed, weaved, bumped, and ducked to get to the spot; otherwise, it was gone in mere seconds. Then it was a matter of waving frenetically to attract a volunteer waiter's attention to come and take their orders. Then another long wait for the waiter in the food lines to the kitchen as the orders were filled. All taking place beneath the intense cone of noise from conversations, food orders, and shouted commands in the kitchen. Not an efficient system, but a longstanding one.

Mrs. Sugiura was one of the women who filled the orders. Rising above the rest, she was resplendent in her full-length gleaming white apron, white cap, and rough, peasant hands covered by blue rubber gloves. Her face was alive with good tidings and laughter.

When our eyes met, I approached her and said, "Hey, Mrs. S! I spoke to Boku...I mean Kenneth."

"Oh, yes," she said. "Let's go to the office."

We snaked our way through the labyrinth of tables and chairs to the cluttered room near the front of the church basement, saying hi to the many familiar faces on the way. Filled with extra furniture, file cabinets, and office machinery, like a defunct typewriter from the 1940s and a Gestetner printer, clean and fresh for use, no one was in the room. Later, volunteers would fill it to count the proceeds for the day.

"Michael, do you think my son is crazy?" she asked in a hushed tone.

"For quitting school? Nah. It's just a phase he's going through."

"It's just that our family believes if you commit to something, you finish it. You don't quit midstream. You keep swimming. Unless there's something...".

"That's just the point, Mrs. S. He wasn't really committed to architecture. He thought he was but, in the end, he knew he was still searching for something in his life. He was playing the detective."

"The what?"

"You know, like he said," I answered. "He's still searching for something in life."

"But what?"

Mrs. Sugiura wasn't particularly attractive, but the lines in her face and the demurely curved eyes gave her a beauty that hinted at a long-ago coquettish girl who charmed with personality rather than guile. On the other hand, she was understanding and compassionate. However, her back was in a slight hunch, as if worrying about Boku was dragging her down.

"I don't know, Mrs. S., you'll have to ask your son yourself."

BOKU'S "PLAN" was revealed to me about one week after Harumatsuri. I received a phone call from Cathy.

"You know Boku's back in town," she said.

"Yeah, we met at the Golden City."

"Do you know why he's back?"

"Quit UBC, the idiot."

"Oh, I thought you support the idea. He said so."

"I kinda do, but I thought it was a total waste. I mean his future was secure, and he likes computers. Now what's he gonna do?"

"I think I can answer that." A long pause followed. "He asked me to marry him."

"Sorry, say again."

"He asked me to marry him."

"He asked to marry you?"

"Yes."

This time I remained silent for a long time. "You aren't fooling me, are you?"

"No," she said with a touch of annoyance.

So that's why he was checking out my status with Cathy. "Hard to believe."

"He was dead serious. He said if I said yes, I would have everything I ever dreamed of... everything we talked about long ago."

"Like what?"

"Split-level house in North York somewhere with a pool in the back. A couple of vacations a year. Two cars. Kids, maybe."

Joanie and Dave's three Cs. "How?"

"He said he had some new plan to get money ... all the money *we* needed. He worked out a new formula for making money on the stock market."

"The stock market? He never mentioned it to me."

"Well, that's what he said to me."

"And you believed him?"

"Not really, but what could I say?"

"Well, are you going to marry him?"

"I don't know. I don't know. He really hurt me."

The proposal seemed very prosaic coming from Cathy. Then again, there wasn't a poetic bone in her body.

18.

March 1991

As I sat alone in the kitchen the next morning, I noticed how cold it was in Uncle's house. The front door wasn't open, but the temperature in the place had dropped considerably. I breathed out a cotton ball of steam. It billowed and curled like a premonition. I shivered.

In order to generate some heat, I put on the coffee and made breakfast for Uncle and me: scrambled eggs, cold rice, and left-over wieners. A little shoyu and ketchup, and the meal was right as rain. Uncle came to join me when the food was ready; I guess the aroma attracted him. He looked older than his seventy-plus years. I suppose I was projecting. His years bent his body into a permanent stoop. He shuffled as he walked, or rather slid, along the floor. His angular head was full of thinning white hair. His eyes eroded with the run of old tears. His skin was rough and furrowed, as if loneliness had him in its grip and was slowly squeezing the life out of him. His once-tall frame was not only sagging, but had shrunk. At least he wasn't fading away like Mom or Naoko.

"Uncle Kunio, what are you going to do with yourself?"

"Do?"

"Yeah, sure, you can't be rattling around this big old house forever." I regretted saying this — it wasn't any of my business — but I was concerned.

"Oh, I suppose not," he replied. "But this was our home, your aunt's and mine. I guess I kinda got used to the place. They'll have to carry me outta here."

"You oughta come to Toronto. For a visit, I mean. Stay at the house, see your friends."

"No...no. Don't want to bother anyone."

"You won't be a bother," I assured, not sure how my mother would react to his coming. "We have plenty of room."

"Most of my friends are dead." He became wistful. "Would like to see the Watanabe family again, though."

"Who?"

"Emiko and her mother."

"I know a Watanabe family. Is there a Dave Watanabe in it?" I asked.

"I don't know, Michael. The Watanabes were very kind to me in the Steveston days."

I had to talk to Dave, though I hadn't seen him in a while.

Uncle paused before continuing. "Strange things happened to the Watanabe father during camp days. He made a deal to get him and his family up to Lillooet. Bet he was sorry he did that. A deal with the Devil. He had to turn against a lot of people — your father and other NMEG people, my gang too. Yeah, he paid a heavy price."

"Like what?"

"Suicide. Your father told me when I caught up with him in Toronto. He had met someone just after the war. Watanabe's daughter."

"This Emiko?"

"No, her sister, Chiemi."

The name struck me like lightning. "Chiemi?"

"Oh, right, you probably never heard of her. Your father was with her a brief time before your mother came into the picture. They fell for one another after the war, though I don't know where or exactly when. Don't really know what happened. As I told you, I lost track of your otousan."

Uncle Kunio didn't know much more about Chiemi. Perhaps she was a dream.

I strained to remember the lines precisely:

She was asleep as she rose into the air and spread her arms wide, poised as if about to fly. Her eyes sealed by the dust of night, she reached upward and began to soar — right through the ceiling and into the open blue. Clouds parted. The sky and stars beckoned as she rose higher and higher.

I called out her name, "Chiemi!"

I knew I had to talk to Dave.

I couldn't continuously badger my uncle for old memories during the rest of my stay, so I decided to look up an old "friend." GiGi Chan, the Yellow Seed woman I had met at Gary Konishi's apartment back in '82 — the one who called me a "jerk." We hadn't parted on good terms, but that was so long ago.

She now worked as a social worker for Tonari Gumi, a Nikkei Seniors drop-in centre in the old Japantown part of East Vancouver.

I called and arranged to meet her at TG, a storefront on Powell Street. I took it as a good sign that she hadn't instantly hung up on me. She sounded like she was happy to hear from me. I was surprised that she was part of the Japanese social service organization.

The building was typical of the area: two rundown floors, a large ground-floor window to the street. Inside was cluttered like the debris of a disorganized mind. Piles of paraphernalia from the Powell Street Festival, the summer festival that celebrated Japanese Canadian art and culture, choked the pathways to the back kitchen and communal area. In amongst the stacks, displays of health and welfare pamphlets vied for the attention of the area's elderly Japanese Canadian Issei with no family, or those whose families had forgotten about them after they had moved back to the area after the war, because that was all they knew.

Down the dark corridor, the place eventually opened to a room lined with Japanese books, a library of sorts, and a rudimentary kitchen at the far end. Volunteer women scurried about like the TBC women preparing lunch or a snack, while others welcomed and then listened to the clients who stumbled in through the front door.

The *toshiyori* appeared contorted like tree trunks tired of their long existence. Many were curved over so badly they could spot lost change in any crevice in the sidewalks of the city. Others leaned on canes or were moulded into their wheelchairs. Their faces were crumpled into permanent squints, contoured valleys and ravines under the smiling eyes. But no matter how humbled, decrepit, crumbled they had become because of age and circumstance, they were...beautiful.

I spotted GiGi sitting in the backroom with one of the old folks, listening intently. She hadn't changed a bit, even her hair was still long and luxurious; she was as attractive as I remembered.

"Mike!" she said, her round face beaming.

"Sorry, didn't mean to disturb you."

The toshiyori man gazed at me with a forgiving smile and turned away.

GiGi took me to a convenient office. "Ta-ke-*san*," she called. "This is my friend Mike Shintani from Toronto. Mind if we use your office for a minute or two?"

A warm-hearted Japanese man looked over, smiled, and granted permission with a wave.

"So why are you working here?" I asked stupidly. It was 1982 again.

"What do you mean?"

"I mean...here. You're, you're Chinese."

She laughed and said, "You're still a jerk."

Turns out she considered herself an Asian Canadian, rather than a CBC, Canadian Born Chinese. Even more surprising, she had an excellent command of Japanese and Cantonese. She was quite a woman. I *was* a jerk.

GiGi was stylishly dressed despite working in such a depressed area. East Vancouver had become a tide pool for the indigent, addicted, and deranged. Sketchy characters reeking of dried urine, sour clothes, and unwashed bodies, their wrinkles, and scars trapping the effluent, crawled along the streets only to come to a standstill when drug fatigue set in. She was the proverbial flower growing on top of the dung heap.

"So nice to see you, Mike," she said in her cool voice. "How are you?"

"I'm fine," I answered, though I wasn't.

Niceties aside, we settled into the business at hand. "What can I do for you?" she asked.

As soon as she said that, I realized I didn't know what I wanted. I stumbled through the story of my father's diary, leaving out the supernatural elements. They sounded preposterous even to me. She listened intently as I then groped for direction.

"Have you ever heard of...a Morry? Here in J-town?"

"Are you talking about Etsuji Morii? He was the gangster kingpin here back in the day."

A gangster? "Yeah, what happened to him? Can I talk to him?" A silly question since my Japanese was so bad.

"When his wife died, oh, I forget when exactly, he went back to Japan. Took her ashes, I think. It was before my time...before TG in fact."

"Approximately when?"

"I'd say the early 1960s, only because some say he died in 1970."

"Some say? Who?"

"The toshiyori here. Mr. Yamada, the man I was talking to knew him." She called out in Japanese: "Yamada-san, you remember Morii-san-ne?"

"Hai, so deso," he said in a craggy old voice. He explained through GiGi that before the war Morii was a criminal kingpin in the Powell Street area. During the war he was in some internment camp and returned to Vancouver after the government allowed the Japanese back in 1949 and led a quiet life as a devout Buddhist until his wife died. He then moved to Tokyo.

Takeo Nagano, the executive director of Tonari Gumi, soon joined the conversation. Takeo-*san* left Japan back in the early '60s only to wind up on the streets of Vancouver's eastside until a social worker took him to the nearest shelter. He was a potter in Kyoto who had had about enough of the strictures of Japanese society. He came to Vancouver in search of artistic and social freedom. What he found was a purpose: taking care of the Japanese Canadian seniors in the area who had no family and had fallen on hard times. He established Tonari Gumi as a result.

"I met and talked to Morii-*san* for little bit," he said in a raspy and accented English. "He didn't say much, but he knew he was going back to Japan."

"Did he mention anything about the Nisei Mass Evacuation Group?"

"No, not that I remember. What is that?"

I didn't answer but, undeterred, he then went on about Morii and his gangland activities: how he controlled all the liquor, prostitutes, and gambling in the Japanese community. How he dictated what was happening in the Powell Street area, even going so far as to setting the curricula at the Japanese Language School and controlling events like Hanamatsuri at the Buddhist Church. No wonder Uncle hated him, and I understood why he left out the man's felonious connections.

Morii was a dead end as far as my father's activities were concerned.

"So which camp did he go to?" I asked.

"Because he delivered the Japanese, he could go anywhere he wanted. He chose Minto, a cozy place for himself. There was electricity, running water, and other things."

He delivered the Japanese. What did he mean by that? I decided to ask GiGi later.

"Where's that?"

"Up Lillooet way."

I would have to look it up on a map, I decided.

Mr. Yamada, who had been listening with eyes closed, then piped in: "You from Toronto?"

My Japanese was rusty, but that I understood. "Hai."

"Then you should see Rikimatsu-san."

Rikimatsu Kintaro was Morii's right-hand man and he was still alive, living in a senior's home in downtown Toronto.

"You should see him. He can answer many questions," Yamada-san said encouragingly.

I THANKED TAKEO-SAN and Yamada-san. I was struck by the idea that the Japanese Canadian community had a gangster in its midst, in fact a gang of them with this Morii as their leader. I grew up thinking we were all law-abiding, quiet citizens, never wishing to call attention to ourselves, let alone commit crimes. Now I find out about a criminal organization. But then there was Boku, the bank robber, and his uncle who slaughtered his family.

I invited GiGi for dinner in gratitude. She accepted after checking with her teenage daughter.

"Brenda? Tell Grandma I won't be home for dinner...with an old friend from Toronto. Don't say that," she said on the office phone.

I heard a laugh on the other end. "What was so funny?" I asked after GiGi ended the call.

"Oh, nothing, she just likes to call me and all my friends *Yellow Power Hippies.*"

"*Yellow Power Hippies*? This know-nothing younger generation."

Isamu's was a long-established Japanese restaurant on E. Hastings Ave. The interior consisted of a dim corridor, one side of which housed many *tatami* rooms, elevated to accommodate a shoe step. Fake woodblock prints, probably from calendars, were housed in cheap frames on the walls; leg space was provided underneath the tables to spare customers' knees. The dominating dark-wood panelling of the hallway needed replacing badly and so gave the establishment a dingy feel. The air was heavy with the odour of stale tempura oil. The two waitresses dressed in kimonos swept their hair up into ponytails and buns and displayed a pleasant demeanour.

"*Oneesan, sake onigaishimasu,*" I ordered. She looked surprised at my cheek at calling her "older sister." GiGi smiled.

"Do you think she was insulted?" I asked.

GiGi stared at me and replied, "No-o-o, not at all."

I looked at her askance.

The food was typical of a Japanese restaurant: teishoku, shrimp tempura, and various *donburi*. The *tekka maki* was divine: deep-red and thick maguro tightly wrapped with springy black nori. And so generous: eighteen *maki* with every order. Nothing like the fresh fish of BC.

The only complaint about the place revolved around the owner Sammy Otagaki himself. A grouchy, middle-aged man, he never supported the Japanese Canadian community even though the volunteers from all the events in the area, from *Obon* to the Powell Street Festival, patronized the place. The Japanese Canadians kept the place afloat, yet Otagaki never bought a program ad, never offered any kind of sponsorship, or even allowed a poster to be displayed. Needless to say, he didn't volunteer in any capacity. He even forbade his staff from getting involved. One did, and was fired for her community spirit.

No one knew why he was so obstinate. GiGi speculated that he had been treated badly by the other Nisei when he was a child. He was getting revenge. It hardly mattered, I thought; the food was good and relatively cheap. And such large portions!

I sipped tea and observed GiGi's face. Her eyes were round and tender, but tended to disappear when she smiled or laughed. Her cheeks supported the eyes once they closed and her mouth was wide and inviting.

We spent the meal catching up. She told me about her career, her love that got away (a California Sansei student leader she had met during her activist days down there), the resulting daughter, and her future plans.

I told her about Naoko and my quest for my father's identity. I didn't tell her about my translator's strange disappearance. She and I simply broke up, much to my regret, was the story.

After dinner, we stepped into the Japantown night and, in the coned light of a streetlamp, a place that existed in dense air, salty sea spray, and time miraculously appeared before me. My parents, my grandparents, my uncle and aunt walked these very streets; my father could have stood on this sidewalk, perhaps this very spot. The same storefronts creaked in recognition.

I walked GiGi to a bus stop on East Hastings and waited. We parted with a hug and as friends when the bus came. She kissed my cheek goodbye.

19.

1984

I ran into Boku a few months after his marriage proposal. We didn't socialize much during that time, but every so often I ran into him at some community event. This time it happened to be the *Bon* Dance downtown.

The incense of the Buddha curled and billowed in the sky above our futuristic clam-shell City Hall. The wisps seemed like the spirits of ancestors coming back for a visit. Kunio Suyama, the perennial emcee of the event, was at the microphone. His Nisei alto voice joyfully gave forth with the instructions for the *Tanko Bushi*, the Coalminer's Dance. If there ever was a universal custom for the Nikkei in the world, it was this dance. Very few in Japan knew it, but every Japanese community in North America and elsewhere, I suspected, came together to dance the Tanko Bushi.

But in Toronto only females joined. It was not cool for guys to participate in a Japanese *odori*. Just not done.

Nathan Phillips Square was packed with Japanese Canadians. The pool in front reflected the faces I had come to love, all the JCs I had ever known in my life: the sad, hangdog look of Fats Nagai; the ironically scrawny Hippo Tanaka; pale Blackie; Tats; Fudge; and Chips; male and female Nisei with stories to tell, but kept secret from their own children.

Reverend Ishiura was perhaps the most impressive, presiding over the celebration in his priestly robes, and his *ojuzu* hanging from his wrists. His shaven head made him more in tune with the Buddha Dharma than anyone else present. His smiling eyes beamed with compassion.

And there were the Sansei girls, refugees from the Girls Club of years past; some dressed in a colourful kimono bought by their mothers from Japan, others in suburban mall outfits, appropriately matched with expensive labels. They waited patiently for the festivities to begin. The Boys were in jeans and collared shirts. They hung around each other making jokes about the girls, something they had done since they were kids. Maturity may catch up with them one day — in their dotage, perhaps.

I ran into Boku by the stage. He was staring at Kunio, the emcee.

"Yo, Boku, what's happenin'?"

"Checking out the emcee gig."

"You wanna be emcee?"

"Sure, why not? It seems easy enough."

"But you don't know any Japanese."

"Why do I need that?"

"So you can communicate dance instructions. Like for the Tanko Bushi?"

"I can fake it."

"Yeah, like what you said to the Issei ladies when we were kids."

"Why? What did I say?"

"You were apologizing for your lack of Japanese," I said, before bowing. "Watakushi no nihongo wa heita-kuso."

"What's wrong with that?"

"Sorry, my Japanese is shit?"

"I didn't say that."

"Yes, you did. They were so upset they flipped their dentures."

"It'll still be cool to be emcee," he said turning toward the crowd.

Seeing little reaction, I asked, "Seen Cathy around? She always comes to these things."

"Yeah, she's around."

"Around? Around where? You don't seem too interested."

"Why should I?"

"I thought she was your betrothed."

"Aww, she drips."

"Whoa, that was harsh. What happened?"

He grew sombre. "Saw her at the Centre after Harumatsuri. She was practising odori with the club there. I was there because I knew she was there. I must say she looked good."

"Yeah, yeah," I said. "What happened next?"

"I asked her to marry me."

"You asked her... well that's great. What'd she say?"

"Well, she was surprised..."

"And?"

"Took a while, but she turned me down."

"She what?"

"She said, 'No,' even after I told her I would give her everything she wanted. You know, the townhouse, the cars, the vacations. I mean, what more does she want?"

We both fell silent.

"Well, she blew it, man. I gave her a chance. I'll get rich and show her, boy, I'll show her."

"I'm not dark enough for you," he claimed she had said. I never knew Cathy to be a racist.

"Now what're you gonna do?"

"I'm just going to have to prove to her I can provide those things."

"I think there's more to it than —"

"Yes sir, that's the ticket."

Not wanting to discourage him, I asked, "You figured out your stock market program?"

"Yeah, something like that."

20.

1991

As I scanned my father's dream diary, I came across another poem in English:

A firedrake dogstar
shone in the daylight heavens,
brighter than Venus in the sky. And at night,
it shone over the Delta like Cassiopeia,
the recumbent constellation (the Buddha reclining,
his right arm at rest next to the body).

The pinpoint lights form the scrawl of His signature.
I watched the dragon lowlying on the horizon,
eastward of Sirius, the Dog Star,
as I walked the slumbering summer fields
at midnight, returning from her arms.

—Summer 1942

A tear came to my eye as the images leapt off the page, pinging and ricocheting in my imagination. I had no idea my father was capable of such beautiful writing.

The layers of obscure references began to overlap and intersect as I contemplated the poem. There were other poems, all in Japanese, and some of the entries were very poetic (according to Naoko), but this was beyond anything that had come before.

Maybe it wasn't original; perhaps it was a poem by someone else altered by my father for some purpose only he knew. Given his circumstances in the summer of 1942, I could see the "Delta" referring to Vancouver and the woman being Chiemi. The Buddha and Cassiopeia were embellishments to be sure. But what was the "firedrake" star?

The encyclopedia told me it was a mythical fire-breathing dragon. What was its significance in my father's poem? Maybe it meant nothing.

I didn't show my uncle the poem as I stood in the front vestibule of his house to say goodbye. The night was cold, lapping at the doorway as my red-eye flight beckoned. I didn't want to linger too long and give him a chill.

His eye rims drooped with sadness; his hunched shoulders emphasized his advancing age. I hugged him; he pulled away slightly as if shocked by my expression of love, but he did not break from me.

"Take care of yourself, Uncle," I said.

Perhaps he saw the concern in my eyes; even so, he didn't say anything except, "Hey, you better go. You'll miss your plane." He sniffled and wiped his nose on his plaid shirt sleeve.

"One last question. Have you ever heard of the word sintamanti?" I asked.

"No, can't say that I have. Spell it for me."

I did.

"Oh, you mean *cintamani*."

"What is it?"

"Some kind of rock. It's a Buddhist symbol or something," he explained and spelled it out for me. "How do you know that word?"

"Oh, I just heard it somewhere," I said as I wrote down the word in a notepad. There was no use explaining my feverish delusions. "Come to Toronto, Uncle. Mom and me'll take care of you."

He nodded and then waved as I entered the airport cab.

THE PLANE RIDE HOME was uneventful. "Relatively crash free," as John Cleese once quipped. It gave me time to think about the recent and distant events of my life. The thin inner atmosphere made me a bit dizzy, but the flight attendant was a nice distraction.

There were people for me to find: Rikimatsu, the gangster; Chiemi; and Naoko. Naoko...there were no more dreams about her after she had said that Buddhist word and "goodbye." Would I ever see again?

I had to find her, but I had absolutely no idea of where to start. I was stuck between two worlds. The burden of history was heavy, its weight warping me.

And then Boku came to mind. I hadn't seen him since his trial in 1987. He was convicted of course. I read in the paper he had been sentenced to three years in a maximum-security facility. His motives for robbing a bank were as puzzling today as they had been back then. After I attended the trial, I found that nothing had been revealed, except that perhaps his mother's suspicions were correct: he was crazy.

But I really didn't think so; misguided, perhaps, but not crazy. He considered Japanese Canadians campaigning for redress "greedy." We had "made it" as he contended. Why would we want "blood money" for something we had overcome? It was shameful to ask. Never mind the human rights issue; never mind the hypocrisy of Canadian racism.

He sounded like a huk, a liberal white-man tired of the argument. We should "move on" with our lives. The internment had happened so long ago with very little effect on my generation. Huks also countered with their own tribulations. Many had suffered at the fists of bullies as well, and they rose above it to become successful, contributing Canadian citizens. Their Sansei partners always became co-opted and toed the line. The couples never took into consideration that in 1942 the "Canadian" part of Japanese Canadian was ignored, and rights were trampled in the panic and paranoia. Everything was taken away, never to be resolved, redeemed, or rebuilt — the torment of loss.

Boku's grandfather was his example of dignity and the higher road.

Still, Boku walked into the bank and demanded $20,000 using the threat of a hidden explosive. That's all he said he did, but did not believe such actions to be attempted robbery. Such was his defence. As he said in court, how could he think he was innocent? Just because he had no intention of robbing the bank doesn't negate the fact that he did. A defense mechanism?

My pal never admitted to being at fault for anything: quitting UBC, robbing a bank, his problems with women.

As I casually gazed out of my airplane window, I marvelled at the constellation of Vancouver below, the Japanese Canadian ancestral home. The edge of black water, forests, and mountains stood in sharp contrast to the stars above. Yet I felt no connection to the landscape: the sting of saltwater, the smell of ocean, and the clean air filled with the spiked aroma of ancient evergreens. Because of the internment experience, I had been hollowed out, leaving me dead, soulless. That was what most huks didn't understand; they saw the redress movement as a grab for money. The constant reminder of past injustices, tedious. More importantly, Boku too was empty inside and he never knew why.

MOM GREETED ME at the front door, and I told her about Uncle Kunio, but little else. Her eyes were downcast as if she was weary. All the remaining energy in her seemed to have evaporated since I was gone. Her lips were pale, her arms thin and nearly translucent. Her face drawn. It was happening again, only more pronounced. I decided she was not disappearing; she must be sick. I promised myself to call for an appointment with our family doctor, Dr. Kuwabara.

"I heard about a man named..." — I couldn't remember so I consulted my notebook I had handy — "Rikimatsu."

My mother's face turned red. Her anger flared as she said,

"What about him?"

"I thought I'd look him up. Ask him about his boss, Morii. I was told they were both gangsters."

She moved slowly, as if in pain, and rose to her feet and said, "No, you will not see Rikimatsu or ask about Morii."

"Why?"

"They are dangerous men. If you go snooping and asking stupid questions, they will come after you ... threaten you ... maybe hurt you. They still have ... friends. Gangster friends."

"Jesus, Ma, I just want to know about Dad during the war."

"You don't need to know that either."

"Then why did you help me get to Vancouver?"

"Never mind." She turned away in disgust.

"Are these men going to threaten me? Or what? Ma? Ma?"

In the ensuing silence, I said, "How old are these guys?"

"Eighty-something, I suppose," she grumbled and shrugged.

I smiled, resolving not to tell her that Morii was dead and Rikimatsu was in a nursing home. "I think I can outrun them."

CASTLEVIEW-WYCHWOOD TOWERS, an imposing red-brick building at the top of Christie Street, was a nursing home with one floor exclusively for Japanese Canadians. It was the only such service in eastern Canada.

Some programs were conducted in Japanese; a Japanese restaurant offered "culturally appropriate food" once a week for free; volunteers and assigned social workers, if not the orderlies, were of Japanese or Asian background. Families felt very secure in leaving their loved ones in such a place seemingly conducive to a comfortable, if not happy, end of life.

The tall towers looked down their long noses at the denizens of Koreatown to the sloped south, filled with crudely put-together restaurants and foreign aromas of spice and oil that enticed passersby. But I wasn't there to visit the impoverished, sad, and condemned. My goal was to meet Rikimatsu. My biggest obstacle was language. As an Issei, the former gangster only spoke Japanese, with very little broken-English. Accordingly, I asked the floor's coordinator, Dick Takeshita, to help me. He knew a little about the man but not much. Thin in muscle and body, Takeshita-san was slightly stooped with fading hair atop his boney head. He looked as if he would soon be a resident himself. The Takeshita family hadn't lived on Powell Street in Vancouver; they had owned a farm in the Okanagan Valley. Dick had come to Toronto well after the loss and exile of WWII to become a social worker and ended up naturally enough at Castleview. He agreed to act as my interpreter, taking me to the man's room and introducing me.

The room was institutional at best, with sickly green walls, a bed, a mirror flat against a wall, a chair or two, and a nightstand. There were touches of home: a small, old radio built by some Japanese company, photographs in frames, a favourite shawl. Takeshita-san said that many items disappear because the residents who could wander in and out of rooms take whatever fancied them. There was no malice intended. Ownership meant nothing to those living with dementia.

Rikimatsu was a shadow of his former self, I guessed. His body trapped by a wheelchair had rebelled against him and curved his back, even more so than Takeshita-san. His arms and legs had thinned out to resemble dried wooden sticks. His face was shrivelled with one distinctive feature: he had no nose. My guide explained that, according to legend, he had lost it to Vancouver Chinese gang members before WWII. Both of us could only imagine why.

Rik-san awoke from a near vegetative state when we entered. With mucus-seeping eyes, he gazed at me as Takeshita-san introduced me. He smiled as we started to converse.

"I know you," he declared, squeezing his left eye as if to bring me into focus. "Shintani? Yes, I know that name."

"You must know my family. My otousan was a banker back in the day. On or near Powell Street."

"No, no, I had no use for banks. I'll think on it for awhile."

He was surprisingly coherent. "Rik-san," I continued, "have you ever heard of the Nisei Mass Evacuation Group?"

After Takeshita-san's translation, he answered with a curt "Hai."

"Then you must've known my father — Shintani Kazuto or Roy."

"Yes, yes!" he said. "Your otousan, you say? He was such a *namaiki*."

"Troublemaker," Takeshita-san translated.

Rikimatsu went on to say the NMEG caused all kinds of grief for the Japanese and Japanese Canadians. They staged sit-downs, protest marches, and riots.

Riots? I was more than a little shocked. The Nisei committed acts of civil disobedience? Unbelievable, my law-abiding, conservative, and quiet father, a dissident, a militant, an extremist, a rabid radical? I suppose my mother and uncle hinted at such. The former gangster was quite forthcoming about his disdain for the group and Nisei in general.

"They were a bunch of dumb-heads. Stirring it up against the government when all they had to do was cooperate. The *Idou* was just a trip to summer camp is all. No one wanted to live in that stinking part of Vancouver."

The Idou was the Issei word for the "Evacuation," Takeshita-san explained.

"And your otousan was in the middle of it," Rik-san said. "I remember the riot in the Immigration Building. One idiot got shot. Don't know how it happened."

"Where were you during the war?" I asked, intrigued.

"Tashme. I was taken care of because I cooperated."

"Can you tell me about Etsuji Morii?"

At the mention of that name, he froze.

"People have told me you had a . . . a relationship with him," I said.

He remained silent.

Takeshita-san observed, "I think the conversation is over."

We moved to leave.

"Hey *bozu*," Rik-san called as we hit the door.

I turned to face him.

"I am just a small man. I used to be big, used to be loved, used to be feared."

I said nothing and stepped through the doorway before I remembered a package of pink, white, and green *manju* I had brought. I left it on his nightstand. Having stopped by Furuya in Chinatown to buy the confection, I was a good Japanese after all, even though I doubted that Rik-san would ever enjoy such a treat with all the thievery on the floor.

AFTER THANKING TAKESHITA-SAN for all his help with another package of manju, I left Castleview to go home. On the bus, my mind went over the scant information I had gleaned from the gangster. For some reason I drifted to thinking about Dave, my car-loving good buddy who once saved my life.

21.

April 1988

Another Saturday night, and Dave and I prowled Yonge Street during the witching hour when all the would-be alcoholics came out to stagger along the streets, often ending up curbside. I had brought along my two-piece, twenty-ounce pool cue on the pretext of bashing about the cherries and colour'd balls in some basement dive on Spadina. We each had bought a custom cue because the ones in the hall had more curves than Highway One on the California coast. But that night we cruised instead.

The drunks could no longer afford to stay in the bars and so spilled out onto the sidewalks. Some pooled with friends rousting about. They howled at passing vehicles, pawing the ground for females. Finding no one.

No matter how bright the neon and incandescent signs, the darkness settled like fog between the pedestrians and lurching cars. The cool breeze hinted at an early autumn, with trees on sidestreets resisting the urge to turn colour.

Dave and Joanie were over. Long over. There were now rumours she had started to see someone else at the Centre — an MBA student at York U no less. Dave said he was all right with it, but I could tell he wasn't. He just wanted to drive, forget pool, forget Joanie, maybe go to Chinatown later. I went along for the ride, to keep him company in case he wanted to talk.

He didn't. He just sat concentrating on the road ahead, even though we weren't moving much. The driver-side window was cracked open so he could smoke, the cigarette flaring brightly with every pull.

I felt compelled to say something. "I hear Joanie's with David Kawasaki," I offered. Another Dave, the irony lost on my buddy.

He took another puff and continued to stare straight ahead. He looked like a fatigued driver on the Don Valley Parkway at rush hour.

"He's just the kind of guy she wants: the nine-to-fiver with a white collar, who wants a career, not a job. He slicks back his hair like he's Al Pacino in the *Godfather II*. Kind of a creepy guy. Don't think it's serious. He knows nothing 'bout cars."

Dave's only answer was to swerve suddenly around the jammed cars in front of us. He jerked his car into a narrow space in the adjacent lane and moved forward a considerable distance before we slowed to another crawl. He then pulled back into the original curbside lane. The manoeuvre told me to shut up. I turned my gaze away and fiddled with the radio.

I rolled down the window and breathed in the stale air. Anxious bodies walked up and down the concrete path; some had stopped to look at store displays; others fell to the ground in heaps unable to fight the alcohol anymore. Old rubbies pissed their pants in alleyways. The young white boys, mostly students from the University of Toronto or Queen's, looked for a fight.

I soon became a target. A bleary-eyed huk spied Dave's car, which stood at a standstill, and wobbled forward.

It's funny how a bad situation slows everything down. The huk, dirty blond and stupid with a decidedly drunk face, stumbled to the car, bent over, and leaned into the passenger-side window. He was so close to my face his fumes grabbed at my throat. "What is this Chinatown? You fuck'n Chinks," he slobbered. "Go back to where youse came from." When faced with raw racism I, like so many of my fellow Asians, usually froze in shock, and did nothing. But this time I reacted automatically for some reason, and swiftly struck him in the face with the butt-end of my handy collapsed cue. The buffoon yelped like a puppy, covering his cheek and fell backward into the arms of his friends. Upon recovery, he struck some preposterous martial-arts pose complete with half-closed eyes, "judo-chop" hands and raised foot. A phony Karate Kid. He was drunk, hurt, and angry.

I instinctively opened the car door and stepped out with my cue at the ready onto the sidewalk. The huk unsteadily moved forward to do battle. I swung my club, missing him, and he fell back to the ground again. At nearly the same moment I heard a loud bang, and a blur of a body crossed in front of me. My head spun with the punch of sound and I fell to the sidewalk. Shouting and screaming all around me.

As my head cleared, I looked over at the body lying in front of me. It was lifeless as a pool of blood formed underneath it and flowed to the nearby curb. It was Dave.

I grabbed him and turned to hold him as I called for someone, anyone, in the crowd that surrounded us for help. Though I had the presence of mind to place a hand on where I thought the wound was to stop the bleeding, I uselessly said — like I was in a movie — "Hold on, Dave. Hold on, you'll be all right." It felt like hours passed before an emergency team showed up. They took over and efficiently stabilized Dave and took him away. The police informed me that witnesses said some stranger in the crowd had pulled out a revolver and opened fire. Dave must've seen what was about to happen and dove in front of me to take the bullet.

THE HOSPITAL WAS HEAVY with that antiseptic smell. It's as if the price of cleanliness was a chokehold on the senses. The lighting was subdued to suppress any hint of brightness and happiness. The brown and green walls, adorned with meaningless art, depressed the spirit as visitors walked through the corridors past darkened rooms exuding a hint of urine and groans of pain and draining life.

Dour nurses patrolled the halls with attendants following and looking purposeful. I noted how many were overweight in fabric-fatigued uniforms. "No look good" as Issei used to say. Doctors were few and far between, though I did see one with a stethoscope around the neck.

I had been dealing with the police the last few days, so I hadn't visited Dave since the first night. They told me it was probably a friend of the young bigot, but there was no suspect or even a person of interest. They could not find the drunk, though they speculated he was from Queen's University; they had found a jacket with a university letter on its breast nearby. I hoped that cost him a lot of money, though he probably had a rich bastard for a father. The night of the incident I was too emotional and shocked to identify anyone. I had held my buddy in my arms until the Emergency Crew came. I remember pushing hands away with my own bloody hands to protect my friend. They only wanted to help Dave, but I didn't know that in my state of mind.

After much wandering of the hospital halls, I finally found Dave's semi-private room. Several machines blinked and buzzed by his bed. A television hung suspended by a flexible arm overhead. It was impotently silent. I couldn't see the wound in his abdomen, but I could sense it as a gaping hole, bloody and vile. Tubes ran from bottles and bags into his arms and other parts. The doctors had placed him in an induced coma.

Joanie sat by his side, crying soundlessly.

I was surprised to see her. We didn't hug or kiss; we didn't have that kind of relationship.

"Joanie, how's he doing?"

"Same as when he came in."

"You okay?"

"Yes."

"His parents been by?"

"Yes."

I did count my blessings to have missed his parents. I didn't know if I could've dealt with the emotion. Not sure if they blamed me for what had happened. Tender mercies were at work.

I HAD MET DAVE a year or two before 1977, the Japanese Canadian Centennial Year. We worked together on the National Sansei Conference in June of '77, which I considered to be the natural follow-up to the 1974 gathering. Richard Yoshida, a Buddhist Church stalwart in charge of the Centennial Sansei Conference programming, recruited me. He in turn was brought on board by the first Sansei Toronto Buddhist Church President, Alan Kai. Al was also on the Japanese Canadian Cultural Centre Board of Directors and was naturally pegged to head up the conference. Good way to raise money for the Centre and fulfill the Centennial mandate.

Rich always wore a suit, tie, brogues, and permed hair. He worked as a realtor. At the Centre, he was in his weekend uniform: a conservative green Polo shirt and neutrally coloured slacks. If I were more cynical, I'd say he wanted to curry favour with the JCCC (nicknamed the Japanese Canadian Country Club) members for business purposes. Yeah, he had sold out, like so many Sansei. At least I was still at university fighting the good fight, I reasoned (fooling myself). Could've used his money though.

Rich came through with speakers, a Get-to-Know-You pub night, and seminar topics, while I found a JC band called Runaway Horses (named after the Yukio Mishima novel) to open the proceedings.

Dave Watanabe really liked working with the band, a ragtag group of folk rockers with an Asian Canadian sensibility. Terry Nakamoto, a volunteer youth worker at the TBC who had been at the '74 conference, had been playing music since the 1960s, first in bands with top-forty rock repertoires and then performing his own songs solo when the singer/songwriter era dawned. He was short, a bit stocky, but with a kind face and friendly disposition that drew people to him. For the conference he cobbled together a band of better-than-average musicians, all Sansei, from around the church. I liked them back in '74 when I was a kid, and I knew Dave would like them now.

After Dave heard them in rehearsal with original songs like "Slocan (I'm Coming Back to You)," "Go for Broke," "Women of the Earth," and "Where Do We Go from Here?" (the conference theme), he was committed to supporting them as a fan and roadie.

Maybe it was too early on a Saturday morning, or it was the classic Sansei reticence, but after Al introduced Runaway Horses to the conference audience, there was a profound silence except for Dave who stood up and clapped. His singular act inspired a smattering of applause. It couldn't have given the band much confidence.

The stage lights came up on the five with Terry standing dead centre, and without saying a word, they launched into "Go for Broke," a tribute to the 442nd Japanese American Battalion and a nod toward the Asian-American ethos of working as hard as you can because the white man will always put you down.

Well, don't you know we have to go for broke,
Every single day of our lives.
You know, we can't provoke;
We've got to be good folk
For White Eyes.
We've got to go for broke.

Movement music to be sure, but every Sansei in the room identified. Still there was a gasp of silence the moment the song ended. I could see Terry gulp in fear. But then the crowd came to its feet and gave a thunderous ovation. They had not heard anything like it before. Runaway Horses was theirs and theirs alone. Terry raised both arms in triumph; the stage lights halo'd him.

Dave had confirmed his commitment to the conference, the band, and the Asian Canadian ideal. Which became a challenge with redress a few years later.

I, too, was captivated by Runaway Horses. They were our Chris and Joanne, our "Charlie" Chin, and so I kept my eyes and ears open for opportunities for them to perform. Dave and I naturally fell into the roles of roadie and manager, respectively. It was a fun time for the next couple of years anyway.

The outcome of the conference that really clicked for me was my relationship with Dave's family. Roy and Kay Watanabe lived in Cabbagetown, in the east end of the city. Roy worked as a middle manager for a Jewish clothier in the Spadina garment district, my part of town. Not so odd was the fact that he hired many Nisei men and women. His generous nature was magnificent. His wife was a housewife.

Roy was like my father — quiet and industrious — but he was outgoing when it came to the Centre. He was one of the "72 Ronin," the Nisei families who guaranteed the mortgage for the building, and so claimed an unstated ownership of the place that was both good and bad. If he wasn't at work or home, he was usually at the Centre. He rose to being one of the most respected and prominent Nisei.

Kay, on the other hand, helped as a volunteer at the Centre but wasn't there "all the time." She had too much to do for that. She spent her days (sometimes with me and Dave in tow) driving around town doing the grocery shopping, getting her hair done or buying clothes and "stuff" for her family. She possessed a charming personality. She was so outgoing she made friends with all the merchants at the St. Lawrence Market resulting in her gaining the best cuts of meat and fish and the freshest vegetables. Uncharacteristic for a Nisei.

She talked shop at the Gaiety Beauty Salon (a Nisei-owned establishment on Upper Gerrard St.) with just about anybody; and she received sizable discounts at Harry Rosen's and other clothing stores. She always promised to take me shopping as her "son" whenever I needed — if I ever needed — a suit.

At home she held court over dinner. She was the "best cook" according to her son. I had to agree. Her table strained with slabs of steak, huge fillets of Atlantic salmon (she disdained BC salmon — either for the taste or her internment past was my guess), and platters of traditional dishes like sushi, *sunomono*, and *maze gohan*. She dutifully prepared and provided the extravagant meals for her family and often invited me and others. I later learned that the first invitation was a test. If you didn't eat copiously and eagerly, she never invited you again. Women were cut a break. No one in her family ate leftovers, so she would have a great deal of food go to waste — hence the invited guests.

I was extremely flattered to be considered family. Other friends observed such; though Mrs. Watanabe always said I was a "friend." She was good at keeping lines clear and sharp.

My own mom was a perfunctory cook — anything and everything to keep the stomach full, and she was not outgoing like Mrs. Watanabe. A Nisei characteristic. Flavour and presentation had nothing to do with cooking a meal.

Joanie came on the scene shortly after the conference. Her Nisei parents were good friends of the Watanabe family. She was a bit of a puzzle for Roy and Kay, or rather their son was. When Dave was born, Roy told Kay "This one will probably marry a hakujin, you know." Imagine that, they were predicting an out-marriage from the get-go.

What they didn't like or abide was politics or anything that smacked of collective socialism. Boku would've made a good Watanabe son. The Centre was a Cultural Centre and not a Community Building. Redress was a no-no for discussion, and talk of drop-in centres and Movement demonstrations were left outside the Watanabe house. I knew which side of my bread was buttered so I never discussed the campaign for redress or any Asian-Canadian political issue or event. But that was a luxury that couldn't be enjoyed forever.

By late 1984, the campaign for redress had gone beyond community discussions and study groups. The National Association of Japanese Canadians or NAJC had gained strength and relevance since its inception in 1947, and had reorganized by setting up chapters across the country. A negotiation committee was assigned the task of talking to the government about compensation for individuals and a community fund. And herein lay the contentious issue for Japanese Canadians. Many thought a payout was demeaning — "blood money" as it were. The NAJC contended it was a matter of principle — a human rights issue. After all, Canadians had been incarcerated, exiled, and stripped of a future in Canada.

I saw friends bicker so much that their thirty to forty-year friendship was torn asunder. Families argued to the point of estrangement. I played witness to the Watanabe family split. Dave's father turned out to be pro-redress; his wife thought redress a crass grab for money. Being in the paper was bad enough, but to ask for money, unseemly. The arguments were played out in the community newspapers. The airing of dirty laundry was such an embarrassment.

One weekend evening, Dave and I had just finished our game of pool, and instead of going to Chinatown, we headed for his home. Joanie was there helping Mrs. Watanabe with a whole fresh salmon. One-pound steaks were also on the menu since she decided to empty her freezer that afternoon. I bet the vendors at St. Lawrence Market waited in anxious monetary anticipation. Such a feast; I wondered how many had been invited, but only Joanie and I were added to the dining table. All seemed normal until I walked into a heated argument in the dining room.

"Why do you want the money?" Mrs. Watanabe asked in a querulous voice.

"They took my parents' farm in the Okanagan Valley," Roy answered. Her face grew taut as he continued. "It broke my father's heart. We spent nearly five years in the wilderness . . . in a shack."

"We're doing okay now," she responded.

"That's not the point."

"Aren't you grateful to this country? We have a nice home; our child is educated, and has a job with a future," she insisted.

"My family was humiliated during those years. I feel so much worse today."

"But it's so *kitanai* asking for money."

"Don't tell me it's kitanai for getting back some of what was taken from us!" Mr. Watanabe shouted, I could see tears in his wife's eyes. I had never seen them so emotional.

I felt extremely awkward listening to all this. I suspected Joanie did too, but this is what families do, I reasoned.

This all proved problematic for Dave. He had to choose which side he supported. He often asked me what I thought. I was working for redress within the NAJC, so my position was obvious. Out of loyalty to me and to the Japanese Canadian ideal, he helped whenever and however he could. Mr. Watanabe, too, threw in his support, allowing Dave to use the company van if stuff needed moving. I don't know if his mother held it against me, but she kept inviting me to dinner.

In that way Dave and I deepened our friendship.

IN THE HOSPITAL room, Joanie and I didn't talk about the "incident," other than to acknowledge the outcome. Her face had changed from when I walked into the room. It was plastered with sorrow and regret; she constantly snivelled into a handkerchief. I sensed that Joanie felt remorse over her break-up with Dave, but she said nothing. And I certainly didn't bring it up. We were both content to sit in silence beside the man we both loved.

The Yonge Street cruises, the Chinatown *yum cha* at Golden City, the Watanabe family gatherings, and our pool games on lonely Saturday nights when nothing else was doing came to mind. If truth be told, Joanie was better at pool than we were on the rare occasions she joined us. But it was the time together that was important, the time when we could talk, just talk. No, it was a moment of comfort when we could be ourselves, relax and just "shoot the breeze."

After Joanie left with a kiss to Dave's forehead, I stood before my friend and closed my eyes as if praying. I wasn't, but I did say to him, "Listen, I know you can hear me. You can pull out of this.

It'll be just like before, you and me, maybe Joanie, playing pool, going to C-town for some *wonton mein*. You hear me, Dave?" I had heard that patients in a coma could hear everything going on around them.

"All of us will die unhealed, but not like this. Not like this."

22.

Beginning of April 1991

I was at an impasse when it came to my father's diary. There was no way my mother was going to open up. I was grateful for the amount she did. Rikimatsu would say no more — not in a million years. Never mind the language barrier. My uncle told me all he could, so that well was now dry. I lost my translator. And then there was GiGi. I could see there was a lot of potential in us: she shared with me a common culture, history, a recent past; I didn't have to explain anything, I didn't have to teach her; she didn't have to teach me; she was socially aware; she was beautiful. But she lived in Vancouver. She also had a kid. I was ill-equipped to be a parent of a young teenager. We promised we would write; I knew we wouldn't. I'm pretty sure she knew it too. My fantasy of a relationship with her was just that, a fantasy. I faced reality: nothing was going to happen.

On the other hand, I was plagued by Naoko's disappearance. Was I crazy like Boku? My head reeled. I had a constant headache. I had had no more dreams of her since Vancouver.

In the sanctity of my room, I stared at the unintelligible pages for hours, hoping for something remarkable to happen. My thoughts drifted to my father. When I was fifteen and the police came to our front door to tell us his plane had crashed and he was missing, I didn't believe it at first; I had never experienced such loss. It was inconceivable. I didn't cry; maybe I should've. I had to live life without a father.

His baffling death wrapped around me like a coat of needles. The thought of having to see him in a coffin and then watching him being buried clawed at my insides. That never happened, of course; his funeral was a memorial instead. I was afraid of death, and the death of a loved one had made it a reality. Fear gripped me more for myself than for him. What intensified my terror was the image of wolves circling the plane wreck. The investigating officials who came to our door told my mother without explanation, although one did say it looked like they were guarding the site. My mother typically offered me no comfort.

I overheard the men who came back a week or two later to report their conclusions. The plane had "experienced a steep impact. A reason could not be determined. The pilot was skilled and experienced with many flight hours to his credit..." Maybe there was more, but I never heard them. My mother destroyed the report and refused to talk about the incident from that day forward.

The nightmare of wolves circling the wreckage plagued my sleep for years thereafter. Always circling, snarling, and pawing at the ground. But what were they looking for? No bodies. Had they dragged Dad and the pilot away, had their fill, and came back? What of their remains? I tried not to imagine my father being torn apart.

The crash itself became a nightmare, too. I saw my father gripping the arms of his seat, not fully comprehending why they were going down. What were his last thoughts? On family? On his reasons for taking the flight in the first place? And on impact, what did he feel? Fire, glass slicing into his face, metal ripping apart? And then death — was it sudden, or did he linger?

I always woke up in a shivering sweat, sometimes screaming.

FRIENDS AND RELATIVES expected me to be brave. "You're the man of the house now." "Be a man." "Take care of your mother. She needs you." "She's your responsibility now." Inane, trite phrases that meant very little. I didn't appreciate the stress, and I was angry. I lashed out at everyone for a time. And I didn't know why.

After things grew quiet, I realized I didn't really know my father. As a little kid, I climbed onto his back many times, and I held hands with him as he walked me to elementary school. As a teenager, I never knew his inner-most secrets, his opinions about people, his take on life. We never talked about what I was going through at high school. Never anything about my future. Yes, he was a quiet man, but he might've taught me some life lessons. Then he was gone.

If I had known him, perhaps I would've understood why he went up north in a small plane. Perhaps I would've understood why the wolves guarded him.

Even when preparing to leave, Dad said very little. "I'm going north of Lake Superior. On business."

Mom later said he was looking for something. She said no more, no less. Her posture told me not to ask further.

With the book and Naoko's help, I felt I had been coming close. With her disappearance, however, my father once again slipped away. The torment of loss is the burden of history. Secrets its weight.

I turned to the journal again and stared at the incomprehensible. It was like some intricate code that needed to be broken. Then I remembered his poems in English. The "Dog Star" in particular. I flipped the pages searching for that one, but inexplicably, I couldn't find it. I even started from the beginning and carefully turned each page until I reached the end. No poem.

I couldn't understand it. I read it in the diary, I was sure of it. So where was it? *Not another problem I couldn't explain.* Then I came across a page with words arranged in poetic form. This had to be it, but it was all in Japanese. How could I have possibly read it? My hands turned white.

Frustration weighed heavily upon me and I swept the surface of my desk clean, spreading debris across the floor. I acted like I was in a television drama or movie. I soon regretted my action and feared the noise would attract my mother's attention, but nothing stirred.

In a sombre and fatigued mood, I closed my eyes and quite unexpectedly a word floated into my consciousness. Cintamani. Yes, Naoko's last message to me. I pawed through the scattered pages on the floor until I found my notepad. What did my uncle say it meant? A Buddhist term. Just as suddenly my next move was clear and obvious. I had to talk to the minister at the Toronto Buddhist Church.

23.

April 1988

None of us really survived the internment years. I've always believed that, even for my generation. I had to agree most of us were well-fed, clothed, and sheltered, most given advanced educational opportunities, many of us became professionals, a few celebrated, honoured, and feted. But I knew all of us were plagued with an empty past; it was like a gaping wound that would never heal. Very few understood or even perceived. We claimed to be Canadian, but none of us was white. Oh, we outmarried, we moved to the suburbs surrounded by "Canadians," but the "Oriental" jokes and the blatant racist attacks kept coming, even in jest, and all any of us could do was "take it." That was the expectation. Even fellow grad students like Jennifer Head would mock me with racist taunts if I brought up issues of race I had learned about at the 1974 conference.

"But there was a war," Jennifer would claim. "The Japs were the enemy."

"So what?" I said, ignoring her insensitivity. "Our parents were citizens. And no one jailed German and Italian Canadians in the same way."

We had attracted a crowd.

"Oh, calm down." She walked away as others in the crowd pulled back their eyes in a slant to mock me.

And the scorn we received for even thinking about redress. We were so Catholic in committing that sin. Some saw intermarriage as a way of escaping racism. That was the real redress.

There was no one to talk to; hell, we didn't even talk to each other. And even if redress was resolved and words of apology came from the Prime Minister himself, we would still be left unhealed and doomed until our dying day. No lofty and penitent words, no amount of money, could bring us back together as a community or build us up as complete human beings.

Boku was my prime example. After Obon in 1984, I didn't see him for a while. There was no point going to his parents' place for Oshougatsu, the sting of his dropping out of UBC was still raw in the minds of his family.

My mother still prepared the osechi for 1985 and thereafter, but since no one came over I escaped the gloom by going to Dave's; his parents always welcomed me; in fact, they expected me. The large, split-level home off Victoria Park Avenue in Scarberia, as many called Scarborough, the family having moved from the Cabbagetown area of town. Kay Watanabe wanted a new house, rather than an old Victorian renovated to within an inch of its life — what the area was famous for. The Watanabes then bit the bullet and bought into a new development. If truth be told, they wanted to get away from the thieving gangs of Regent Park to the south. The new house had everything Mrs. Watanabe wanted.

Their New Year's tradition included a parade of well-wishers throughout the day and night, well into the early morning. Each guest was assigned a time. I was afforded prime time, given my friendship with Dave, I suppose — six o'clock.

The spread of food was amazing. With a mountain range of Alaskan King Crab legs, boiled shrimp and lobster, it had to be the most extravagant home-cooked meal in town. Add to that the large, fresh salmon; all the traditional Japanese delicacies with a healthy amount of sushi and maguro; and a variety of desserts, including Jell-O shots, cakes, and pies.

Dave had spent most of the morning slitting the lobster and crab pieces to make it easier to get at the meat. When the first guests arrived around noon, he parked himself at the table and ate to his heart's content. There was always enough.

I felt right at home, even though I would never be family

unless I married in, and that wasn't going to happen. Mrs. Watanabe's nieces, though smart and very attractive, lived too far away and so bought into the mediocrity of suburban culture. Besides, they'd in all probability marry a white man.

As the campaign for redress continued, the arguments between Mr. and Mrs. Watanabe subsided and then disappeared and all returned to normal. I thought they had declared a détente.

BOKU, I ASSUMED, had continued his epistemological detective role, forever looking for a cause. It must've been about that time the idea of robbing a bank came into his head.

I started going back to the church. Don't know why; perhaps I needed to get back to my roots, or I was trying to stay in touch with my friends, though I didn't see many of them anymore. In any case it seemed like a natural thing to do.

Gossip around the place had it that Boku had given up on Cathy and everybody else. Goats Goto, the current Boys Club coordinator, told me there was talk of a fling or two with hakujin women and a "brown" woman, but I said nothing. After coming home, Boku, it was said as a final condemnation, kept working at odd jobs, sometimes for his old man, and lived in the basement of the family home until everyone forgot about him.

But what Boku said back on Oshougatsu 1984 kept surfacing in my brain: "History must be ascertained and not studied."

I concluded he was investigating the truth from a philosophical standpoint. Maybe an objectivist's truth since he seemed to be impressed by Ayn Rand. And the year before, we had talked about redress. He was dead set against it and his mother, at least, was for it. So how were redress and epistemology connected?

Redress was a battle for my truth. In my humble efforts to contribute, I chose to explore and then to disseminate the truth. I was my own truth detective. Ever since the late 1970s, I tried to convey my emotional reaction to the internment photographs I saw in 1974. I talked at student workshops put on by the National Association of Japanese Canadians; at public gatherings sponsored by the *Sodan-kai*, a group formed to facilitate discussion amongst Nikkei; and in private conversations with friends and their parents. I could feel my father's presence; I was not sure if he would've approved or dismissed my involvement. But Boku's reasons for robbing a bank to redress the injustice done to his grandfather were unfathomable.

24.

April 1991

The Toronto Buddhist Church was built in the 1950s as a Nisei beachhead on Bathurst north of Bloor and northwest of the Japanese sector of town centred around Spadina and Dundas. The Issei had agreed that the congregation needed a new building. It would be better than sitting in the cramped main floor of the Huron Street Church, Reverend Tsuji's semi-detached house in my neighbourhood. Or renting the Ukrainian Hall or the Legion Hall on College Street between Bay and Yonge every week for services and special events, like funerals and weddings. But they didn't like the notion of taking out a mortgage to do it. Better to save the money first. The Nisei, however, prevailed, mainly because they could speak English and knew the modern financial system. They took over the responsibility of a mortgage, and that was agreeable. But that meant the church elders gave up a considerable amount of power. All important decisions were taken out of the old guard's hands. The Issei were relegated to providing the grunt work for various fundraising events and religious celebrations. All decisions now came from the new Nisei dominated Board of Directors.

The Building Committee hired a Nisei real-estate agent, a Nisei architect, a Nisei contractor (Boku's father, I believe), and even a Nisei concept artist to design the altar. The result was a magnificent building: a multi-level structure with a foyer with stairs leading up to the hondo; a library; offices and meeting rooms; social area and kitchen in the basement. Even an adjacent Japanese garden that would be seen through the side windows of the hondo. The place was constructed mostly of blond maple to represent Canada. The hondo soared high into the heavens with arched buttresses of layered wood — a Japanese technique. The focal point was the *butsudan* at the head of the hall, with a scroll with *Namu Amida Butsu* in *shodo* reverently displayed.

As soon as I stepped through the double wooden doors, I stepped back twenty years or so. The ever-present perfume of incense filled my nostrils, reminding me of the presence of the Buddha. The statue of Shinran Shonin greeted me, and I felt immediately at ease within the familiar.

I walked upstairs, across the large landing, and through the open doors to the expansive hondo. It was empty, but I met the spirits of all those who had come before me. Guilt soon replaced my reverie as I approached the minister's office to the left of the butsudan. I hadn't been to service in a long while. Like most my age, religion didn't play much of a role in my life, but events of late made me turn to the Buddha.

I stood in *gasshou* before the altar, bowed, uttered the *Nembutsu*, and then went to the Minister's office. I knocked and checked my watch. I was a few minutes early for my appointment.

"Ah, Michael, so nice to see you again," greeted Reverend Mitsui. His black robes rested nicely over his body. "Enter." There was a formality about the man that I found charming.

Reverend's office was clogged with books, a metal desk and chair, and a few tables creaking with framed pictures and stacks of paper. Mitsui Sensei had been at the Toronto church a long time, but he was the latest in a long line of ministers dating back to Reverend Tsuji, the "Founding Father." His kind, open face told me he was truly glad to see me. He didn't chastise me for my absence — Buddhists weren't like Christians. Perhaps that made me feel all the more guilty.

He first asked after my mother and then said, "What can I do for you, Michael?"

"Well, Sensei, I've come across a word that you may be able to help me with."

"Oh?"

"Yeah, do you know the word cintamani?"

"Not offhand."

"I believe it's a Buddhist term."

"*Jodo Shinshu?*"

"No, I don't think so, but I'm not sure."

"Let's look it up." He reached behind him for some text. After checking, he read aloud: "A cintamani or *chintamani* is a wish-fulfilling stone within both Hindu and Buddhist traditions."

"Oh, I remember," he added. "It may be Tibetan." He continued reading: "Buddhist tradition maintains that one attains the Wisdom of Buddha, able to understand the truth of the Buddha, and turn afflictions into *Bodhi* through the stone."

"How?"

"I suppose by holding it or rubbing it like Aladdin's lamp," he said with a smile. "Not really. I believe it was one of four objects that fell from the sky. The Buddha's bowl, the jewel, a *mani,* or stone with a mantra carved into it ... oh, maybe they're the same thing. Sorry. I can't remember the exact objects. It's said to come from the Sirius star system. That's how the Dharma came to Tibet."

"It's a myth, then," I concluded. I kept mum about Dad's poem mentioning Sirius, the Dog Star.

"I suppose it's like a four-leaf clover or a rabbit's foot. Or maybe the Philosopher's Stone of Western tradition. I suppose it is a wish-fulling stone," Sensei explained. "But I'd have to say it's more like a metaphor for the Buddha Dharma."

I mulled over what had been said before I recalled the stone in Dad's box marked *Moose Jaw.*

"Michael, how did you come by this word?"

"Hmm, oh, I just heard about it from one of my students. He wanted to know ... " The words *firedrake star* entered my mind. I made my excuses and left abruptly.

I DIDN'T MEAN TO BE RUDE, but I had to get home. I'll apologize to Sensei later, I promised myself. Once I arrived, I made a beeline for the basement. I found the box where I had left it, in the shadows behind the furnace. I pulled out the stone. It was smooth, like it had endured a metamorphosis, like atmospheric friction. It was blank, with no inscription. Was this rock a cintamani forged by the heat of a star — a firedrake star — and fallen to earth like the Buddhist myth claimed? It was more than a little far-fetched.

"You're a wishing stone, are you?" I said aloud. I held it in the palm of my hand; the smooth surface felt good against my skin. I closed my eyes and in a whimsical moment made a wish: *I want Naoko back. Here and now.* I opened my eyes and looked around. "Nothing. You're no help," I scoffed. *Silly. What am I doing?*

I trudged upstairs with the rock in hand to my bedroom. It was something I could ask my mother, but she was having a nap as she usually did at this time of day. I flopped into my bed to contemplate the stone. It certainly was smooth with no jagged edges and composed of non-descript minerals. It wasn't perfectly round, more oval than anything else, and it was unusually heavy. Or was that my imagination? My hand holding the artifact slowly dropped to the bed. My consciousness began drifting.

That is not what you really want. A familiar female voice quietly echoed about me in my half-sleep. I tried to answer, but nothing came forth. *Your wish is not what you want.*

Who's there? The thought called out silently. *Who are you?*

Look deeper and realize what it is you really want.

I woke with a start. I was alone, the rock in my hand, inert as ever. "Naoko?" I called out. "Naoko, is that you?"

"Michael?"

"Yes?" I said expectantly.

"Michael?"

It was my mom. "Yeah," I said irritated.

"Who were you calling? I heard you shouting."

"No one, Ma, no one. I wasn't shouting," I complained.

She appeared at the door, more tired than I had ever seen her. She still had that overcoat of transparency. The one I had noticed before. Her hair appeared stringy and straggly, universally grey, her arms and hands weak and thin, translucent in pallor.

Ignoring her condition, I held up the cintamani. "Ma, do you know what this is?"

"A rock?"

"No, I mean, yes. I found it in Dad's Moose Jaw box in the basement."

"Well, then it belonged to your father."

"I know that, but why would he keep a rock?"

"I have no idea," she said as she turned to leave. Maybe she was sensing what was coming next.

"Ma, stay a bit."

She stopped and turned to me.

"You gotta tell me something more about Dad. Not knowing is driving me crazy." I felt the sweat rise on my brow; I must've looked desperate.

"Nothing more to tell."

"Stop that! I know you know. You know lots of stuff. Come on, don't leave me in the dark like you have all my life. I need to know. I have a right to know."

If I had shocked her with my outburst, I couldn't tell. She just stood there with her usual stoic look about her, but she did come into my room to find a convenient chair. "What would you like to know?"

A bit startled at the turnaround, I stumbled. I decided to ask her a question she had already answered. "Okay, okay, where was Dad during the war?"

"Angler."

So far so good. "Why was he there?"

"He was a ganbariya. And don't ask me what that means. You know already. I told you before and Uncle Kunio must have told you."

"What happened to him after the war?"

She fell silent, again.

"Not this again. Come on, Ma, what's the harm in telling me?"

"He protested the war."

"I said after the war."

"That's right, he was protesting after the war."

"What? Why?"

"Things hadn't been settled. He and the others wanted justice."

"For how long?"

"I don't know for certain. Someone told me two years."

"Two years? Protesting the war? But it was over."

"Yes, but the injustice wasn't."

"Who was with him?"

"I don't know...really, I don't know. I don't know much about those years. I met your father in Toronto in the late 40s."

"How did you meet?"

"At a Nisei dance. Hagerman Hall, I think, behind city hall. It was a Harvest Dance and the hall was decorated with bushel baskets and leaves. Someone made a scarecrow for the night," she said smiling. "Your Uncle Kuni and Aunt Marion dressed up as matching pumpkins." She laughed with her hand to her mouth.

Nice to hear her laugh, but before she fell too far into nostalgia, I had to bring her back. "How do you know about Dad protesting?"

"He told me a few things."

"Like what?"

"I just told you. There's nothing more." She stood.

"Ma, please," I said. "Listen, I appreciate what you said. I really do. Why you couldn't have told me years ago baffles me."

"You didn't need to know. I mean, no one needs to know about that stuff."

"One last question: what's Moose Jaw got to do with all this? Was Chiemi from there? Did he travel there?"

With a terse "I don't know" she became as cold as stone. The hall darkness quickly swallowed her as she trundled out the door.

THE NISEI WERE HARD DONE BY during the war. Most were children when they were ripped from their homes and dragged to isolated camps buried deep in the mountain wilderness. Some like my father had come of age, but that sense of betrayal must have eaten like acid into their core as they became Enemy Aliens rather than Canadian citizens.

Robbed of their souls, they spent so many years trying to regain what they had lost but not really knowing how. They were up against a huge, faceless government and feared it could strike again for the same capricious reason.

It took the Redress Campaign by Sansei, some Nisei, and the support of compassionate Canadians of all walks of life to regain a sense of justice, a sense of belonging for all Japanese Canadians. And yet, the negotiations, the protests, and the words spoken and in print could never bring back what was lost: our connection to the thick and knotted trees of BC, the crisp, fragile mountain air, and the unfathomable black depths of the ocean.

I couldn't blame my mother for her silence, her reticence to reveal the family history. It was, after all, a legacy of shame and secrets. *Don't air our dirty laundry.* But she never realized I was an empty vessel without it.

Naoko's voice (if it had indeed been her voice) came back to me: *Look deeper and realize what it is you really want.*

The answer was in Dad's diary and the cintamani. Had to be.

25.

Summer 1988

Just before the trial, Boku had one more surprise.
"I told you I don't want a lawyer," Boku stated to his parents
in the living room of their suburban home. Mrs. Sugiura had
invited me to the house for moral support — for her or him, I
couldn't tell. "I already dismissed one. And I'll fire the second."

Mrs. Sugiura's face shrivelled. Her son was becoming more
of a burden than when he was a baby. "You have to have a lawyer."

"You need a lawyer," I added.

"No lawyer can say what I want to say," he said defiantly.

"*Bakayaro*," his father cursed.

Boku's otousan, Herb Sugiura, was now sole owner of a construction contracting company that did very well, a far cry from
the days he was interned in New Denver and his parents were in
Lemon Creek.

Herb Sugiura had wandered after the war, working for some
lumber company in Northern Ontario before coming to
Toronto. His mother had died in the camp, and his father Haruo
had become, according to some, half the man he was before:
bitter, weak, and mute. Eventually Haruo made it to Toronto
where he recovered somewhat, and father and son, after recon-
ciliation, had established the contracting business. And then
there was Herb's younger brother Daniel, Boku's uncle, the one
no one talked about. I knew the rumours, but I did look him up
in the newspaper collection at the Central Library. Seems he
went berserk one day and slaughtered his family. No reason was
ever discerned. He was imprisoned in a jail for the criminally

insane. But no one talked about those events, so they somehow didn't happen: the Great Japanese Canadian delusion.

In Toronto, Herb met and married his wife and went into business with his father. He was probably considered a "good catch," since he had a future in the contracting business. They worked hard to save enough money to buy a home and start a family — the Great Canadian Dream. That's when they moved to the Danforth and Greenwood area, and then Scarborough. Haruo stayed in the Spadina and Dundas area until his death.

But now Herb discovered he had a kichigai son, perhaps genetically like his younger brother, Daniel. At least, no one had been murdered.

"You need a lawyer," Mr. Sugiura insisted. "We hired one for you. He got you bail and you're home now."

"But I didn't ask for bail. I wanted to stay in jail."

Mrs. Sugiura turned away crying.

I stood against the wall to avoid embarrassment, for both me and the parents.

"*Damare*! Appreciate what's been given you. You've done enough to hurt your mother."

Boku shut down with that.

I HAD NEVER BEEN IN A COURTROOM, never mind attended a trial. The massive, squat provincial court building was behind City Hall. Within its dark corridors was Room 9A, where Boku's case would be settled. 9A featured a high ceiling and polished floors. Every piece of furniture consisted of gleaming wood; the setting was right out of an episode of *Law and Order*.

I came late, so sat in the back and observed the proceedings, taking out a notepad and pen. I saw Boku with the family's lawyer sitting behind a table, while the prosecutor sat at an adjacent table. Boku's family was nowhere to be seen.

I also noticed Frank Morimoto, an estimable columnist for *Maclean's Magazine*, sitting in the audience. Covering the trial, I assumed. Mr. Morimoto had started at *The New Canadian*, our community newspaper, as a cub reporter before WWII. He was a cherub of a man: short, five-foot-four at the most, "spherical" as Wodehouse would say, with a constant smile on his face. He was an eloquent man who, many said, had been a "wiseacre" as a young man. Some even said he was a "cocky S.O.B.," though I could never see it. He was always charming and approachable at community events and gatherings.

The judge was a serious man hunched over his papers. He wore a glum expression as he heard the charges without looking up. Once the charges had been heard, he asked the prosecutor for opening remarks. It was then the defense attorney stood and addressed the court: "Your honour, pardon my interruption, but my client wishes to represent himself and has therefore dismissed me."

The judge peered over his glasses and asked, "Is this true, Mr. ...um...Mr. Sugiura?"

Boku stood slowly and said, "Yes, your honour."

"Well, are you aware of the possible consequences of your action?"

"Yes, your honour."

"Then so be it."

And so the trial began. The facts of the case were presented forthwith by the prosecutor. It was obvious Boku was guilty. Witnesses, like Mrs. Roberta Flaxman, the bank manager; bank employees; and Detective Sgt. Gill came forward to testify.

The detective sat on the stand and referred to his own notepad. He recalled that he had stepped into the interrogation room of the Dundas Street Police Station at about eight o'clock the evening of the incident. From my seat, I could see that he was all business. His grey hair at the temples gave him a distinguished air; his Armani suit was expensive; his gold Cartier pen and undersized Rolex watch spoke of a successful, and I assumed corrupt, career. He reconstructed the exchange he had with Boku from his notes.

He said that Boku spoke first. "I'm not guilty, sir."

"That's not up to me to decide, son," he replied.

"I know. I know. I just wanted to make it clear."

"I have the facts in front of me. Do you want a lawyer?"

"No...no thanks."

"You're entitled to one. Didn't you understand your rights?"

"I won't need one," he said.

He then stated, "Well, then, you had better tell me your side of the story."

"I am innocent. No matter what that file says. I mean, I had no intention of robbing that bank, and that makes me innocent."

"How so?"

"In my mind, I had no desire to rob the bank."

"But you did."

"But I didn't want to. No, I was recreating the circumstances of my grandfather's arrest."

"Your grandfather is a criminal?"

"Yes...no, I mean not now. During World War II, he was interned like all the Japanese Canadians."

"Oh, yes."

"He was taken away for no good reason, other than because of his name and face. He spent years in the backwoods and mountains of BC, only to be released and exiled."

"Yes, I know the story, I read the *Star*. But what does that have to do with you?"

"Don't you see? I am wrongly accused of robbing a bank now just because you think so, the bank thinks so, and society thinks so. But did I take any money? Did I try to run away from the police? Did I resist arrest? The collectivists all have conspired to put me in jail. Just like they did in 1942."

"Settle down, son."

"Once convicted, and I know I will be, and after I get out of prison, I will work to be the best that I can be. Just like my grandfather did after the war."

"That's all well and good, son, but I recommend you get a lawyer."

AFTER GILL HAD finished,. the prosecutor called Kenneth Boku Sugiura to the stand.

"Isn't it true, Mr. Sugiura, that you walked into the Canadian Imperial Bank of Commerce at Spadina and Dundas with the sole purpose of robbing it? You demanded $20,000 in fact."

"That...that is..." Boku stumbled, "what you think."

"Now why did you need the money?"

"I didn't need the money."

"You said it was compensation for what your grandfather lost during WWII."

"Now, that wasn't true."

I was confused, but the lawyer wasn't; he ignored the statement.

"Yes, it wasn't true, was it? You wanted the money to start a new company employing a computer program you devised to predict stock market trends."

"No."

"Another misperception, perhaps?"

"No, it simply is not true."

And so the cross-examination went, leading to the prosecution resting his case. As the judge declared a recess until the next day, I thought it did not look good for my friend.

FOR HIS DEFENSE, Boku did not call any witnesses; instead, he read from papers he had prepared. He sighed and gulped before he began. I could see his forehead was wet with sweat; his voice trembled.

My grandfather was my role model. He above all others was the supreme example of egoism. He was taken into custody in 1942 and exiled to a camp somewhere in the BC mountains. And for what? Because he was Japanese, a member of the Buddhist Church, of the community, yet he was arrested and put away out of a malicious collective belief: it was racism, pure and simple. The Canadian government acted with catastrophic results.

But did my grandfather resort to criminality? Did he rebel against society? Did he give up and die? Did he at the very least remain bitter for the rest of his life? No, he rose above it all. After his release, he worked for years to prove himself a good man. His ego was placed first and foremost to become the success he was in the end.

I did what I did to recreate the circumstances that put my grandfather in harm's way. You think I robbed a bank, but I know I did not. You therefore persecute and now prosecute an innocent man. You will find me guilty, of that there can be no doubt. I am therefore willing to take any punishment you mete out. But within my own self, as I said, I know I am innocent. And when I am released, I will work the rest of my life to prove I am a good man. Just like my grandfather.

My example will be a beacon for all the true individuals in society who are selfish for themselves and not an altruist for the "greater good." To be an altruist is simply folly. In order to do so, I sought to ascertain history, not simply study it. I truly became my grandfather in 1942 — a man, a simple man, with no criminal record who was suddenly arrested, stripped of all his basic rights and incarcerated because of the way he looked and nothing else. I placed myself in an analogous situation to prove what I suspect is true — I live in a slave society. Do what you will, I am ready. I am an epistemological detective, and, like all private investigators, I am on the outside looking in.

When he finished reading, he looked up and pointed out the fact that he asked for $20,000, the same amount as the NAJC is demanding as redress. He also wore his grandfather's old shirt under his own Applebee shirt and stored his grandfather's old passport and wartime identity papers in his second gym bag.

"Why would I do these things?" Boku said. "The second gym bag completed my tribute to my grandfather. I knew the police would find and bring the artifacts to my trial. Everyone would see why I did what I did."

"But why hide them?" the judge asked.

"These documents were useless to my grandfather in 1942, and they will be useless at this trial. But they serve as a reminder of the false accusations against my grandfather and me."

"But you asked for $20,000. You just said so."

"True, but my demands were false. They were a denigration of the NAJC's demands. I want everyone to see how that organization is an example of collectivist greed. Blood money that is not needed or wanted by Japanese Canadians. The NAJC is a parasite of contemporary Canadian society."

I could see the judge was not impressed and the prosecutor was sharpening his knives. As I watched, I concluded that my friend was truly delusional. It was the only way I could explain his actions.

In closing, the prosecutor stood, straightened his suit jacket and spoke: "Your honour, the defendant obviously invented his ludicrous story in order to hide his real motives for robbing the bank: he wanted the money to start his own company. The 'epistemological detective' ploy is just a smokescreen, a red herring. Does the defendant really believe the court will accept such a cock and bull story when so many felt their lives threatened?"

That was the precise moment I knew Boku was a condemned man.

26.

April 1991

Night crept slowly past midnight and well into the small morning hours as the gloom steadily grew heavier in the house. My eyelids drooped with sleep deprivation, but I willed them open with every pull to the dark horizon. I caressed the cintamani stone's smooth surface. It did offer some comfort. At the same time, I stared at the pages before me. Buddha only knows what I was searching for — an answer to emerge, no doubt.

The recent events confused me to no end. Surreal moments caused doubt to drip into my insides, like sludge in a drainpipe, plaque in an artery. There was no one I could talk to — certainly not Glenn — and I hadn't seen Dave since February. My head started to spin.

At some point, the remarkable happened. At first, I couldn't believe what was going on. I blinked and then rubbed my eyes. I thought about splashing my face with water, but I couldn't turn away from my father's notebook. On every page, the *kanji*, each ideogram, unhooked and the parts began moving, trembling at first and then swirling in concentric circles. I turned away, but then returned to the notebook. So compelling. It must be a hallucination: it was the hour, the state of my brain, my need for sleep. But the characters kept moving and shaking like in an earthquake. I stared and tried to understand. My head reeled with confusion and fear.

Finally, the swirling parts coalesced, forming English words. Quite miraculously, the poem I had been looking for appeared on the page:

A firedrake dogstar
shone in the daylight heavens,
brighter than Venus in the sky. And at night,
it shone over the Delta like Cassiopeia,
the recumbent constellation (the Buddha reclining,
his right arm at rest next to the body).

"What kind of trick was this?" I said silently, rubbing my eyes to rid myself of the illusion. I didn't want to touch the book, but I eventually examined it, cautiously, front, back, spine, inner pages, to see if there was a mechanism of some kind driving the metamorphosis. Nothing. *Is someone playing a trick on me?*

Not only had the one page changed, but the entire text was slowly converting to English. I could now read it all without Naoko's help. Was this the enlightenment she had promised? What was going on?

I stayed up the rest of the night contemplating and reading, stewing in my bewilderment, and revelling in my new-found comprehension.

Another poem had emerged:

The galaxy of a million stars
clouded her eyes yet
I could feel her gaze penetrate &
cut me to my core. As if
galaxies were ripping at
my sense of being,
splattering it
upon the ground before me.
– February 1942

The words took my breath away. February 1942, the beginning of the Idou, the internment. Yet the imagery was reminiscent of Naoko's effect on me. Was there a parallel between

Naoko and Chiemi? Before I could answer that, I had to find out more about Chiemi. I decided to leave the narrative and do some further investigating. I suppose I was taking a chance on the type reverting to Japanese, but really, I had no choice. I had a hunch Chiemi's identity would not be revealed in the book. There were too many variables.

My uncle had told me Dad had met Chiemi just after the war. If she was the one and the same, she had a profound effect on his life. But there were inconsistencies. His writings contained dreams that happened before and during the war when he supposedly didn't know Chiemi. *Was she a premonition?* I wondered. Uncle could've been wrong, so I wondered where they had really met and what the circumstances were.

There was the Watanabe family Uncle Kunio had told me about; I had to call Dave. In the meantime, I had to talk to Mom; she was the only connection easily at hand, but I couldn't bluntly throw the name in her face. I had seen her reaction the last time. I had to be subtle, but there was something she wasn't telling me.

AT DAYBREAK, I found Mom in her sewing room; she appeared like a hunched Tolkien creature labouring in the corner. I was relieved to find she had solidified somewhat. Maybe she wasn't fading away after all.

The piles of cloth rose behind her like the coastal mountains of BC. She had vowed to organize everything before she died. I quipped that she would live forever since there was so much stuff.

As usual, she called me baka.

It always came back to Mom. She always claimed she was protecting me from the truth. *How bad could it be?* I wondered many times throughout my life. When my grandfather died, the house became a labyrinth of whispers throughout my childhood. I was only eleven, and I could hear my parents talking very softly to each other in the hallway downstairs. I thought I heard Mom say her father had asked forgiveness of her mother while on his deathbed.

"Forgiveness for what?" I had asked her later.

"*Aho*, you don't need to know!" She was surprised that I had overheard the conversation.

I now resolved to talk to Mom again. From the doorway of the sewing room, I called softly so I wouldn't startle her.

"*Naniyo*," she chastised. "Don't sneak up on a person like that."

"Sorry, Ma. I just want to talk a bit."

"Again?" she slammed. After a pause, she relented, having no other option. "Oh, all right, talk." She returned to her work, knitting a sweater. She still appeared sickly; her face drawn with more lines than a withering tomato. Her hands were rivered with veins ready to burst their constraints. Her legs slightly bloated.

"Is there really nothing you can tell me about Chiemi?"

She stiffened again.

I was frustrated and tired of her anticipated obstinacy. Fatigue was also getting to me. I had to know. I feared my time was running out. "C'mon, Ma, Uncle Kunio told me Otousan had met someone named Chiemi after the war. You know that don't you?"

With a heavy sigh, she looked at me with her sad, eroded eyes. Pain chiselled the expression on her face and guilt corroded my resolve, but I waited.

"They were together in camp," my mother finally said.

"Angler?"

"No, after the war."

"Oh, right, after the war. There was a camp after the war?"

"In Moose Jaw."

My brain flashed to the box in the basement. I didn't know there was an internment camp there. "I thought all the camps were closed at the end of the war."

"It wasn't an internment camp like the rest. It was a...a...a military base."

The words hit me hard.

"What was he doing there?"

"He was part of the Ganbariya Group."

"I know that. You told me."

"Yes, well, they continued protesting after the war. Two years after the war."

"In Moose Jaw?"

"In Moose Jaw. I don't know how many there were. Couldn't have been a big group, the leftovers from Angler."

"And Chiemi was at Angler?"

"Baka, no women there. She came to Moose Jaw after leaving East Lillooet, I think."

"But why? She could've gone anywhere, not another camp."

"I don't know. I just know her father died mysteriously."

I turned away, happy for the glimmer of truth, but not sure I wanted to sink deeper into the mud of the past.

"You know Chiemi's family," my mother added.

I swivelled in astonishment. "I do?"

"Your friend, Chiemi is his aunt."

"Dave...Dave Watanabe?"

"No, that's a different Watanabe. No relation. Your other friend."

"Who?"

"Boku Sugiura," she said with finality.

27.

April to October 1988

1988 was a memorable year. The Redress Campaign came to a head. What started the movement toward resolution was the Ottawa Rally, organized by the NAJC. It was April, cold and windy, accentuated by a steady rain. But there I was standing at Yonge and Sheppard outside the subway entrance in the northern part of the city, with several Nisei and a smattering of Sansei at 7:30 in the morning, waiting for the chartered bus. Some smoked to chase the chill away; some drank coffee from thermos bottles; others stamped feet to keep warm. I flapped my arms.

"Last time I did this, we were being taken away to Sandon back in '42," a Nisei man quipped. "That was a hell of a ride to a worse-than-hell place."

I listened, chuckled in agreement, and sipped my coffee given to me by a kindly Nisei lady who knew me from the church. I knew nothing of Sandon other than it was initially a Buddhist internment camp. The government in its wisdom decided to segregate the Japanese Canadians by religion. The whole thing backfired, when they realized that the majority of the community was Buddhist.

The bus finally came. We all boarded and sank into the warm, *kimochi* air. The Greyhound rendezvoused with another from Hamilton at Scarborough Town Centre, the city hall of suburbia. A similar convoy made its way to Ottawa from Montreal and environs. The atmosphere inside my bus was filled with anticipation, reminiscences, and the prickle of adventure, underpinned by a sense of doing the right thing, especially with the toshiyori. Emotion rippled across their furrowed and chilled faces.

I sat in the back with some of the many placards and ribbons, which proudly displayed names of the deceased and the elderly who just couldn't come due to health constraints. I found my father's name on one ribbon. I wondered how it got there. Maybe one of his friends, I decided. I liked to think he would've been proud of me representing him.

The skies over Parliament Hill were cloudy, as if gathering to make judgement over what was happening below. To me, the huge gothic towers and block of buildings glared and scowled like mythic giants at the tiny creatures forming a procession of protest. What right did we have to protest? The "made it" argument by hakujin again. Blah, blah, blah; split-level, five-bedroom houses; two cars; and expensive vacations twice a year. How dare we demand compensation for a justifiable act against an enemy of the state? All was past. All was dead and buried. *All was prologue*, the expression went. *Never again*, the real theme of the Redress Movement. I could see that every Nisei bore the burden of history and were exhausted by the questions. It was in their crooked bodies and aging faces.

Joined by other Japanese Canadians from across the country, we walked around the quadrangle's circular driveway, placards adorned with slogans hoisted above. I suddenly noted the solidarity I felt with so many Nisei. These were not the same adults who called me "rebel," "troublemaker," and "aka" when I ran with the Yellow Seed North Sansei and Canadian Born Chinese. Then again, our critics were Cultural Centre Nisei, a totally different breed from the Nisei on Parliament Hill. The "Country Club" kind were much more conservative and afraid of authority, afraid of losing their favoured status as a charity.

I also noticed only one RCMP cruiser was stationed to watch us. Don't know if I was insulted, or grateful, because I saw at the foot of the steps to the Peace Tower wooden barricades set in place while dozens of Mounties, police, and military milled about waiting. It turned out a Native-Canadian protest was planned for after we finished. I suppose we weren't considered to be a danger. We were a law-abiding people after all. Look what happened during World War II.

Though the placards screamed "Justice Now," "Enemy that Never Was," and "Redress in Our Time," we walked in peaceful and quiet protest. I was spurred to action. "Come on people, we got to let them know we're here!" I began chanting, "Hey, hey! The War Measures Act has got to go! Hey, hey, ho, ho!" Fortunately, some joined me, but not enough to draw any ire from the "peace officers." Many others responded when I yelled, "What do we want?"

"Redress!"

"When do we want it?"

"Now!"

The chant didn't last long. I suspect some were embarrassed and looking forward to getting inside the West Block to hear speeches, enjoy performances (especially by Terry Nakamoto, the star of the 1977 Sansei Conference), and listen to Nisei testimony. As everyone walked in, the smiles and words of good cheer turned to expressions of seriousness and determination.

The room was cavernous, panelled entirely in a dark wood. It smelled of privilege and white history. Rows and rows of metal chairs filled up the space, and a large podium stood at the front of them.

"We don't have much time left!" bellowed Gary Konishi. His index finger pointed to the first row of survivors. "You probably won't see redress from this government. But we have to fight on." The NAJC had invited him and flew him to Ottawa from California, where he had moved.

The Nisei bristled and grumbled their displeasure at the man. And I was called a *jerk*?

I hadn't seen Gary since the Yellow Seed days during the early '80s. He looked the same with a round, full face and intense glare that warned anyone not to challenge him. At least, he had discarded the dashiki for a collared shirt and slacks. He had moved from Toronto to San Francisco to find his roots in Asian America.

He had been elected President of the Japanese American Citizens League.

Terry Nakamoto, with guitar in hand, stepped up to the podium by himself and performed *New Denver*, a song dedicated to his parents.

> *Internment camps in BC's wilderness*
> *Are all I recall.*
> *And all I can offer you is a lifetime of hardships,*
> *My love.*
>
> *Maybe love's not worth much*
> *In these troubled times.*
> *But it's the only thing*
> *We can live on,*
> *On the outside, in the snow.*

There wasn't a dry eye in the house. Not sure if it moved the politicians in attendance as they glad-handed afterward and then disappeared into the catacombs of the Parliament Buildings.

DURING THE SUMMER, President Reagan signed the Civil Liberties Bill authorizing redress for Japanese Americans. In order to encourage the Canadian government to follow suit, and to bring media attention to the movement, the local NAJC organized a "friendly demonstration" in front of the US Consulate in Toronto.

A hot day, University Avenue was crowded with lunchtime office-workers scurrying to find sustenance. About fifty of us stood in front of the Stars and Stripes waiting, since several RCMP officers confronted our leaders. They wanted us to break up before we even started. Now they were afraid of us. Once the police permit was waved in front of their faces and a few elderly

Nisei claimed we only wanted to thank the US government, they allowed the demonstration to proceed. The Consul refused to meet any of us. Too political, I reasoned, but the media came out and gave the cause more publicity than was warranted.

The day was a rousing success even if I had to wring out my shirt, saturated with sweat, afterwards.

ON SEPTEMBER 22, 1988, the Redress Agreement was finally signed by the Conservative Government of Canada. Prime Minister Brian Mulroney read the Acknowledgement and terms in the House of Commons in the morning. That evening, the community gathered at a reception in the ballroom of the Sutton Place Hotel in downtown Toronto.

The place was brimming with jubilation and anticipation. Gerry Weiner, Minister for Multiculturalism, was scheduled to address the crowd to announce the fact of the agreement. In the room gathered the agitators for redress, the fence-sitters, and the redress opponents with hangdog expressions on their faces. Despite the hard feelings toward opponents, the victors magnanimously forgave, but they resolved never to forget.

At some point before the Minister appeared, the room began agitating. I waded through the crowd to find out what was wrong. The hotel had displayed the Canadian flag crossed with the Rising Sun. Outrageous. After all the fighting, the negotiations, the political machinations, the press coverage, we were still seen as Japanese citizens and not fully Canadian. A few Nisei leaders found a government official who was quickly apprised of the situation. He understood and without argument had the offensive flag removed.

As Gerry Weiner, a tall well-dressed politician with a compassionate look to him, spoke, I saw many around me start to cry.

"This is a momentous day," he began.

Others were too stunned to speak as he went on to apologize.

It was as if all of us were transforming, changing as it were, into Canadians.

Then began the "silly" season.

At Lawrence Park Collegiate in the north end of the city, the National Association of Japanese Canadians held an information session in the red-brick building about post-settlement redress. It was a warm fall night filled with colour, the tree leaves in full decline, and the smell of burning leaves and rotting pumpkins in the semi-darkness. Hundreds, maybe thousands, of Nisei came that evening.

"Where were these people when we needed volunteers?" asked a young NAJC member.

Where indeed? I saw the many detractors: the kind that didn't want to accept "blood money"; the kind that split their own families over redress; the kind that made it their life's goal to discredit the campaign and the leaders of the movement. And yet there they all were, eager to get their hands on the $21,000 (one more thousand than the US settlement) for each living victim of the internment.

I did see friends of my parents, church members, and Dave's parents. Boku's family was not present. I guessed all was forgiven among them. I knew some really needed the money though I wasn't sure it was enough to keep them in rice for too long.

I was there to represent my mother and watched with great interest.

The NAJC president, a thirty-ish Sansei in suit and tie, took to the microphone in the school auditorium to announce to everyone that the money would soon be distributed once proof of internment was sent to Ottawa. Everyone had kept their government-issued ID cards and other papers from the 1930s as bitter reminders of a sad time. They could give the documents to the local NAJC to forward. If they wanted weekly updates of the redress progress, they could pay $5.00 to be on the NAJC's mailing list. It was not a membership fee, he emphasized.

Still, people complained. "Why should I give you money?"

said Akio Ikebukuro, a grey-haired Nisei with a curve to his back. He was a distant cousin of Dave's mom.

"For postage to mail you the newsletter," explained a young volunteer sitting behind a small table.

"What? You should be sending me the newsletter for free!"

And he stormed off just as the volunteer shouted, "But we don't know your address!"

A lot of pain and resentment there. I guessed $21,000 was hardly compensation for what he had lost. Or he was just cheap. To my mind, he was a contrarian, but a cowardly contrarian. He was nowhere to be found during the fight for redress.

ON THE OTHER hand, there was a wonderful turn of events: by late October, Dave Watanabe was out of his induced coma and talking.

"How you doing? You okay?" I asked in that antiseptic hospital room.

"Yeah, I'm okay," he said in a groggy voice. He struggled to sit upright.

"I hear you'll be out soon."

"Who told you that?"

"Joanie. Saw her at the Centre last weekend."

"She tell you anything else?"

"No, not really."

"We're back together," he said with a satisfying smile.

"No kidding? That's great."

"Yeah, I promised to change and so did she."

"Like how?"

"I'm going to college."

"That's great. How's she gonna change?"

"Let me hang out in Chinatown with you more," he said.

I was glad to see he still had his sense of humour.

28.

September 1991

I hadn't seen Boku or his family since the trial in 1988. He was found guilty, of course. His sentence: three years in a maximum-security prison. Some in the press and many Nikkei lawyers felt it was a bit harsh, especially for a "first-timer," but at the time, the judge wanted to make an example of him in light of the four Armenians who tried to blow up the subway with a homemade bomb.

What exacerbated the situation was the fact that Boku didn't want the automatic appeal. He was entitled, since he had acted as his own counsel, but no, he would take his punishment as he had declared in the courtroom. And so, he was quietly put away.

About a week after the verdict came down, an article in *The New Canadian* caught my eye. It was by Frank Morimoto, an opinion piece about Boku. He had not been at the trial for *Maclean's*, but rather for *The New Canadian*. I bet the Nisei editors welcomed new work from one of their own.

Mr. Morimoto first outlined the facts of the case. On a hot summer day in 1987, Kenneth Sugiura left his suburban home for his old neighbourhood of Spadina and Dundas carrying two gym bags. He walked down the back lanes of nearby Huron, Sullivan, and Phoebe streets. The old home of Boku's grandfather, Haruo Sugiura, who had been a prominent member of the Toronto Buddhist Church, was located nearby. In a lane behind his grandpa's place, he stopped and placed one of the bags in the space between garages. From there he proceeded to the bank.

Inside the Imperial Bank of Commerce on the southwest corner of Dundas and Spadina, he asked to see the manager,

Mrs. Doreen Flaxman. In an enclosed office, Kenneth threatened to set off a hidden bomb if the bank did not give him $20,000.

The manager calmly cooperated, but surreptitiously pushed a silent alarm. The police soon arrived and searched the building, finding no explosive device. Detective Sgt. Gill questioned Kenneth, asking if he had a bomb on his person. He did not. Determining it was a hoax, the detective placed Kenneth Sugiura in custody.

Given that Mr. Morimoto's reach into the family (he even managed to talk to the parents), the community and the police was considerable, he provided several bits of information. Boku, for instance, wore a second set of clothes under his street clothes, tied down with several belts. He outlined the bus, subway, and streetcar route Boku had taken.

Detective Sgt. Gill talked to Boku for hours and managed to extract a confession. A court-appointed lawyer, Helen Chao, negotiated bail at $100,000 before being dismissed by her client. Boku wanted to stay in jail. His parents hired their own lawyer and got him released under protest.

In Boku's police statement, he said he robbed the bank "for respect. To honour his grandfather and to redress the money and property lost because of the WWII internment." Because $20,000 and sentiment mirrored the National Association of Japanese Canadians' demands of the Canadian government, Frank Morimoto said, "Kenneth Sugiura attempted to corrupt the very ideals of a sincere effort to gain compensation for wrongs done."

How Mr. Morimoto ended the article intrigued me. He concluded that the Sansei were victims of the internment as much as the previous generations. "In the final analysis, Kenneth Sugiura's act was not an aberration, but a reflection of the Sansei state of mind," he wrote. "As a result, we have all been injured by the experience, and we will all die unhealed."

DESPITE THAT INSIGHT, I couldn't solve my problem about how to approach Boku's family with my mother's revelation. She had stunned me with the fact that Chiemi was Boku's aunt. I made her laugh when I asserted, "He's not a Watanabe!"

"He has two sides to his family," she answered with a smile.

"Ma! Why didn't you tell me this in the first place?"

She shrugged her shoulder and turned away. "No need."

I perceived that she was ashamed about the whole thing. Not sure what she knew about Dad's relationship with Chiemi, but she had an inkling about her. I mean, Uncle Kunio said so. In any case, Chiemi was important to Dad. Not wishing to cause any more pain to my mother, I stopped asking her. She was right, there was no need.

It then occurred to me that I didn't know Boku's grand-mother's first and last names. There was never any need to ask; no one in the public calls Obasans by their full name. Even contemporaries call her "Obasan."

In any case, I couldn't just walk up to the tranquil suburban house under clear blue skies and a canopy of television antennae, telephone wires, and the slow but sure invasion of cable lines and invite myself in unannounced. Their shame had kept them away from their beloved Buddhist church and every festive occasion at the JCCC. I had not seen them at any of the community picnics or Obon. They did not observe Oshougatsu the way they used to. I had no wish to disturb them, but I had to know about the link between our families.

Then I got lucky. I spied Mrs. Sugiura at the Buddhist Church Fall Bazaar. After a few years away, she had returned to the chaos and Nirvanic smells of tempura, teishoku, and chicken teriyaki.

The basement bustled with the familiar. Like every year, the young scampered around and in-between the well-worn and scarred wooden tables, constructed by Issei and Nisei men dec-ades before. The young girls with trays and aprons with pockets filled with hashi and napkins acted as waitresses; the boys bus boys with wipe cloths. The patrons, mostly Nisei and Sansei with their babies and toddlers — the next generation — vied for seats and planted themselves in place with no intention of ever leaving. The Issei were sadly no longer present.

The menu was simple: teishoku set or a la carte shrimp tempura or chow mein. Drinks could be had at the "youth table:" tea, orange drink, and pop. Hot dogs, too, with mustard and relish condiments. The attendants seemed proud of the array of homemade sliced pies. Mrs. Tsuruoka made the best lemon meringue; Mrs. Sasaki apple; and Mrs. Nakamura cherry and blueberry. The sugary and fruity desserts sat on the counter calling out to all who passed.

Ordering took place at the small ticket table at the entrance to the basement. The narrow hallway from the staircase to the dining room funnelled everyone into an irregular but organized line. Everyone cooperated as Nikkei do. It was always nice to see Mrs. Kondo or Mrs. Ikebata stationed there. Either one would give me an extra shrimp plate to accompany the tempura dinner plate.

The Nisei women who recognized me all asked after my mother. I hesitated to tell, though they seemed to know anyway and expressed their sympathy. The grapevine expanding from Castleview was that good.

ON A DECEPTIVELY pleasant day last May, I came home early in the evening. The house was dark. I didn't think anyone was home, though I had no idea where Mom would've gone. In any case, I announced my arrival according to Nikkei and Japanese tradition: "*Tadaima*."

No answer, so I proceeded up to my room. I heard a low moan somewhere deep in the house. I called again, "Mom?"

No answer, but I retreated to the front hallway quietly. "Mom, are you home?"

The low groan again.

I hoped that it was Naoko, but I instinctively knew it wasn't. I moved quickly to the sewing room in the back. My mom was lying in a heap on the floor breathing irregularly, barely conscious. I slid to her and said something stupid like, "What happened? You okay?"

I called 9-1-1 immediately.

The paramedics said it was probably a stroke, but couldn't be sure. They took her to Emergency at Mount Sinai, the best place for the elderly. I spent eight hours at the hospital. The doctor who finally saw me in the early morning confirmed that it had been a stroke.

"With time, therapy, and luck, she should be back to near normal."

I didn't ask what that meant.

After a few weeks with my mom still in the hospital, I became determined to place her in Castleview-Wychwood Towers, the nursing home where I had visited Rik-san. He was no longer there; I was told he had passed shortly after I had seen him. I knew Mom didn't like it, but I had no choice. I couldn't afford homecare and she couldn't take care of herself. She could barely move or talk.

I must admit to feeling extremely guilty, but I convinced myself I had no choice. My heart broke as I watched her lying immobile in her new bed, in her new and unfamiliar surroundings. Her face was blank from the stroke, but the eyes gazed at me with disappointment, misunderstanding, and perhaps love. I suppose every child goes through the same thing with his parents. *Lucky was the child whose parent died early*, I cynically muttered to myself.

The house settled into its ghostly murk once Mom was fully moved out. It was happening all over again. My father had left me with no answers and a black hole at my core. With Naoko, the hole doubled in size. With Mom, that hole grew deeper and blacker. The silence enveloped and suffocated.

Maybe it was natural, something to be expected, but I started to think about my mother's passing. I did not want it to happen; I just couldn't help myself seeing her so debilitated. An image of her materialized before me: she lay within the Realm of Hungry Ghosts, her rotted graveclothes hanging loosely on her wasted body; the air was filled with the sweet smell of incense and burning wood. Her breathing was erratic, muting her voice; it smelled of wet ashes. I shivered with horror, especially when I heard her disembodied laughter.

I couldn't take it anymore and shook my consciousness clear. I retreated to my room and the dream diary, but I had no desire to study it further, or to even open it; instead I thought about my okaasan, my sad and beautiful okaasan. The guilt I felt for digging up old secrets.

I TOLD THE LADIES she was happy in Castleview, walking in her way, but not talking. I visited her once a week when the Japanese dinner was served, or more often when the staff informed me that she needed something. The Nisei declared that I was a good son. Didn't feel like one, but I didn't disagree.

Mrs. Sugiura choreographed the women in the back kitchen. The Nisei in long white aprons danced in a complex ballet, avoiding each other as they moved pots and fry pans to the stovetops, as they took out the hot trays of food to let them cool in the steamy air, as they called for more clean plates and platters from the dishwashing Nisei men in the nearby boiler room. None of the women looked particularly attractive since they wore hairnets, as the city food inspectors had demanded. Mrs. Sugiura, however, looked none the worse for wear; she was in her element. No one would ever mention her son's folly in her presence. Everyone knew and gossiped about him behind her back, but no one wanted to embarrass Mrs. Sugiura. I supposed Boku wasn't a "good son."

I caught her eye and she smiled at me.

Sometime between the chaos of lunch and the wonderful anticipation of picking raffle winners, I caught up with Mrs. Sugiura in the front office — the room where she had asked me if her son was kichigai.

Mrs. Sugiura was sitting at a large table, sorting through the ticket stubs for the Dana Ladies Draw. Someone was about to win a twenty-six-inch Sony Vega television set.

"Michael, how are you?"

"Good, Mrs. Sugiura," I answered. "You look well."

"For an old lady, you mean," she replied with a smile.

"No, no, not at all. You look good for any lady." I felt a little ill at ease, but I then blurted out my question, "How's Boku?"

I could see a slight shade of embarrassment come over her face, but she must've anticipated my asking. "I haven't seen him in a long time," I added. I quickly realized how stupid my question must've sounded. "I mean...I..."

"It's all right, Michael," she assured. She knew of my discomfort and wanted to lighten the moment. "I haven't seen him in a long time, too."

"Mrs. Sugiura, there is something I want to ask you. Not about Boku." It was my turn to assure her.

"Oh yes?"

"Your mother's name is Watanabe, right? Your maiden name?"

"Yes."

"What's your first name? I mean, I've never known. I mean, why would I?" I stumbled around the room.

"It's Emiko."

"Do you have a sister? Her name is...she is...?"

"Chiemi."

Don't know why I was so reticent asking her about her family, since she didn't seem to mind. I was being Japanese Canadian, I guess. I could feel myself sweat a bit. "Did she know my father?"

"I don't know, did she?"

She sounded genuine enough; she wasn't being coy, but I did perceive an anxiety, a flinching of the eye.

"My uncle said she did."

"Who's your uncle?"

"Uncle Kunio...I mean...Kunio Shimizu."

"Ah. He's a good man. He must know what he's talking about."

"Then you don't know...I mean...about your sister and my father."

"I never saw her again after the war."

"Why is that?"

She didn't answer immediately. She drew in her breath and breathed out sadness, a gust of air full of regret.

"I'm sorry, Mrs. Sugiura, I didn't mean..."

"It's all right, Michael. I was just remembering. My father died in a peculiar way near Lillooet during the war. He just walked out of camp one night and we never saw him again."

"He just disappeared?"

"Well, the search party found him, but my sister and I weren't allowed to see him."

"What happened? I mean how did he die?"

She paused before saying in a soft voice, "Suicide." I knew that took a great deal to admit. "Hanged himself."

The words fell with a thud. My uncle had told me, but hearing it from the victim's daughter was profound. I was really impressed with her candour. After a swelling and crescendo of bazaar noise coming from outside the office, I ventured, "What happened to your sister...after that, I mean?"

Mrs. Sugiura straightened her back and averted her gaze. "We were in East Lillooet for the Duration. When we could leave, Chiemi decided to go off on her own. Okaasan was too much in shock to care, so my sister left for some place in Saskatchewan... Moose Jaw, I think."

"Why Moose Jaw?"

"Don't know, she never said anything to me about it."

"You didn't go?"

She shook her head. "I took care of my mother."

"My father was there. Perhaps that's where they met."

"Oh? I guess so, but I don't know." She next said in a solemn voice, "She died there." She lowered her eyes. "Okaasan and I received a letter from Ross Thatcher when we were in Hamilton. He was a new MP back then."

"*The* Ross Thatcher? What did it say?"

"Not much, just that my sister had died. She was sick. And that he was sorry."

A sudden remorse came over me. I hadn't meant to cause Mrs. Sugiura pain. A hard luck family. I knew not to press her about Boku, though I was curious about him. I thought myself a jackass for bringing him up in the first place.

"One strange thing about my father," she mused. "I heard some of the search party men talking afterward. There was a pack of wolves circling around his body. They seemed to be guarding him. Never asked my mother about it, but that has been with me my entire life — probably until the day I die."

THAT EVENING BACK IN MY ROOM, I revelled in the comfort of the dull light of my desk lamp. I put Santana's first album on my handy CD boom-box and sank into the Latin rhythms and '60s counterculture. In my head, I went over that afternoon's conversation with Mrs. Sugiura. A pack of wolves again. They circled her father's lifeless body and my father's downed plane. What's the connection? Is there one? The implications unnerved me well into the night.

Eventually I picked up my Father's notebook and hoped against hope that the English had not reverted to Japanese. I slowly opened it. I sighed a moment of relief: the English was intact.

Naoko's last words came back to me. *Look deeper and realize what it is you really want.* That could've been a figment of my feverish mind, but I didn't think so. What did I want? Naoko: her sense of compassion; her classic good looks, especially her captivating eyes; the supernatural events surrounding her. I wondered if she had even existed. My eyes followed a trace of words on the page before me.

> *the warm- press*
> *of her figure.*
>   *wind*
> *serpenting thru the woods*
>
> *until i knew her*
>   *her nostrils flaring,*
> *her diamond eyes*
>
> *cutting the dark skies with fire*
> *and*
>   *then she disappeared.*

Father's words burning on the page expressed exactly how I felt about Naoko. She was what I was looking for. I needed her physicality back in my life. But how? Maybe she was in Japan and I had to go there as my father did. I remembered the transparency of her body, and my mother's. Both had disappeared from my life, Naoko physically and Mom spiritually gone.

I turned to the diary. About halfway through, the narrative suddenly turned to a coherent prose. I was wrong about the book not revealing anything about Chiemi. The story unfurled before me as if the dead had been resurrected in front of my eyes.

29.

October 1988

It was raining hard the night I met Glenn. The streets of Nighttown were greasy as its denizens crept their way home. At least the stench of commerce had been tamped down by the weather. The piles of cardboard boxes outside each darkened store had begun to collapse.

I sat alone in the Golden City. Before Glenn showed up, I thought about Dad. I wondered why he had gone north of Lake Superior in the first place. Maybe Angler had something to do with it. Perhaps he was looking for the original site, perhaps to find something left behind, perhaps to talk to ghosts. I just didn't know.

I wished I could spend one more day — an hour, a few minutes — with him, to talk. My bones ached.

Glenn came in looking tense in his Nike tennis shirt, blue jeans, and runners. He slung his wet windbreaker around the back of his chair. The dripping jacket formed puddles on the floor.

"No date tonight?" I asked.

He gazed at his hands and matter-of-factly said, "Met Cathy for a coffee."

"Cathy? Boku's Cathy?"

"Yeah. Hey, nothing to it. She just wanted to talk. She'll be calling you soon."

I closed my eyes.

"So Boku's gone?" Glenn asked.

"Yeah, three years in Millhaven. That's hard time, my friend. Maximum security."

"But he's a first offender."

"True, but he had no lawyer and he refused an appeal."

"Why?"

Why indeed. That was the question that plagued everyone. The Girls incessantly talked about him, speculating to no end why he did what he did. I had no answers for them or anyone else, though I could've mentioned Ayn Rand, but to what end? Although I knew he was influenced by Rand, I couldn't explain how much to myself, never mind to anyone else. *He was an objectivist detective.* I knew he blamed me and his mom for embarrassing him during Oshougatsu back in 1983, but I refused to take the blame and feel the guilt. I didn't force him to rob a bank. Was I starting to talk like him? He, after all, couldn't answer any of the arguments we presented for redress. Now he felt he could, I supposed. Such extreme lengths to win an argument — throw away your life to make a point?

I could see Glenn was badly shaken by Boku's crime and fate. It was far removed from his career and serial dating. He loved and respected his parents; he would do nothing to harm or embarrass them. What Boku had done was the greatest sin — he had shamed his family, his parents especially.

"If I explained things to you, Glenn, you wouldn't understand. Trust me, I don't understand it myself."

"You're just as bad as Boku. You think I'm stupid or something."

"That's not true."

"Shut up," he snapped. "Why would he betray his family? Why did he turn his back on all of us? He was bright enough to get a good education. It didn't have to be architecture. He was good at computers. He could've been with Cathy. Why did he give it all up?" His lips started to tremble.

I was startled by his outburst, but I understood. "Come on, Glenn, buddy, I didn't mean to insult you. I'm sorry if it came across that way. You're the smartest guy I know. I told you I don't fully understand why Boku did it myself. And that's the truth. He told me he did it to be like his grandfather. If you get that, then explain it to me."

Glenn calmed down, wiped his face with his shirt sleeve, and looked away. "No, I don't get it. Is he crazy? You know I heard about his uncle."

We ate our rice plates in silence. Even Radar went about his business without a word. He just gave us the bill and disappeared into the back kitchen.

"You leaving?" I asked as Glenn moved to stand.

"Yeah, I gotta see my mom."

"Yeah, for sure. I should be getting home, too."

"You up for a game this Sunday? After church, I mean."

"Touch football?"

"Yeah, the Goatman called. He's trying to get a game going at Hart House."

Gary "Goatman" Goto, one of The Boys, was the organizing jock among us. "Yeah, sure. Meet you at church?"

"Right. I'll be there at the end of service."

"As always."

Radar slinked out of his hole just as Glenn left, and I was about to. His white jacket was soiled with crimson char shiu juice and his hair was as slick as ever. He bore no smile, no charm, just a perfunctory grunt as he scanned the table for the tip. A huk couple walked through the door.

"Number 6 with egg roll," Radar said. "Two?"

"Yeah, that's right," the tall man said astonished. "How did you know?"

ABOUT A WEEK LATER I sat in the Golden City again. A different table, but with the same view of the front of the restaurant. Don't know why I felt nervous, but I was, my palms sweating even in the cold.

I gazed into my teacup trying to remember the significance of tea-leaf patterns. Just trying to kill some time. And then she walked in. The clicking of her heels led straight to my table. I thought I could be cool by kicking the chair away to allow her to sit, but I wasn't James Dean.

"Hello, Michael."

"Cathy. Nice to see you." As she sat down, I noticed just how attractive she was. Her long hair accentuated her high cheekbones, her delicate skin invited touch, and her large, unadorned lips made her appear vulnerable. Her back was a straight edge as always. And there was something different about her: she wore high-heels and not runners. "You wanna order something?"

Radar materialized tableside, startling me. That was something I could never get used to. "Beef and green on rice?" he asked without irony.

"Yes," she said. "In a bowl and not a dish. And a fork."

"You can get it like that?" I asked.

"Yes."

"Never knew that. You learn something new every day."

Radar bowed his head, clicked his heels, and squeaked away.

My nerves had calmed down, but I still searched for words. "You had coffee with Glenn." This was ridiculous. How long had I known this woman?

"Yes, I did."

"Isn't that unusual?"

"Why? We're friends."

"Yeah, but... not friends in that way." I fell silent. What was the use of this small talk? I finally spoke: "You talk about Boku?"

Her face compressed. Radar brought her beef and greens on rice in a bowl, and my wonton noodle soup. I didn't bother ordering anymore since Radar always knew my choice.

Cathy squirmed a bit as she picked up her fork to eat. "Yes, we talked about Boku. But you knew that. No answers, that's for sure. It was good just to talk."

"Yeah, Glenn's pretty upset... broken up about Boku. Have

you seen him, Boku I mean, since the trial?"

"No, but he wrote me a letter."

"Really? When?"

"Before his trial. Maybe just before."

"What did he say?"

"Romantic stuff."

"You mean to tell me he wanted to get back together?"

"Not really, but he did say . . ."

"What? C'mon Cathy, give."

She frowned at me.

"Sorry, Cathy, I didn't mean to be — "

"He did say he would be getting everything I expected," she interrupted. "So we could be together again."

"What did he mean by that?"

"No idea. But he was persistent even if I turned him down about marriage."

We spent the rest of the meal in relative silence, though I did ask what she was up to. I hadn't seen her in a while and really hadn't paid any attention to her life choices.

"Working at Monarch Park Secondary."

"Oh, yeah, doing what?"

"Gym and geography teacher. Might as well put my education to work. I . . . I met someone there. Bob Sinclair. You should meet him. He's a nice guy. We're dating."

And so it went. We ended the evening with a hug and a peck on the cheek after I walked her to her car. The last thing I said to her was that I would like to meet her new boyfriend (even if he was hakujin).

BOKU WAS GONE, put into a maximum-security prison. I felt the Redress Settlement had proved him wrong and, in fact, made a mockery of his "detective work." The hell of it was not knowing how he felt.

His parents were devastated. I heard they gave or threw away all his belongings. It was like he never existed for them. Boku's friends remained confused and eventually stopped talking, and presumably stopped thinking, about him.

Like Glenn I was angry that my pal, with whom I had grown up and who had so much potential, had thrown it all away on a wrongheaded whim, no matter his reasons.

I thought about Cathy. Could the bank robbery be a way for Boku to assuage his guilt for not giving her all she wanted out of life? Was the punishment, three years of hard time, his way of paying for it? I didn't believe it. Or was the act a way of proving his devotion to Objectivism, as a true believer. Maybe he truly hated the NAJC and redress.

I could ask him, I supposed, even though he'd probably deny everything or give me some obscure answer. I could possibly see the truth in his eyes. But that would be impossible now; no real trace of him remained, and I had a morbid fear of jail. Boku had vanished; Dave nearly died, and I rarely saw him. My father was an unsolvable mystery. I suspected many more people I had known would simply cease to exist in the years to come.

30.

September 1991

My father's words shone on the page. I was thrilled in the anticipation of what I was about to learn, yet I feared the implications and secrets unearthed; a chill hung in the air. Death seemed to touch my shoulder as I read:

Early Autumn 1945
A cold day. Raining hard when they announced the end of the war. I didn't believe them. They lied to us about Hiroshima. How could one bomb kill 70,000 people? About the Emperor capitulating. He would rather die for Japan. He was Japan. Only the traitors believed. How was any of that possible? Then they released us. I warned the traitors: if you leave Angler, you will die unhealed.

But they left, running out on us and leaving the seven of us to carry on the battle. We were the genuine article, believing in Japan's just cause. The Ganbariya. We alone stood as a bulwark against the deceit of the Canadian Government. We alone would bring honour to our families. We alone would win. We stayed as a protest.

1946
Told to leave in no uncertain terms. Tosh said, "We gotta vamoose."
But we said no. Even if the gates are wide open, the machine gun towers empty, and the barbed wire cut in places, we were staying to fight the good fight. Even if they dismantled the camp around us.

Summer 1946

*Jimmy Isojima, Takashi Kawai, Daniel Sugiura, Tamio
Tanemitsu, Bullet Gotanda, Tosh Umeda and I were herded, at
gunpoint, onto a train headed west. We were still at war — the
rifles proved that. We weren't the only ones. About 130 others
from around Ontario came along.*

*The train was meant to carry freight. The floor was bare
wood covered with a thin layer of hay. Slivers plagued us. Bugs
bit us. The sliding doors were shut tight. Dust particles flew in
the air, choking all of us. Between the slats, I could see the landscape slowly moving past. We were like cattle.*

*We finally came to a stop and detrained in the middle of
nowhere, at a place called Moose Jaw, a hick town if I ever saw
one. We threw around the question, "Why here?" It made no
sense. We had to get used to Saskatchewan.*

*The military boys took us to an installation four miles south
of town. The sign above the camp identified it as RCAF Station
Moose Jaw, established 1940. The locals, as I later learned, called
it the "Moose Jaw Hostel." It was just another prison camp to us.*

*The training airbase was well guarded with double barbed-
wire fences. We were greeted by the Hostel supervisor Jack
McKillop. I didn't know his connection to the military, but he
was the head honcho, that was clear. This was a man who
wouldn't take any guff from the likes of us. His posture was as
straight as a grain elevator, his gloved hands large, solid like
rocks I imagined. He wasn't tall, but he wasn't short. His stocky
build gave him the appearance of height. It was clear from the
outset that he did not want to be bothered with us, but those
were his orders. In other words, he was like every popinjay
Commandant we had met along the way.*

*"I understand you don't want to be released," he said to us.
"The war's over, you know. You look like intelligent men. Why
don't you just get on with your lives? I'm sure we can accommodate you and quickly. Provide transportation, provisions, and
even some money."*

Well, he came to the point anyway. As for his question, I might have answered by asking, "Where can we go? We can't go back to Vancouver; your boys have seen to that. There's a new law..." But I remained silent, as did the rest of us.

We were assigned barracks, and we kept out of trouble.

It was a different place from the prisoner-of-war camps of Ontario. The living quarters were about as "comfortable," small rooms inside metal cans — Quonset huts, I believe they were called — instead of wooden barracks, but there were very few guards and the ones who were on duty were friendly, more or less. They didn't keep their distance like in the camps back east.

The most remarkable feature of the Hostel was the library. A library! I hadn't seen a book since walking down Main Street on a Sunday afternoon back home. I savoured every volume I came across: Flaubert, Zola, Dylan Thomas, Orwell, Fitzgerald, and Hemingway; the sacred, the profane, the lovely, the disturbing. Then I came across it, the holiest of holy: The Dubliners by James Joyce. A collection with my favourite story: "The Dead." Such was my joy.

About a week later, something extraordinary happened. Members of various families from the BC camps started trickling into Moose Jaw. My father wasn't one of them. He had written to tell me he was going back east to a place called St. Catharines. He had pleaded with me to join him; I was his only family left since my older sister had disappeared into the woods. She was lost to us.

One night we all met and mingled in the large central hut, its lights dimmed to provide "atmosphere," and even food was provided by the military! Hot dog wieners and buns, but they were like fancy canapés to us. Maybe Jack McKillop wasn't such a bad guy after all. At least we had a day to relax and savour a bit of hope.

My father had a sister? I had an aunt? Another secret, another dilemma. Why the hell wasn't I told? My parents never said a word. They could not have been "protecting" me. What would've been the point? What is the shame of knowing?

I was also surprised to learn a Daniel Sugiura was there. Was that Boku's uncle, the one no one talked about? I was pretty sure Boku didn't know; Mrs. Sugiura would know, but I wasn't willing to put her through more discomfort. My father didn't seem to find anything abnormal about him back then. Did something happen after the war?

"Mom!" I screamed in frustration, but there was no one in the house except me.

I assumed my aunt was dead. I didn't know why or how. And there wasn't any way I was going to find out, unless Dad talks about it later in the diary. There were photos, but unidentified. My aunt could've been in them, but hell if I knew.

I continued to read. I wondered where Chiemi was.

31.

Fall 1946

About three hundred of us occupied the Moose Jaw Hostel, an intermediary stop for people moving east. The Moose Jaw Hostel was now a Dispersal Centre. The weather turned cold, the days shorter, the light more sombre, but I was in high spirits. Everything was as good as could be, despite the situation. And then I saw her. Chiemi walked into the Hostel. Man, what a sweet damsel.

She was a Watanabe. I had had run-ins with her father. He was an inu, a traitor of the highest order. Chiemi was a bit thin, but then we all were. She brought a touch of beauty to the drab military surroundings.

Chiemi, with long black hair, slim build and long legs, was the one for me. I knew it from the start. But there was something strange about her. She never looked anyone straight in the face; she always averted her gaze. But then I saw her, I really saw her, when the sunlight, meagre though it was, caught her just right. Her eyes were not aligned as normal eyes were. One seemed to be slanted below the other. I couldn't stop looking at her until I made her uncomfortable and she turned away. I tried to follow her to her barracks, but was thwarted by her friend, Michiko Abe, a woman I remember from Japanese school days.

"You'll have to forgive her. She's just a bit shy."

"Sure. Sure. I meant no harm."

Once the war ended, I learned through gossip, the Watanabes had left East Lillooet, a self-sustaining camp for Japanese families with money, to head east. The Watanabes had gained a place in the camp through the father, who named Japanese nationals and Nikkei troublemakers. His victims were immediately imprisoned in Ontario. I knew some of them in Petawawa and Angler and some made it here. He paid for it with his life. The family became sharecroppers in Alberta, south of Calgary, when Chiemi decided she wanted to do something more. She was angry and bitter over the government setting up that whole self-funded camp idea in the first place. When she heard of a protest being staged here with the remnants of the Angler Ganbariya, Chiemi was convinced that this was the place to be. Her sister, Emiko, tried to point out the folly of her plan, but Chiemi would have none of it. "You got some moxie, girl," Emiko said to her sister as a parting shot. Her mother objected but could not stop her from leaving. Emiko committed to staying with her mother to protect and help her. And that was how Chiemi came to be in Moose Jaw.

LATE OCTOBER 1946

I finally got to know Chiemi at a Nisei dance. Things were quite a bit looser than in the Ontario POW camps of Petawawa and Angler. A Nisei Social Committee formed and put on a Fall Harvest Dance in the Mess Hall. Michiko Abe, a spunky go-getter and Chiemi's friend, was in charge. Don't know how she and her cohorts did it, but the place was decorated with orange and black crepe paper, a few pumpkins scattered about, some balloons suspended above and piles of hay here and there. The place looked like a magical fantasyland. Michiko sure was a spitfire of a gal. Music came courtesy of Supervisor McKillop. He hauled out his record player and some of his men provided the records. The crowd was good, loud, and bustling. The organizers were afraid they'd run out of food, but McKillop, bless him, ordered his men to bring in leftover sandwiches from the Mess Hall. He was an all-right guy.

A small group of Japanese strangers came in through the door. Young guys, locals, they were farmers and long-time residents. They looked friendly enough, with bright eyes, unkempt hair, and sun-baked skin. Everyone knew by their names they were Okinawan Japanese. Their last names (Kohatsu, Yamashiro and Higa) and their rough looks gave them away. What brought them to these parts was beyond me, but they caused a stir. Okinawan Japanese were the untouchables, since they worked with pigs and leather. Some of the fellahs warned the girls not to dance with them; some wanted to kick them out, resort to violence if necessary. I reasoned with the ruffians that it was absurd, given the reason we were all here in the first place. In the end, peace reigned. Michiko broke the ice by asking one of them to dance. Higa was perhaps shocked, but he willingly obliged. She was a real friendly gal. That wide, toothy smile of hers! They looked good swinging around the floor to Benny Goodman's "Stompin' at the Savoy." Higa, a regular jive bomber. I decided it was good the Okinawans had settled here, rather than face a double whammy of discrimination in Vancouver.

A little later I spied Chiemi from across the room, like so many romance novels and scenes in Hollywood movies. "Moonlight Serenade" came on and I made a beeline for her. Maybe I was a little anxious, since I startled her into laughing nervously. I wasn't in fancy duds, like a suit and tie, but I tried to look my best. Better than some of the guys who still wore their grey Angler uniforms with the large red sun on their backs (targets for the guards in case of an escape attempt). I had on a clean, white, collared shirt and black trousers. In any case, she seemed happy to see me after the initial shock and accepted my invitation to dance.

We floated on the wave of saxophone and trombone chords and harmonies across the floor awash in coloured lights. For me, her simple dress transformed into a gown of chiffon, silk, and lace. Her perfume clouded my senses and I felt intoxicated with her presence. I was mesmerized by her eyes, like they had some mystical power. I felt a rapturous surge of light emanating from them, enveloping me in a glow that was at once effervescent, warm, and familiar.

I remember our first conversation like it was yesterday.

"Where're you from?" she asked.

"Oh…um…Angler."

"No, before that, silly."

"Oh, Vancouver, originally. I was working as a clerk in a bank there. On Powell Street. You?"

"Steveston. My father was Secretary to the Fisherman's Association."

"Oh, yeah." I remained mum about what I knew.

WE WERE INSEPARABLE from that moment onwards. There wasn't a whole lot to do in camp, but we managed to fill the time. The Ganbariya met in secret, or held community meetings to remind everyone of the "cause," but really everyone was settling into life as best as we could. There was really no use in protesting anymore.

Chiemi and I held hands as we walked the perimeter of the place, keeping away from the airfields. We respected the prohibition. All I wanted to do was to be with my girl, maybe make plans.

"Chiemi, you and me, we're copacetic, right?"

"Yes, I suppose so."

"Maybe we ought to think about getting away from here. You know, start our lives."

That didn't sit too well with her. Not that she didn't see a future with me, but she had a purpose in being in Moose Jaw. As she put it, she wanted to "make amends for my father."

I didn't understand until we were confronted one day by Jimmy Isojima. There he was, the once-young fisherman from Steveston with a creased, tired face, thinning body and madness in the eyes, blocking our path during one of our daily walks together. He was seething with anger, like a predator confronting an enemy.

"You!" he bellowed as he pointed accusingly at Chiemi. "I know who you are. You can't fool me."

"Isojima-san. Of course, you know who I am. You came over to our house several times. You and my otousan —"

"Don't talk to me about your father. That *ketsuno-ana* was responsible for killing my family. My father committed *hara-kiri* because of him. And Gladys...Gladys..." The name caught in his throat. He couldn't go on, and he crumpled before us like paper caught on fire.

"Take it easy, Jimmy," I said, stepping between him and my girl. He stopped momentarily, but I was ready for violence.

Other Ganbariya led by Dan Sugiura came and helped Jimmy to his barracks. I pulled Chiemi away as well. In a private and dark corner of the camp, I asked her what that was all about. Most of what she confessed I already knew. Her father in order to get into the self-sustaining camp became an informant for the BC Security Commission and the RCMP. It cost $1,800 per family to be assigned to one of those camps, a sum very few could afford. There was no other way for the Watanabes to remain together. One of the father's victims was Jimmy, leaving his family to fend for themselves. Jimmy was sent to Angler while the rest went to Tashme. Under the thumb of the Morii gang members, Gladys, Jimmy's younger sister, fell victim to an outrage by a soldier. She died in the attack. Jimmy's father, a stroke victim, dropped into such a depression that he committed harakiri. Chiemi's own father was filled with remorse; guilt drove him into the nearby woods to commit suicide by hanging.

Chiemi had joined the protest in Moose Jaw as a gesture toward making amends for her father's treachery.

"I should talk to poor Isojima-san," she said.

"No, no, you shouldn't. He's not right in the head. Hasn't been for a long time," I explained. "Let me try. Maybe I can get others to help."

She just nodded. Her eyes and cheeks were damp.

32.

Spring 1947

Supervisor McKillop announced employment opportunities in the surrounding area for us. Official word had come down from the Commissioner of Japanese Placement, JF MacKinnon. Anyone who took the deal, however, would have to leave the facility.

Tak Kawai reminded everyone in a meeting why we were here. Tak started out in the Nisei Mass Evacuation Group, but became a Ganbariya in Angler. His anger kept him going; his youth had evaporated with his greying hair and crow's feet. His fanaticism was rekindled by the offer.

"No one leaves. Get me? That's just what they want, for all of us to forget what they did to us, our families, our community. Don't accept these jobs! They must be well beneath us anyway. Stay the course and remain here. We will win in the end." Many applauded.

Tak's speech did the trick. He as representative issued a flat refusal to the offer of employment.

MAY 30, 1947

The powers-that-be issued a notice to vacate. We were to be out by the end of May for parts unknown. Several of the older Issei, and those who had been debilitated during the war, were deemed unfit for work and so were loaded onto trucks and taken by train to a nursing home for the aged in New Denver, BC. Japanese Canadians were still prohibited from returning to anywhere along the West Coast.

Supervisor McKillop tried to persuade more, and most left the Hostel until only about eighty remained.

My own resolve was starting to go. I liked the hakujin stationed at the base, especially the supervisor. Sure, he was an S.O.B. at the beginning, but I understood. He was kind and even compassionate underneath it all. He was caught between a rock and a hard place — between duty and understanding.

Maybe the softening of my attitude had to do with Chiemi. I knew she was where my future lay. She would carry me through to better times. But she was determined to stay, "to make amends" as she said. How was anyone's guess.

SUMMER 1947

The Department of Labour set a final closing date of August 13th for the "Enemy Alien Hostel". If no one left, then food supplies and services would be terminated.

On the 6th, three more Issei were deemed unfit for labour and sent to New Denver. They screamed at the officials, "I'd rather die than leave." Mounties stormed the barracks and forcibly took all three out to an awaiting truck. They were dragged out, the heels of their bare feet scrapping the wooden floors. The sound was sickening.

It was afterward that an advocate stood up in Ottawa on our behalf. Ross Thatcher, as good a man and politician as ever there was, always appeared in a suit and tie, and kept his thinning hair neatly combed. My initial impression was on the side of caution. He was perhaps a simple man, but, as I was to later learn, he was well educated.

As a CCF MP for the federal riding of Moose Jaw, he addressed Parliament shortly after the three Issei were taken out against their will. His speech was reprinted in part in *The New Canadian*, our community newspaper:

We must undertake collective action for the betterment of the political, social, moral and economic welfare of Canadians of Japanese ancestry...and work toward the development of a true Canadian democratic social order wherein fundamental civil rights and liberties are accorded all citizens.

The Mess Hall was closed, food services suspended. More people left. About sixty remained: eighteen single men (including us Ganbariya) stayed in one barrack; a few women, including Chiemi and her friend, Michiko Abe, in another; and six families in the oversized fourth.

Thatcher again called attention to the situation, this time to the Prime Minister himself in a telegram. I read about it in *The New Canadian.*

> *Strongly protest forceful evacuation of residents of Japanese camp at Moose Jaw by RCMP. Believe order stopping food may result in damage to dozens of children and old people. Democratic rights of Canadian citizens apparently endangered by strong-arm tactics. Urge immediate investigation to avoid trouble at camp.*

And there was trouble. The Red Cross turned against us and refused our pleas for food. Bullet Gotanda yelled out in a meeting, "Damn, dem sons of bitches! Is they trying to starve us to death? What I wouldn't do for a Blue Plate Special at Ernie's."

"Heck," I said. "All I want is a good cup of joe."

Again, Ross Thatcher came to the rescue. Don't know what got into the man, but he was a good one. I mean, I understood McKillop's actions, though I didn't condone them. He was under the gun to obey orders, but what was in it for Thatcher? In the end, I decided he was just a good, kind man.

Thatcher canvassed local store owners, sympathetic townsfolk, and Japanese to give us food and they came through.

One such Japanese resident was the owner of the Star Rooms, a modest boarding house of six rooms in the centre of town at the far end of Main Street, the poor side of Moose Jaw. It was two storeys high with a wooden staircase outside. Small, basic rooms with functional furniture, nothing to shout about, but the place was like a refuge from the chaos that surrounded us. It represented the old days, when we could count on neighbours for help and shelter. I never learned Iwakichi Sato's story, how he, a short man with a few teeth missing, came to settle in Moose Jaw, how he managed to learn English to woo and marry a white woman, and how he managed to start the hotel, but we were grateful for his help. Remarkable man really.

Sato-san came through with one hundred pounds of rice! I teared up as Chiemi cried.

From town the Endo family, Kiyooka family, and even the Okinawans gave us fresh vegetables. I guess they felt grateful we had accepted them as our own. Fumiko Endo, the sixteen-year-old daughter, came by occasionally to enjoy, I guessed, people who looked like her. She probably had never seen so many. Her wide smile, open face and sparkling enthusiasm were always a welcome sight. I didn't want her mixed up in this fight and told her so, but she came by time to time. Such a brave, compassionate soul.

After political pressure from the CCF, the Department of Labour backed off on their threats. For the time being.

33.

Beginning of February 1948

A "final" warning came in a letter from the Dept. of Labour. Tak right away called for a sit-down strike. It started outside McKillop's office, but after two days, everyone left for their barracks to initiate a hunger strike.

It was exhilarating at first. I held Chiemi in my arms as we sat for hours in her room. The smell of her hair was intoxicating. Though we grew hungry quickly, we held strong in our resolve. The bastards allowed the cooking smells from the Mess Hall, open again and staffed by military personnel, to waft into the hallways. My impression of McKillop started to turn sour, especially when he ordered the water, electricity and heat shut off. We shivered by candlelight as the temperature plummeted to sixteen below zero. Was he really a fat-head, doing the bidding of his superiors?

MARCH 1948

The days turned into weeks. I worried for everyone's health, Chiemi's especially. She wasn't strong to begin with. She worried about things all the time. She constantly pulled at her hair, which came out in small clumps. Though we had enough water, I could see her weakening day by day. I imagined her face growing thinner with each moment. Her body became steadily skeletal. Only her resolve didn't thin out.

Weeks passed and Chiemi was confined to her bed, still refusing to eat. I wondered if she forgot how. She gazed at me with her magical eyes, their spark dimming. I was by her side, ignoring my own hunger pangs. She was skin and bones like the prisoners in a Nazi concentration camp. Her arms were like stunted tree branches in a desert. But she refused food, even a little bit, even if I implored her, to maintain her conviction that we were doing the right thing.

Finally, I went to Tak and begged him to stop this foolishness. "We can call on Sato-san for food. Maybe Thatcher-san will come through for us. Man, people are going to die here."

"Baka!" he growled. "Small sacrifice for the honour we bring to the Emperor. Our cause is just. We will hold the line."

I could see it was useless; madness had taken over his reason.

The hunger strike ended after three weeks, but the damage had been done. Chiemi was bedridden.

JUNE 1948

Chiemi, my poor Chiemi, died during a bright, balmy day. Her body just gave out. Her spirit blinked out like a distant star.

I asked McKillop for permission to bury her.

On a star-filled night, after the heat of the day rose to the heavens, I buried my beloved with the help of McKillop's men. Her lonely grave lay outside the front gates and away from the Hostel with a humble wooden marker. Reverend Scott, a local Christian minister, performed the service. Though Chiemi was a Buddhist, I felt she wouldn't mind. Only I, the minister and McKillop stood with lanterns as mourners.   ·

I stood beneath a shining, blue-night heaven. Just then a shower of stardust cascaded across the sky. Chiemi was saying goodbye.

I THOUGHT OF my mother once telling me in a letter that she had a premonition that she was going to die. She saw herself surrounded by wolves. Vicious and snarling wolves, they attacked her and dragged her into the woods. Her face, she said, was full of sorrow, not horror, or agony, just sadness. I dismissed it at the time, even after I heard she had died in Japan.

Then I remembered my prewar dreams; I described some of the significant ones in this diary.

I retreated within my grief; in fact, I did nothing but cry for days. Something I had never done in my life.

JULY 15, 1948

Four vans arrived and twelve movers stripped our possessions from our barracks. They unceremoniously dumped everything in a field north of the Hostel. Heartless bastards.

The Sheriff and six deputies then gave us a half hour to vacate the premises. Tak yelled at them and ordered everyone to defy the authorities. That did it. The officers raided our quarters, and pulled and pushed everyone out. Tak and Isomura, the last Issei among us, remained defiantly in their bare beds. The deputies grabbed them, pried their hands from the frames and dragged them, barefooted and in night clothes, outside, across the grounds and unceremoniously dumped them outside the gates. The two screamed all the way.

Tragically, one deputy manhandled Michiko when she was unwilling to move. She screeched and twisted and turned to maintain her grip on the bed. Jimmy immediately leapt to her aid. He shrieked, "Let my sister go!" And with that he pulled out a hidden kitchen knife, lunged, and stabbed the assailant in the abdomen. Blood spurted in an arch and splattered everywhere. Several deputies jumped on Jimmy and beat him senseless.

I had never witnessed a killing. I gagged at the sight of blood and fell to my knees, retching and emptying my stomach with the little digested food that was within.

Jimmy had obviously had a psychotic breakdown and mistook Michiko for his sister, Gladys, who was murdered in her internment camp back in BC. Jimmy Isojima was arrested, confined, put on trial, and convicted of murder. He was sent to a prison for the criminally insane.

WITH ARMED GUARDS posted at every gate, and nine deputies watching over us, we sat in the open outside the gates, but then Ross Thatcher appeared with pup tents for us a day later. That was the first time I met the man. His face beamed like the Buddha as he stood before us in casual attire and floppy hat. We didn't say anything to each other, but he did smile at me and gave me a knowing wink. Gratitude flushed throughout my body. Maybe Canadians were all right.

I couldn't help but feel this was a mistake, though we continued to receive food and water from local benefactors. Fumiko Endo came by with *onigiri* made by her mother. Her twinkling eyes told me she understood what was going on. Her round, innocent face was beautiful. Still, my grief for Chiemi turned everything black.

AUGUST 1948

I, seeing the futility of continuing, left for the Star Rooms in Moose Jaw. Eventually most in the protest departed the area and settled elsewhere.

Bullet went to Winnipeg. His girlfriend had resettled there. Tosh and family settled in the Lethbridge area. Not sure what happened to Daniel Sugiura. He just left without saying a word.

I decided to go to Hamilton, Ontario, since Toronto was off-limits to us. Its City Council had barred Japanese Canadians from settling there. I could've gone anywhere in Southern Ontario or even Montreal, but maybe I had Chiemi's family in mind; I found out they had moved to Hamilton from Alberta. I never ran into them. I kept tabs on the Moose Jaw situation through Sato-san of the Star Rooms and *The New Canadian*. Only Tak and Isomura stayed behind to continue the protest. Tough sons-of-bitches. One hundred and thirty-six days after being forced out of the Hostel, even they lost their conviction and agreed to be transferred to New Denver. Tak was too young for the rest home there, but he had aged badly during the Moose Jaw ordeal. I heard he died a few months later. I guess the hunger strike had done too much damage to his body.

LATE SUMMER 1948

The night before I left Moose Jaw, I visited Chiemi's grave one last time. "I must leave, my darling. There's no future here. I feel my destiny is somewhere else. Will you forgive me? You once said we'd meet again, and I believe you. I don't know how, but we will. That I know."

At that moment, I heard a strange noise above me. I looked up to see a sizzling fireball heading straight for me. I fell backward and rolled to avoid it just before it hit the ground. It fizzled out almost immediately. I crawled to the smoking, glowing mass.

After half an hour, the smooth, oblong rock had cooled enough to touch. I picked it up and a surge of energy tingled throughout my body. I passed out. After I don't know how long, I awoke to a brilliant light. It enveloped me so that I had no idea where it was coming from, until I realized it was emanating from me. Was I imagining it? I was confused, but filled with a sense of well-being. Thoughts entered my consciousness: Chiemi, like her father, was being protected, by what I didn't know, but I had the feeling she was happy to be...home.

She was with loving ancestors in a strange and wondrous land with rivers gurgling and twisting toward the horizon, white clouds gently raining, a rolling landscape of fragrant fields and soaring mountains. Perhaps Japan, perhaps Nirvana.

Everything eventually returned to normal. I lay conscious, but weak, puzzled. I had no explanation for what had happened. Perhaps it was a hallucination. Maybe it was a *hinotama*, Chiemi's soul come back to me.

A stone from a firedrake star.

Hamilton, Ontario
Fall 1948

34.

September 1991

My brain buzzed like a hornets' nest. I became feverish and my hands trembled. The book ended with the firedrake reference — a touch of hope. Only blank pages followed. Dad had found the love of his life and then lost her. My mom chose to ignore it, keeping the secret inside her, like some undisclosed disease.

My parents never expressed affection for one another: they never hugged or kissed; they never casually touched one another; they never addressed each other by name, never mind a pet name. There seemed to be no passion between them, unlike Dad and Chiemi. Yet I knew my parents loved each other.

A LONG-FORGOTTEN INCIDENT came back to me. It was just before Dad left for north of Superior. Might've been the morning of his flight. An argument between my parents. I don't know what it was about, since I was in my room in the far reaches of the house. They were in the kitchen. It scared me, I was fifteen and had never heard them so angry, or at least my mother was.

I had sneaked down the stairs and peaked over the bannister. They faced each other, my mother quite animated in both Japanese and English. My father stoic as ever.

"Why do you have to go?" she asked.

"You know."

"And you know what I know . . . my dream! Don't go. No good can come of this."

Dad did not reply; he just stood as silent as a tomb in front of her.

She slowly bent before him, as if bowing. She looked like she was crying quietly into her hands. At least, I think she was. I was too far away to tell.

As Dad turned to leave, I scurried up the stairs. I don't think he heard me, but I couldn't be sure.

Later when Dad was about to leave, he did a remarkable thing. He and Mom were in the front hall facing each other; Dad rigidly stood still while Mom was bent over, her eyes closed, and her hands clasped in front of her stomach. He unexpectedly raised her face with a finger. He smiled and cupped her face with the palms of his hands. He then leaned in and kissed her forehead. She opened her eyes and smiled. He turned to me, smiled broadly, and waved his hand. And then he was gone. The entire episode was bewildering.

PARTS OF MY LIFE started to solidify, but there were several mysteries yet: Boku, Naoko, Mom, Dad's death. Am I cursed? Am I crazy, going out of my mind? What did it all mean?

Alone in my home one evening when the shadows intruded and took over, I felt my hands roll into fists. I squeezed till they were white, anger oozing between my fingers. All the mounting questions, all the frustration of not knowing, and all the supernatural phenomena playing havoc within me came to a boil. I screamed. My mom knew all along why Dad had gone up north, probably knew all about Angler, Moose Jaw, and Chiemi. And all the family secrets. But she would never tell her bakatare son. *You don't need to know.*

My face contorted with anguish and rage, and I suddenly rocketed to my feet and bolted down the hall. I was filled with insecurity, the fear of the unknown, the dread of death. It surged up my spine to my brain. I could do nothing but run. As quickly as the ominous sensation came over me, I slowed to a stop; I couldn't out-run it. The terror disappeared. There was nowhere left to go, nowhere left to explore, and nowhere to seek answers. I was lost, and I knew it.

I realized I had to see Mom, again. I hadn't seen her for a while. Not to ask questions, not that she could answer them. I hadn't told her I loved her, or kissed her, or hugged her since I was a kid. I couldn't let that happen. I hadn't told Dad I loved him. And then it was too late. In my heart of hearts, I wished I could see Dad one last time to tell him. I would see her tomorrow.

Returning to my room, I began to reason through my situation. What to make of my father's journal? I still couldn't explain the paranormal elements, like the Japanese characters floating and reforming into English. Or the cintamani. There were no answers in the book. Was Naoki responsible? I clung to the fact that she was real, but I couldn't explain her ghostly appearances.

But I did see my father's sense of justice, his passion for what was right. He used slang a lot, probably because he was a young man. He loved James Joyce. It explained the lyricism of his images. I was impressed since he never talked about the great writer.

I also loved Joyce. Something beyond the complexity really drew me to him. The stunning imagery, the use of language and the intellectualism of *Ulysses* was beyond belief. His short stories, too, inspired me. "The Dead" was my favourite, like my dad.

Around midnight I peered into the darkness and saw a gathering of shadows. Night coming together into a solid figure. I wasn't asleep, so it wasn't a dream. I gazed in amazement and curiosity as the seeming emptiness began to pulsate. I could see a faint glow at its core. It slowly grew stronger and stronger until a bright light blinded me momentarily. I rubbed my eyes and saw a tall figure emerge, obscured by an indefinite outline. Then I heard a voice.

"So now you know what you want."

It was deep, resonate, and familiar. Not Naoko, but my father. I knew it instinctively, yet I had to ask: "What? Who are you?" I pulled back in fear.

"I'm here as you wished."

"Dad, is that really you?"

"Search inside yourself and you will know."

"How can it be? You're dead."

"I live inside you. I always have. I always will."

"But how...?"

The vision started to fade, but the face became clear.

"It is you! Wait, don't leave. Don't go..." I reached out, hoping to keep my father with me just a while longer. I called out in desperation, "Dad! Dad, I love you!"

Just before he disappeared, he turned and smiled at me, just like the day he had left us. And then I found myself sitting in the dark, feeling robbed like I was fifteen again.

I heard the rain outside. There was no moon, but the gentle tapping against my window kept me in the realm of reality.

What had just happened? Like everything else I was experiencing lately, I couldn't explain what I had seen. I suddenly understood that he had gone north to retrace his journey. He would have probably turned left from Angler and headed for Moose Jaw. Maybe revisit Chiemi's grave.

I thought of Naoko. How did she put it? "Look deeper and find what you really want."

Maybe Dad was looking for what he really wanted.

35.

October 1991

We sat in silent communion. What could be said? My mother's eyes were glassy, quivered now and then with a faraway look. Her hair was long, grey and straggly, framing her shrivelled face in a chaos of forest tendrils. The left side of her body was petrified. The arm hung limply by her side. She wore a body-length pajama top with no pants, and worn slippers on her damaged feet.

Her room was like all the others at Castleview: boxy, pale green, and sparsely furnished. The one window with a thin curtain looked out onto railway tracks leading nowhere. Her side table held a plastic pitcher of water with a matching cup beside it. I had brought a rudimentary AM radio during a past trip, but it was gone.

But we had no need for music or water or whatever. I wanted to be with my mom, my okaasan. Just to be near her was enough.

She was hunched over, like some woodland animal. I lifted her head to look at her. The left side of her face was frozen. Her mouth drooled a bit, so I cleaned it with a handy tissue. The copious wrinkles around her eyes had deepened. The face was filled with kindness, perhaps regret, certainly melancholy. I gently cupped it with my palms, and I whispered, "You knew ... you knew all about Chiemi, all about Dad's search up north, what he was looking for, everything. Why wouldn't you tell me?"

There was no reaction; I didn't expect there to be. Like Dad, I leaned over and kissed her forehead. I thought I saw a smile; at least I'd like to think she smiled. Moisture brimmed her eyes as I whispered "I love you" in her ear. Emotion overcame me and I started to quietly cry. It was then I felt her good hand move and touch my forearm.

We sat for a good long while. I said nothing; there was no longer any need.

36.

Spring 1992

I moved out of my mom's house, my childhood home, in April 1992. I sold it to pay for Mom's expenses at Castleview as the government required. I then resolved to get my act together. Get a PhD, maybe, and a real career (my lecture and tutoring position was going nowhere); find a woman I could cherish; and take care of my mom, visit her at least once a week. I knew that forgetting the recent past was impossible, but I thought I should try. I saw an advert in NOW *Magazine* for an upstairs apartment on Bloor near Brunswick. Naoko's old place? I called and got an appointment.

As it turned out, it was the same building, the same grizzled old caretaker, the same man who had discovered me sleeping on the floor. He had the same haphazardly shaved face, the whiskers grey and spotty. His body was stooped and tired. He examined me with one bulging, cockeyed eye.

"Hey, don't I know you?" he growled.

I turned away as if distracted by the street traffic.

"Yeah, you're that fellah I found sleeping on the floor upstairs," he concluded. "Could never figure what you was doing there."

"Oh, I don't know," I said, not wishing to bring up Naoko.

We fell silent as we proceeded up the stairs to a second-floor apartment. That tingle again. Something inside me. It was Naoko's room. The door yawned open and the caretaker watched me as I walked inside. It was fully furnished as it had been. Same posters, same kitchen utensils and pots and pans, same records, same books, same furniture, same everything. It was as if Naoko had just stepped out for a minute.

"What's going on?" I demanded. "What're you trying to pull here?"

"What?"

"Whose stuff is this?"

"Yours. I mean if you rent it. The apartment comes fully furnished."

"It can't be. This all belongs to my girlfriend." That sounded strange as soon as I said it.

"You talking that crazy talk again?"

I stopped myself to regain control. "No, it just looks so familiar somehow."

"Sure thing, young fellah. You want it or no?"

"Yeah, sure. Gives me a sense of symmetry."

"Simple, what?" he asked.

"Nothing. I'll get the first and last to the landlord."

The caretaker gave me the key and left me to my own thoughts. I half expected Naoko to return sometime soon.

AFTER I COMBED through the LP collection and found Joni Mitchell's *Blue*, I put it on, and her soprano blues filled the air. I sat down on the floor in the middle of the apartment and gazed around the place. I sensed a mist rising through the wooden floorboards, curling around.

A lyrical passage swirled in my mind.

Her face unknowable yet becalming in her fearful nearness; her stormwarnings and the calm of her crooked eyes; the stimulation of her light, her motion and her presence; the prevalence of her curves, her arid seas, her silence. Her absolute beauty when present; her devastating and aching attraction when invisible.

Could have been Joyce, Murakami, or my father. I closed my eyes and waited for another ghostly visit.

37.

1992

It was a beautiful June wedding, the weather perfectly sunny, the bride resplendent in her gleaming white gown, the groom nervous in his smart tux. Dave and Joanie seemed destined for the happiness of a suburban couple living for their three Cs: children, condo and cars — plus a luxury vacation. All this contingent on Dave's college education and Joanie's career as a technician (I was never sure what kind).

I was in the wedding party — not the best man, but a groom's man for sure. Dave's cousin filled the honoured position. I wasn't complaining, since they had known each other their whole lives.

Dave had not fully recovered, but at least he could drive, his car his true home away from home. He stood at a slight stoop as if the now absent bullet had bent his posture. He told me he still needed painkillers and rainy days were the worst. He was one of those guys. The doctors, his bride, and family, if not he, were optimistic. I could see pessimism in his face, but I chalked it up to the stress of his wedding.

Yes, it was a Buddhist wedding; Joanie's prediction had come true. Her family was Christian, but the wedding was a gesture in light of Dave's condition. The church itself was all adorned in white ribbon, the incense held to a minimum. Reverend Fujita was all smiles and well-wishes as he took control of the ceremony. His black robes luxuriously folded around him, he caused tiny gusts of wind wherever he walked.

The hondo overflowed. Who knew the extent of friends and relatives both families could boast? It seemed all of them had been anticipating the union for a good many years. Guests came from Vancouver, parts of Alberta, and even Japan. I was impressed someone would pay that much money to witness the happy occasion (to be honest, the Japanese had plans to visit Niagara Falls and then PEI — for *Anne of Green Gables*). And it *was* a happy occasion.

The reception was naturally at the Cultural Centre, the auditorium decked out in satin with the Nisei-built tables covered in white cloth; each featured a round mirror and centerpiece of orchids and balloons. Joanie had done a fine job of planning everything to the smallest detail.

Dignitaries included the Consul General of Japan, various heads of Japanese corporations, and Cultural Centre Board Members and Administration. I didn't know Dave's father had such reach, but there it was. So much so that the best caterer in town agreed to provide the food at a substantial discount. Apparently Ryoji-san owed Mr. Watanabe for covering up some indiscretion in the distant past.

A traditional roast beef dinner with Yorkshire pudding, potatoes, a green salad, and vegetable soup kept everyone satisfied until the real food came out at eleven o'clock. Of course we had to suffer the speeches, though the best man's was quite funny: "I've known Dave since he was a kid. This is the first I've seen him without a pool cue and Mike by his side. Guess there's no Chinatown tonight. Well maybe ... if Joanie doesn't mind. What else does he have to do? Can't have a day without grease!"

At 11:00, the platters of sushi, shrimp tempura, and other Japanese delicacies graced the serving tables. Can't have a Nikkei wedding without soul food.

The DJ was Dave's youngest cousin with an ambition to turn pro. He played the hits of the day and the first dance: "Time, Love and Tenderness" by Michael Bolton. Not to my taste (nor Dave's I suspected), but it was Joanie's show. Ten years before, a disco tune like "I Will Survive" would have played and the blessed couple would have done a dance routine on the floor. Thank the Buddha it was the '90s.

Everyone had a wonderful time.

I didn't have much time to speak to Joanie, only a brief conversation in the reception line. We just joked with each other as we usually did. I was able to talk to Dave in the waiting room before the ceremony.

"You okay, man?" I asked, sensing something.

"Yeah, yeah," Dave said, his eyes darting nervously from side to side.

"So, you're getting married. How do you feel, man?"

"Oh, I don't know. I suppose...I'm more worried about after."

"What do you mean?"

"You know, the college thing, not working for my old man anymore, getting a real career. Stuff like that."

He sounded like he was a teenager again.

"Hey, come on, man, you've got a bright future with a fine woman, right?"

"Sure, sure. I guess I got to grow up. Looks like no more pool or Chinatown."

Even I knew that. "Had to happen sometime, I guess. I'll say hi to Radar for you."

I supposed from that day on, I would only see Dave with Joanie (never solo) — more if I were married, fat chance of that happening any time soon — and at an occasional Watanabe family gathering with its legendary feasts, the reasonable replacement for Saturday-night cruises up and down Yonge Street. The Buddha was right: change is constant.

38.

Summer 1992

From the real to the surreal. One evening about a month after the wedding, when the rush-hour tide flowed through the Bloor-Yonge subway station's upper level, I stood on the southbound platform and quite unexpectedly I came face to face with Boku Sugiura as he stepped off the train.

"Mike! Hey, close your mouth, I'm not a ghost."

It took a moment for me to recover.

Boku laughed at me.

"What're you doing here?" I asked awkwardly.

"What d'you mean? Did my time. They let me out."

I realized it was true. Why would he lie to me?

"They didn't break me, Mike," he stated.

I had no idea what he was talking about. "When you get out?" I asked.

"Last year. I kicked around Kingston for a while before coming here."

Boku was cordial enough, remarkable considering what he had gone through in the last three years. However, he wasn't the same. He wore seriousness like an overcoat, not one he could take off, either. I noticed a few new age lines at the corners of his eyes; he seemed thinner, a little more fragile. Despite everything I was happy to see him.

He invited me to his hotel, the Windsor Arms, off Bloor east of Bay St. The establishment was as its name suggested: homey, elegant though old-worldly with décor from Toronto's Edwardian era. Fortunately it had been renovated recently. In general, the rooms were well kept, but a little dark. Boku's was cramped. I assumed he was used to such small spaces. It contained a small bed, a smaller table with a compact Underwood typewriter sitting on it, and a perfunctory chair. He was flush with prison cash and spent it on himself.

He informed me that he had saved all his prison money, every penny he made working there, nothing spent on frivolous comforts like cigarettes, magazines, or chocolate bars. Once out, he had rented a place in Kingston. After he had finished his "business" there, he came to Toronto. Curious, I thought, but didn't say anything.

He checked into a hotel for a week. He needed a little pampering and picked the Arms because he always had a taste for luxury, even if his room was "undersized." At least, he dined in high style in the Courtyard Café, one of the finest in the city. I wondered how it compared to Bumpkins, our student haunt.

"Did you call your parents?" I asked.

"They don't even know I'm out. They never visited me."

"They didn't?"

"I told them not to. Don't think my mom could've stood it."

"I suppose."

"Don't think they wanted to see me, anyway. I know my dad didn't."

I paused for a few beats, letting the implications of that statement dissipate. "What did you do in Kingston…after you got out, I mean?"

"Wrote a movie script."

"A movie script?"

"Yeah, is that so unusual?"

"No…no, I guess not."

"I spent a week here to polish it," he said, holding up a thick manuscript and smiling.

"What're you going to do with it?"

"Make it into a movie, you idiot."

"You? You know how to make a movie?"

"No, a film company does."

"Which one is gonna do it?"

"Don't know yet."

"What?"

"They've haven't found me yet. When they do, they'll come and make an offer."

"What? You've got to send it out, so they can appraise it."

"No, I don't. I said they'll come to me."

"So what, you're just gonna wait?"

"Nope. I'm leaving tomorrow."

"Where're you going?"

"Some place away."

"But what about your script?"

"They'll find me."

"But —"

"Will you stop . . . don't worry about me."

I could see there was no use arguing. What fantasy world he was living in now I would never know. He wasn't budging from his stand. I let it go, and said goodbye, making sure he would write me at my new address.

"Mike, you were the only one to understand. I had given up on all my friends, my family. But I should've known I could count on you. Remember when my grandfather died, and you sent me a poem? I never told you, but I was blown away. I stayed up all night reading that poem and thinking about my grandfather, what he meant to me. I had taken him for granted, but not that night. I want to tell you I cried. It took the death of a man I loved very much. Thank you, Mike. You put me on the path I walk today."

With that I left. I confess I barely remembered that poem, and I certainly didn't know I had that kind of effect on anybody with something I wrote. Something about "white ashes," based on an old Buddhist proverb. We may be happy in the morning, but we may be white ashes by the evening. It put me in mind of my father.

I walked through the gathering humidity, contemplating Boku's strange attitudes and behaviour and the mysteries that plagued my life.

Boku had obviously come out of hell with his delusion intact. He really believed he experienced what his grandfather, and I could only assume, his grandmother, parents, my parents, Glenn's parents, and every Japanese Canadian Issei and Nisei had. But he did attempt to rob a bank — that was the uncontestable reality. But not in his mind. He was simply arrested, tried, convicted, and incarcerated for no valid reason.

He had "ascertained history" with no need to study it. To me, without study there can be no understanding, no insight. But he had his cause, like the Nisei in Moose Jaw, I suppose. He would now live to be the best he could be. But where?

And then there was the case of his uncle, Daniel Sugiura. I'm not sure he would've liked what his uncle did early on — I mean joining a collectivist group of rabble rousers to demand justice, even after the war. I was sure Boku would simply have said they should've risen above it and observed from a distance.

I received one letter from Boku shortly after I ran into him. It was from Prince Edward Island, some obscure place called Chintamani. The word echoed in my brain, but I was more interested in the content. It was a blank sheet of paper with a signature: Beaucoup Sugura.

I could only think that it was symbolic of his life being a blank, and that he was starting over to fill it. As for "Beaucoup" and the misspelling of his last name, I guessed that he was now totally estranged from his family. They had no desire to know where he was and how he was doing. He no longer existed.

Opponents of redress stated without a doubt that the Sansei were not affected and therefore had no right to demand it, especially on their behalf. *You weren't there. You didn't suffer. You've made it: intact families, good upbringing in nice suburban homes, excellent education, good careers, and a degree of wealth, acceptance, and prosperity.*

Boku with his advantages gave it all up to proceed in the mistaken belief that he could replicate his grandfather's life. His past was a vacuum, as was mine. For all intents and purposes, he and

I believed our grandparents had come from Japan, lived for a while on the coast, and eventually bought a house in Toronto and began life. Their silence negated us.

He mailed me a copy of his film script. I read it only to discover it was not so much a drama, but a diatribe against collectivism and a declaration of his objectivist values. It was called Ego, named after the central character. It was his trial statement verbatim. His opening monologue was his day in court:

Ego:

My grandfather was my role model. He above all others was the supreme example of egoism. He was taken into custody in 1942 and exiled to a camp somewhere in the BC mountains. And for what? Because he was Japanese . . .

EPILOGUE

The Petticoat Creek Conservation Area hugs the shore of Lake Ontario just outside Scarborough, out Pickering way. The plentiful but well-spaced trees provide ample shade for bedroom-community visitors relaxing on Sunday afternoons before heading home to barbecues and a Blue Jays game. The thick grass easily yields under the blankets and backsides of picnickers. These are not the working-class immigrants of Kew Beach in the city who want to escape the drudgery of a construction job and the mysteries of the English language. They constitute the comfortable middle class. They drive Toyotas, they shop at the Scarborough Town Centre, and they take the Go Train to the downtown canyons of Bay Street or University Avenue to white-collar jobs. Lunch baskets, plentiful and bulging with food, are perched on copious numbers of wooden picnic tables scattered around the park.

The Wakayama Kenjinkai Community Picnic was in full swing by the time I arrived, well after lunch. The kenjinkai were established shortly after Toronto's prohibition of Japanese Canadians was lifted. The clubs served the Japanese from the same prefecture of Japan to find each other, to keep in touch, to help each other, and to keep up their unique dialect. Some of the organizations were quite powerful in the JC community. The Issei elders could arrange marriages, represent those in trouble with the law, oversee funerals, and provide money through a *tanomoshi* to buy expensive items like a house or one of those Toyotas, maybe a luxury model. Over time they diminished in influence, until the annual picnic was the only evidence of their existence.

My family wasn't from Wakayama-ken, but all were welcome. Besides, I liked going to this picnic because it reminded me of the halcyon Movement days when I met the wonderful brothers and sisters from the West Coast. The community picnic was embedded in my soul, in all our souls.

The bountiful meals were the highlight, but there were also pick-up football games; badminton nets for a match or two; a baseball tournament; and organized games like races, hit-the-watermelon, and the messy, but fun, egg toss, for everyone from toddlers to the toshiyori. Prizes were provided by community sponsor businesses and handed out courtesy of the organizers. The highlight of the afternoon had to be the *mochi* toss. Volunteers piled picnic tables on top of each other into a pyramid and someone, a brave or reckless volunteer, would climb to the top with trays and trays of the pounded rice cake. Once there, he would toss the round white treasures to the crowd gathered below.

And the mob scrambled for the treats — soft, moist mounds of rice pounded to a smooth consistency and sometimes flavoured with sweet bean paste in its centre. Everyone from little kids to the most senior of seniors vied for them. The old ladies were the most aggressive, elbowing competitors aside to gather the prize; it didn't matter that the pure white, powdered surface was grass- or dirt-stained. It was all for fun and the mochi, after a little cleaning, were good in *miso* soup or fried with shoyu and sugar in a pan that night.

At the end, the volunteer produced rectangular slabs of mochi and threw them in a twirl into the air, like massive and awkward helicopters, for the lucky ones below. One had to be quite agile and strong to catch those mid-flight. The toshiyori had retreated from the battle by that point. No one, luckily, was ever hurt with the clamour for the delicacy.

I was content just to watch. When I was a kid I would rush and grab for them, scoring several for my mom. How she laughed and prized my booty. Damn, she was happy then. But no more. Okaasan was in Castleview, half-knowing her circumstances and not enjoying it. She could talk a little bit. She always asked in her slurred and garbled way when she was going home. My heart broke every time I had to say, "In a little while."

These days the obasan and oji — too old and ailing — no longer participated. They amused themselves with some maki sushi, and noted how grown their grandchildren had become. At least, those who came. Most young people spurned the past, not wishing to be uncool, indulging in traditions that no longer held relevance in their lives. Japanese culture was anathema to their sensibilities, especially an old Japanese culture that didn't exist in Japan anymore. But the Issei, with wrinkled faces, stooped posture, and failing eyesight, were beautiful in their decrepitude. The young were the truly blind.

Glenn wasn't there; Boku was long gone, buried by the shame and alienation of family and friends. Dave and Joanie had another family gathering to attend, always something on weekends. I heard Joanie was pregnant with twins, but that was a rumour. If true, I was very happy for them, even though I yearned for the days of the midnight Chinatown run. I wondered if Dave was singing the two-bedroom-condo blues in Don Mills. At least I saw them at New Year's when Mrs. Watanabe continued her tradition of great cooking. I was to be "Uncle Mike" to the kids, though I would probably not get to know them, and vice versa.

Neither The Boys nor The Girls came to the picnic anymore. I thought I saw Cathy, but I was probably wrong. I didn't go looking for her. She was Cathy Sinclair now. She married a Monarch-Park colleague (his *alma mater*) in the Geography Department; he coached the junior football team. He hadn't graduated from a collegiate like Jarvis, Malvern, or Riverdale, but a secondary school; it was good enough for her.

I got to know him, a little bit, over dinner at Bumpkins. The restaurant had moved closer to Yonge Street, on Gloucester Street. It wasn't the same, but we enjoyed a good meal. Bob was tall, kind of thin, with robust thick hair. A nice guy, friendly, and outgoing. They and their two *hapa* kids made for a good-looking family. Just what she wanted. Yes, these days I was content to play witness to my fading childhood, the slow death of my community.

I decided to leave early. Some families invited me to have dinner with them. I knew better. It was a trap. If I had accepted and ate a fine meal, I would've been the subject of gossip around town. Not that I had any family that would be embarrassed, but it would be mortifying to run into Glenn or Dave or worse, some Nisei somewhere, like at the church, and be asked what I was thinking going to the Wakayama picnic without my own food. I would forever be known as a mooch. I probably was the subject of gossip anyway for showing up alone, without food, and leaving early.

So I drove down the 401 toward home in my rented car, planning to take the DVP to the Bayview Extension, swing up to Bloor and then cruise along the crosstown artery to the Annex part of town where I lived. Naoko's old place.

Somewhere near the Highway Two cutoff, I took the exit and headed for Kingston Rd. I drove into a cobweb of empty streets. It was still bright out, but the streetlights came on in anticipation of the approaching dusk.

I pulled over and got out. I needed fresh air. It was cool; a slight breeze rivered up to meet me. I greeted it with an open heart. The asphalt had lost its daytime heat. I noticed the streetlights were that much brighter, the evening sky darker. I hadn't noticed the passage of time.

I turned my gaze to the streets and roadways surrounding the plaza. The landscape was flat, as barren as Scarborough could be. With the whizzing of a limited number of vehicles, I saw how alone I was. There were no pedestrians. Solitary, detached, bungalows sat in the near distance, some with a light or two on, most mute and dark.

I wondered what to do next. Maybe I'd go to Japan, a place I had never been to. And search . . . for what? For her?

GHOSTS: EVERYWHERE I LOOK, everywhere I go, even places I don't go, ghosts are everywhere. Lovers, friends, relatives, community. The spirits within ghostly jails, empty internment camps and ghost towns, on dead streets and fields where Japanese Canadians gathered as a visible community. At the Powell Street Festival, the Bon Dance, community picnics, I talk to and walk amongst ghosts. Fields of celebration, fields of *matsuri*, fields of ritual, ceremony, fields of my youth, my nascent adulthood, fields of alienation, of loss, fields of mourning.

I looked up and saw a multitude of pale stars twinkling against the canopy of night. Then I saw a shooting star, or maybe a hino-tama, streaking across the sky. I began to sweat; an itchy film covered my face. My nerves frazzled. I stared at it, tracing its path until it disappeared into the inky horizon. The deep darkness expanded across the sky and pressed down on me. I desperately tried to penetrate the galaxy above by staring as hard as I could. I began choking, gasping for breath. My knees buckled, and I fell to the ground. I felt ensnared in the coffin of night. My hands started vibrating. I began losing consciousness. Will I dream? If so, will I dream of Naoko, Otousan, Kaasan, and Chiemi?

In the last moments, I heard the distinct, but faint and comforting howl of wolves. In my steady loss of consciousness, I thought of my father with Chiemi in the deep woods of Ontario. Together, safe, and in love. Maybe reality is a hallucination. Maybe nothing is real...

We will all die unhealed.

age-zushi	sushi rice wrapped in a "bag" of bean curd
aho	stupid
Aka	a red, Japanese Canadian slang for a dissident
baachan	grandmother (colloquial)
bakatare, baka, bakayaro	a fool, an idiot; or, as in the expression, "You idiot!"
bento	packed lunch
bocchan	young master, a term of affection
Bodhi	enlightenment or awakening
Boku	Japanese for "I"
bousan	Buddhist minister
bozu	term of affection for a young boy
Bussei	Young Buddhist Association; short for Bukkyo seinenkai
butsudan	Buddhist altar
-chan	a form of -san used for young children and female family members
Chankoro	derogatory term for Chinese person
char shiu	barbecue pork
cintamani	mythical stone said to have come to earth from Sirius, the Dog Star
Damare!	(vulgarism) "Shut up!"
Dana	Buddhist women's club
dashiki	a loose, brightly coloured shirt or tunic, originally from West Africa
denbatsuke	Japanese radish pickle, said to have been invented in New Denver, BC

dharma	the teaching of the Buddha
donburi	bowl of rice with meat and vegetables on top
Edo	Edo or Tokugawa Period from 1603 to 1868
enka	popular Japanese music said to resemble traditional music
Fujinkai	Buddhist Senior Women's Club
futomaki	a large sushi wrapped in nori
gaijin	foreigner, non-Japanese
ganbariya	member of the Perseverance Group
ganko	stubborn, obstinate (adj)
gasshou	pressing hands together in reverent respect
gatha	Buddhist hymn
gesha	monthly tuition fee
hachimaki	stylized headband, usually with a *hinomaru* emblazoned on it
Hai, so deso	"Yes, that is so."
hakama	loose Japanese trousers
hakujin, huk	Caucasian
Hanamatsuri	Festival of Flowers, associated with the birth of the Buddha
hapa	a person who is partially of Asian or Pacific Islander descent
hara-kiri	ritual suicide
hashi	chopsticks
Harumatsuri	spring festival
hinomaru	the symbol of the red sun; flag of Japan
hinotama	fireball; spirit of the recently deceased

Hondo	main temple hall
honto	true
Idou	Issei expression for the Nikkei exile during WWII, euphemistically known as the "Evacuation."
inu	dog; used as disparaging slang
Issei	first (immigrant) generation of Japanese Canadians
Jodo Shinshu	Buddhist sect common in Canada
-ka	participle; added to a word to signify a question
kai	club
kakimochi	rice crackers
kanji	ideograms
Kawaiso-ne	How sad.
kazunoko konbu	herring roe on seaweed
ken	Japanese prefecture or province
kenjinkai	prefectural association
ketsuno-ana	(vulgarism) asshole
kichigai	crazy
Kika-Nisei	Nisei educated in Japan
kimochi	feeling comfortable
kitanai	dirty
Kodomo no tame ni	"For the sake of the children"
konbu	seaweed (kelp)
maguro	tuna
maki sushi	sushi roll
manju	sweet rice cake
matsuri	festival

matsutake	a type of mushroom highly prized by the Japanese
maze gohan	mixed cooked rice
mezurashi-ne	unusual, rare, precious
miso	soy bean paste
mochi	pounded rice
-mura	village
namaiki	troublemaker
Namu Amida Butsu	a Buddist expression: "I rely on the Buddha of Infinite Light and Life."
naniyo, nanja	(expression) "What?"
ne	an expression used for confirmation: "Well, you know."
Nembutsu	an expression of gratitude to the Buddha (recitation of Namu Amida Butsu)
Nihonjin, desu ka?	Are you Japanese?
Nikkei	Japanese living outside of Japan
Nisei	second generation Japanese Canadian (first generation born in Canada)
nishime	a braised vegetable dish
noren	fabric divider hung across the top of a doorway
nori	treated seaweed
ochazuke	cold rice submerged in green tea, accompanied by Japanese pickles
obaachan	grandmother
obasan	an elderly woman
Obon	summer Buddhist Festival of the Dead
odori	folk dance
ofuton, futon	Japanese comforter

Ogenki desu ka	expression: "How are you?"
Ogochisou-sama	expression said at the end of a meal to express appreciation
ojiichan	grandfather
oji	elderly man
ojuzu	Buddhist rosary
okaasan, okaa, kaasan	mother
Oneesan, sake onigaishimasu	"Big Sister, some sake please."
onigiri	rice ball
osechiryouri, osechi	New Year's food
Oshougatsu	New Year's Day
otaku	obsessive individual
otousan	father
salarymen	businessmen in Japan
-san	honourific: Mr., Mrs., Miss
Sangha	men's club in the Buddhist church
Sansei	third generation Japanese Canadian
sembei	rice crackers
Sensei	teacher, master
shikataganai	(expression) "It can't be helped" or "I have no choice"
shin ijusha	new Japanese immigrant
shodo	art of traditional Japanese calligraphy
shoyu	soy sauce
Shusho-e	first Buddhist service of the New Year
Sodan-kai	study group
sunomono	cucumber salad
tadaima	(expression) "I'm home."

Tanko Bushi	Coalminers' Dance
tanomoshi	savings and credit association
tanuki	shape-shifting racoon
tatami	straw floor mat
teishoku	meal set
tekka maki	tuna roll sushi
toshiyori	the elderly
tsukemono	pickled vegetables
wonton mein	noodle and dumpling soup
Yamato	"Spirit of Japan"
yum cha	snack, a small meal (usually with dim sum)
zabuton	Japanese cushion

Author's Note

Dream

Thanks to Tane Akamatsu, Bev Ohashi and Ken Noma for encouraging me to write about the Sansei.

Ian Cockfield, Brian Kaufman, Karen Green: thanks for helping me make this book a reality.

ABOUT THE AUTHOR

Terry Watada is the author of the novels, *The Three Pleasures* and *The Blood of Foxes*, a collection of short fiction, *Daruma Days*, four books of poetry, two children's books, the nonfiction title *Bukkyo Tozen: A History of Jodo Shinshu Buddhism in Canada 1905 – 1995*, and two manga style comic books. Terry is also a musician and recording artist. Mr. Watada lives in Toronto.